Echoes from Annwn

Paula Aspin

Leaf by Leaf

Published by Leaf by Leaf
an imprint of Cinnamon Press,
Lytchett House, 13 Freeland Park, Wareham Road, Poole, Dorset, BH16 6FA
www.cinnamonpress.com

Print Edition ISBN 978-1-78864-856-1
British Library Cataloguing in Publication Data. A CIP record for this book can be obtained from the British Library.

In the EU, we are fully compliant with GPSR (General Product Safety Regulation). Our EU GPSR Authorised Representative, via Inpress Books, is LOGOS EUROPE, 9 rue Nicolas Poussin, 17000, LA ROCHELLE, France E-mail: Contact@logoseurope.eu
Designed and typeset in Adobe Caslon Pro by Cinnamon Press.

Cover Design Adam Craig.
Cinnamon Press is represented by Inpress.

Acknowledgments

Heartfelt thanks to my family. Vicki and Steven, for your ongoing support. To Jack and Sarah, who together purchased a laptop for me when mine broke. Without which, I couldn't have finished the book. Also, to your respective partners. Andy, James and Sam. A special mention to Millie, who never failed to ask about the progress of my writing. To my husband, Stuart. For your love and support, offering me the time at home to write. I am blessed by you all, and your unwavering belief in me. To Barbara, who has always been, and continues to be, a wonderful friend through all the highs and lows. Equally to Janet, for your listening ear and decades of friendship. Special thanks to Sylvia, for reading the first draft, and reiki. To Peter, Marylin and Claire at Latchygors. Having stayed in your restful holiday cottage numerous times I now consider you friends. Deepest gratitude to ACW and Tenby, where it all began. A big thank you to Jan, for your blogs, Kith, mentoring and editing. Kind encouragement and generosity. You have touched my heart with your personal story and opened my mind with ideas. Also, to Rowan at Leaf by leaf. Your editing and way with words have made all the difference. Not forgetting Adam, for the beautiful cover design. Final thanks go to my parents, who continue to touch my soul with their love and guidance from beyond the veil.

About the Author

Paula Aspin began writing as a coping strategy when her mother was diagnosed with dementia. With a diploma in metaphysics counselling and a reiki master. words, written, spoken, or thought, and their influence on the health of mind and body, are the fundamental principle at the heart of all her endeavours.

Echoes From Annwn is her first novel, drawing on her Welsh ancestry and love of Tenby, which began in her teens with three summer seasons working in a local hotel.

Paula is mother to four grown up children and a grandmother. She works with children and lives in Lancashire with her husband.

For Mum

A gossamer veil invokes a tale.
Hidden truths, which shall prevail.
Open your heart, seek and find.
We are never apart, our hearts entwined.

Echoes from Annwn

Chapter 1

Lockhart

Pale light sifts through the shuttered window slit, shadows clinging to the walls in familiar silhouettes. In black breeches and doublet, falling band collar at my neck, goosebumps peppering my skin like a plucked bird doomed for the pot. Pulling the musty moth-eaten blanket tighter around my shoulders, reluctant to leave its warmth, I cross to the window; the cold stone floor seeps through my boots, grasping at my feet with icy fingers. The shutter, warped from the onslaught of Atlantic weather, opens after a sharp tug. An oblique pink-grey sky dawns a new day beyond the castle wall. Captains holler to crews of fishermen, setting their sails, manning the oars of boats, moored in the small inlet harbour, bobbing hypnotically on a shifting tide. Milk-white waves lap their hulls and the base of Goscar rock—an arresting stack of jagged siltstones erupting from the golden north beach. A dragon in my youth, slayed with childhood friends, sticks for our imagined swords. The memory warms me on this spring morning, much like any other, except, snippets of the night's journey leaves me awry.

A loud knock at my door, the daily call to rise, returns me to the present. "I hear you, I'm awake." I rake my hand through waves of dark hair. Reluctantly discarding the blanket on top of the wooden chest. It contains all I own, bar the three-legged stool which belonged to my father, waiting, as if for his imminent arrival by the unlit fire. But he will not come again.

Descending the curved steps built into the stone wall, the leather soles of my boots echo around the confined space. In the hall, fellow soldiers huddle at the long table, facing the crackling flames in the large stone fireplace. Grabbing a pewter bowl, I wink at the serving maid; her blush gaining me an extra-large dollop of potage. It always works. Merek slides further along the bench granting me a seat beside him.

"Aelwen has been driving me to distraction with wedding plans," Merek is saying to anyone who cares to listen, "I asked her, what's it got to do with me? As far as I'm concerned, I just need to turn up on the right day looking presentable, the rest is up to her."

A tapestry of a golden phoenix with open wings presides over us. A silver sword clasped within its claws, a serpent of rainbow colours twisting around the blade. The hilt of my own backsword is fashioned in similar, though simpler design.

"You appear preoccupied," Merek acknowledges, shovelling food into his mouth, dribbles of slop spilling into his beard. At times I find his habits grotesque, but we are brothers in all but blood.

"Just admiring the needlework." I cringe at my phrase, and Merek lifts an eyebrow.

Emlyn's valet crosses the hall, stealthy as a rat with his eye on prey, coughing to gain my attention. "Governor Edwards wishes your attendance, immediately, Sire." He is scrawny, serving his master with unashamed grovelling. I ignore him. "He made it quite clear; I should fetch you at haste."

"As you can see, I am eating." Spoon halfway to my mouth.

"Do you wish me to go and tell him that?" Gethin asks haughtily.

Plonking the spoon into the bowl, contents splosh onto the table, and I deliberately position myself in Gethin's personal space as I stand, forcing him to step back, before I head out of the hall.

Gethin's face reddens from the exertion of keeping up with my long strides, and I reach the study first, surprised the door opens and a man emerges. Gethin scuttles inside and closes the door.

"A good meeting Sire?" I frown. Tom Griffiths` demeanour stiffens at my questioning tone, small dark eyes, shifting. The Tenby councillor has made clear his distaste for Emlyn, believing him unworthy of such an eminent position, proclaiming with conviction he should be evicted from the castle. So, what is his motive for meeting so early in the morning?

"Yes, Sire, a very good meeting." Pulling the brim of his hat low over his brow, he pushes past me.

My gut tightens. A warning, or hunger? "A man cannot even enjoy his breakfast," I grumble. The door reopens and instinctively my shoulders pull back, chin aloft, habitual before entering Emlyn's study. A solid stance gives me confidence and height; one of my few advantages. I have learnt in my two and twenty years, I need all the help I can muster dealing with my older brother.

Emlyn's bulk fills the oak wainscot chair, stomach paunch barely contained within tight breeches. Senior by six and ten years, his lank black hair peppered with grey, drapes his face, mostly hidden behind a bushy beard. The corners of his cold grey eyes wrinkle as he surveys me, and insolently I stare back. I find him irritating, occasionally intimidating, an underlying unease in his presence. His fingertips drum the mahogany desk.

"Finally, what took you so long?" The fear instilled by voice alone, serves him well. "I expect you to arrive promptly to our meetings."

"Accept my apologies, brother, I…"

He dismisses my words with a flick of his wrist. "I am in no mood to listen to your meagre excuses, Lockhart. Information regarding your recent commission is what I require."

I find the continual drumming of his fingers distracting and consider if the meeting with Tom Griffiths is cause for such behaviour, but have no time to pursue the thought before Emlyn snarls, "Well speak up man, I trust your expedition was a success?" He folds his arms across his chest. "You returned with the coin owed to me from Dai Thomas?"

I stiffen, my sword to Dai's throat, threatening eviction. Contrite at my bullish behaviour and confused why, I recount, "I warned him of the consequences but gained no coin."

"No coin!" Emlyn rebukes. "You must have returned with something, pray, anything?" He raises an eyebrow.

"He had none to give, how can he be expected to pay what he does not have?" I challenge. "The rain over wintertime took most of the crops."

"You cannot seriously think I care about the dilemma which Dai Thomas finds himself in." Emlyn flattens his hands against the desk, leaning forward. "And brother, I am aware of the weather, it is hard not to be in this damp hellhole, but a debt must be paid, as well you know. I cannot believe you are even questioning such a thing."

I am not sure either. Speaking in defence of a peasant farmer, making my opinion known, is out of character.

Emlyn moves from behind the desk, pushing my shoulder with the palm of his hand. "I knew it was a mistake to send you alone, you have proved, yet again, you are nothing but a pathetic excuse for a man. Tell me, what exactly am I paying you for, if you cannot even accomplish a simple task?" He does not expect an answer, and I look over his head, focusing on the deep-set window nestled into grey stone, which adds a small band of light to the dreary room. The back of my legs are burning from the heat of the fire, tongues of gold reflecting onto the glass. "Do you have nothing to say for yourself brother? No version of events to clarify?" His forehead wrinkles. "You appear to have lost the use of your tongue."

There will be consequences to arguing back, but today, remaining silent is proving difficult. "I can only reiterate; he had nothing to give."

"A horse," Emlyn suggests condescendingly. "Which you could have relieved him of? Or a child, I could put to work to pay the debt."

"His twins are mere infants, and I believe the horse, his only hope of a meal."

"How dare you speak to me in such tone. It seems to have slipped your mind that you work for me. When I send you on a mission I expect results. Is that too much to ask, you ungrateful brat? After all I have done for you, Lockhart, is it not time you showed some gratitude?"

I am no longer listening, staring at the dark wood panelling lining the walls, and the portrait of Emlyn, dressed in a deep purple doublet with silver buttons, which hangs beside the desk, seeing with fresh eyes. No expense has been spared on Emlyn's office and chambers, whilst everyone for miles struggles to pay the extortionate rent and taxes he increases year upon year. Thinking on it further, his lack of care for the castle is evident in its deterioration. Damp seeps through walls, timbers rotting, and outer walls crumbling, putting the castle in danger of attack. Emlyn claims hard times, and even poverty, to cover his lack of interest in keeping the building maintained. However, I am aware my brother gains a good profit, and not just from taxes, but wine, spirits and salt, smuggled from ships, through secret tunnels. It hasn't gone unnoticed by the locals, either, that his fine clothes and expensive goods have been paid for on the back of their toil and drudgery. A sediment of silt in the small harbour town stirs with unrest.

Returning to the security of his desk, Emlyn fiddles with something in his pocket. He does this often, leaving his fingertips punctured or bloodied. I speculate it must be sharp.

"Are you listening?" he bellows, bringing me back from my reverie. "Rumours abound of cattle rustlers, spotted close to Llandovery, Irish vagabonds or such sort, no doubt. Ride out tomorrow, check my land. Interrogate the peasants and yeomen for any sign of wrongdoing, I don't trust any of them. Do you think you can manage that?"

Hackles rise at the patronising remark, nails digging into the palms of my fisted hands.

"If you discover so much as one of my cattle missing, I suggest you do not return without capture of the perpetrators, is that clear?"

"Did Tom Griffiths inform you of this?"

"What does it matter to you?" Emlyn frowns. "Where, and from whom, I get my information, is no concern of yours. Just do not cross me, or you may have to keep an eye open as you sleep."

Boldly I lean across the desk. "Is that a threat, brother?"

Shock momentarily lights his eyes at my audacity, pushing back his chair; the wooden legs scrape loudly against the stone floor. "Take it as you like, I am governor of this castle, your superior, you would do well to remember that."

My brow furrows. "Why do you believe I would cross you? What ridiculous ideas has Tom Griffiths put in your head?"

"I will not be made to look a fool by anyone, especially Kin." Emlyn's yellowed teeth snarl.

"What are you accusing me of?" I scowl back.

"Just prove your loyalty, and get the job done. That is an order." Emlyn refolds his arms defensively. "You can go now; I have more important matters to attend to than arguing with you." I harden my stare, delaying a moment longer before turning to the door. "Lockhart, one other thing, before you leave." Emlyn announces to my turned back. "I almost forgot to say, I am to be married again." I twist around, a smug look curls his thin lips, and I am unable to hide my shock.

Angharad bore two daughters, calming Emlyn in a way no other could. Her death had broken him. Unable to even look at his daughters such was the resemblance to their mother, they were packed off to live with their maternal grandparents in Aberystwyth, residing there ever since. Whilst I took the brunt of his grief, his rage unleashed in both words and penance, and henceforth, a heavy cloud hung around Emlyn, which his second wife, a petite Irish girl, had been unable to penetrate.

"Who…" I attempt to keep the contempt out of my voice, "is the lucky lady this time?"

Emlyn grins salaciously. "The youngest daughter of the wool merchant Cedrych Davis, though I believe he loses more coin than he gains." He scoffs, and I eye my brother sceptically.

"Why would you marry into an unprosperous family?" Emlyn's thunderous stare indicates my misdeed, which I promptly gloss with a question, "Have I met her?"

Emlyn pulls a face. "I shouldn't think so; I barely know her myself. A pretty little thing though." He rubs his hands. "I am looking forward to her siring me a few sons."

My stomach turns. "It's just, I have not heard you speak of her before, brother, are you not being hasty? Niamh has only been gone, what, three months." Unable to live up to the memory of Angharad, the young girl suffered greatly at Emlyn's hands, living but a year after their wedding. Dying in childbirth, along with the son Emlyn so desperately longed for.

"What does it matter to you who I wed? Her father and I have come to a satisfactory agreement, and it is imperative I waste no more time. You know I must have sons, Lock. One of us must continue the family name, and I cannot see you making headway in such matters." Emlyn replies irritably, "Is it not time you found a woman to share your own bed, instead of concerning yourself in my affairs?" He raises an eyebrow. "No one interested, Lock? But then I guess you have little to offer. Money, status, and power make a man, do they not, and you possess none." He assess me with distaste. "Off you go, little brother."

The watchtower sits central to the courtyard, offering unrivalled views across Carmarthen Bay, Worms Head, and the Gower peninsula. Seldom manned these days, but in times of old, when the castle was deemed an important fortification, it was an ideal lookout point. It saddens me to see the castle left to fall into disrepair, when it must have taken years for our forefathers to build the battlements with notched parapets, defence for arrow men shooting through the small gaps. Now the roof leaks, and the east wall is crumbling. All that remains of what was a chapel is a rectangle of stone, the rest carried away to build houses in the town. No one wants to live in a draughty castle anymore. Beyond the archway, too low to pass in the saddle, the horses wait. Caprice is there, my black Welsh cob, an unexpected gift from Emlyn when Angharad was alive, and he was almost bearable.

"Where is he?" My patience wears thin, and I approach Edwin the young groom, idly kicking the dirt with the toe of his boot. "Go and find Merek." I snatch the reins from his hand. His eyes fall and my heart lurches. The boy hurries off in too-short breeches, tunic tied with string around his thin waist, slipping from his waif shoulders. He reappears with Merek moments later, who ambles as though he has all the time in the world.

I shoot Merek a cutting glance. "We were meant to leave at dawn."

He yawns, dismissing my irritation in his nonchalant way. "I know, I know, but the light is in our favour at this time of year, we will still get a fair way today, if the weather holds."

Heavy clouds perch on distant hills like Captain hats. "Well, let us hope you can stay awake for the remainder of the day; you need more sleep than a baby."

Edwin helps me alight, and I ruffle the boy's hair, redemption for my previous harsh words. His shoulders visibly relax at this small kindness, and I am recompensed with an internal amity. Settling into the saddle I tug the reins, applying slight pressure with my calves and clicking my tongue, as a whistling wind pulls at my cloak and hat. The fortification is separated from the town by a narrow isthmus, the horse's clop across the wooden bridge, the formidable town walls encasing Tenby residents in a stronghold of protection. Timber framed shacks with turfed roofs cluster around the harbour, overshadowed by merchants' dwellings of imposing height and structure. St. Mary's church, central to the town, encompassed by an array of small shops. The cone spire, a landmark for trading ships, protrudes through grey cloud, racing across the dreary sky.

Riding at a moderate pace we head north, pathways sodden and slippery after the heavy rainfall overnight. Lush green terrain, droplets of dew, sparkling in morning sunlight. By late morning we pass Carmarthen. In 1188, Gerald of Wales claimed it to be Merlin's birthplace. Past the oak tree, where Merlin is said to have prophesied. "When Priory's Oak shall tumble down, then so will Carmarthen Town." Pregnant with new growth despite its age, surviving another harsh Welsh winter. We cross the green slutch of Merlin's hill, the last place he was said to have been seen, watching over the river Towy. I find myself surreptitiously scanning for a cave, his possible resting place. Where, according to legend, he is locked in bonds of enchantment by his lover. Some say they hear his chains clanking still.

There is a month in age between Merek and I, he the slightly older. Brought up as brothers, his mother Enid was my main caregiver, after my own died in childbirth. We are opposites. He thickset and strong, I, tall and lithe. But our differences serve us well, attested by many brawls in Tenby over the years. Our skills as soldiers thus far, remain untested. Tenby, being on the trading route of the Bristol channel, is always susceptible to attack. The five arches tower was added to the west walls a little over fifty years ago, fearing assault from the Spanish Armada, which luckily failed to materialise, but the threat of invaders from across the sea remains. For now, our days mainly consist of running errands for Emlyn and tracking down people for non-payment of taxes.

By mid-afternoon, clouds chased away by the breeze have left clear blue skies. A bright spring sun lightening my mood. Small flies hatch in the puddles along a rough road.

A man up ahead walks with a stick and an Ass, pulling an empty cart. Merek shouts to him as we pass by. "How far to the next village Sire?"

The man squints, his eyes a clouded milky film. "Not far." He points back the way he has come. "Just over a mile."

"Is there an Inn or Tavern?" Merek asks hopefully.

"Yes, on the left, before you reach the houses."

Merek jumps from his horse, pressing a coin into the man's hand. "Thank you Sire, we are most grateful." I hide a smile.

A wooden sign nailed above the door of a ramshackle hut, simply reads, Tafarn, in weathered black paint. Tavern in Welsh. Although English is spoken fluently by many, a necessity with the influx of cattle drovers passing on their way to London, Welsh remains the main language, and we speak very little in our neck of the woods, a few words, an odd saying, hence the reason we are often referred to as little England beyond Wales. Wilting daffodils skirt the perimeter of the tavern, the most redeeming feature.

Ordering two ales, Merek takes a large gulp of the mud brown beer and pulls a face. "Not the best, is it?"

I take a sip. "Tastes like pigs' water," I shudder. "Don't think we should complain though, we don't want to cause a scene, those two fellows by the window look a nasty pair."

Merek glances their way. "Look alright to me."

Instinct tells me different. Glancing out of the window, I spot an old woman hovering around the horses, tied to a wooden post. "Come on, let's go." I indicate to Merek.

A basket gripped tightly in weathered hands; she is muttering to herself as we approach. "Your sacrifice is for a higher purpose, do not fear."

"Can I help you?" I untie the reins.

The woman smiles at me; a front tooth is missing. "Lavender," she offers, rummaging in her basket.

"Not today." I mutter, trying to dodge round her.

"You need luck on your journey." She attempts to hand me a dried sprig.

I ignore her and alight the horse, sitting high in the saddle. "Be off with you, old woman."

The remainder of the day passes uneventfully, colours fading in evening dusk, basking the landscape in shadowy shades of grey. Merek leads the way through a wooded glade below a hillside, an ice white waterfall cascading into the river, visible through the trees. Coming across a felled log and remnants of cold ash, we settle for the night. The horses drink greedily by the water's edge, and I collect twigs for the fire. Merek rummaging in the saddlebag is delighted to find a heel of pie, and we eat in comfortable silence, shadowed by the firelight, darkness enveloping the sky, interspersed with silvery stars, a waxing moon high above treetops.

"Do you think we are all there is?" I consider aloud.

Merek pokes the fire with a stick. "How do you mean?"

"You know, only the earth. Do you think there are others like us, living on the moon?"

Merek shakes his head. "You come out with some strange ideas my friend, of course we are the only ones."

"What of the book by Bishop Francis Godwin?" Merek looks at me blankly. "It is called *The Man in the Moone.* The story tells of a Spaniard, who journeys there and finds a place of beauty."

Merek scoffs. "Utter rubbish in my opinion. Anyway," he says smirking, "since when have you been interested in books?"

Having never confided in Merek the reading lessons received from Angharad; I am piqued at the reply. "I just believe we should have an open mind to such things."

Merek shrugs, picking at remnants of crumbs from the muslin wrap and shoving the last piece of pie whole into his mouth.

"Aelwen has no idea what she is letting herself in for, she will spend all day trying to fill you." I can never stay angry with Merek for long.

"Cooking for her man, best place for a woman anyway, is it not? Well, there or the bed." Merek grins mischievously.

"Come on, out with it." I probe. "I know you have some secret; you are grinning from ear to ear."

Merek whispers, "I went a little further with Aelwen last night, than I perhaps ought."

"You lucky old dog!" I push Merek's arm. "No wonder I could not rise you from slumber this morning, basking in the afterglow of illicit fornication no doubt." Merek sighs with an irritating contentment. "So how did you persuade her?" I inquire, though I have little interest.

"I simply explained it hardly mattered; we are betrothed and will soon be wed." Merek smiles brazenly, no doubt picturing Aelwen's dark brown eyes, the tight curls of her chestnut hair, and swell of her ample bosom. Having no one special to share my life, a twinge of jealousy burns in my chest.

We are a few miles short of Llandovery, following a line of hedgerow, and slow the horses to a trot. Easterly gusts bend and sway branches, budding with bright green shoots. Compared to yesterday, it feels nothing like spring, and I huddle deeper into my cloak.

"We need to watch them first," Merek says, planning our strategy for capturing the rustlers. "See how many there are, before we make a move."

"Yes," I agree. "It is imperative we..."

Out of the bushes, two men, shouting and waving their arms, startle the horses. Caprice rears, whinnies in alarm. "Whoa," I try to bring her back in line, but the man wields a stick, begins beating her haunches, and she kicks backwards. I try to kick him away, but he grabs my ankle, pulling my leg, and reaches for the reins, tugging them from my grip. I fight for control. Caprice rears again and I am thrown backwards, landing heavily. The jolt sends shockwaves through my body. The attacker is quick to react, already astride me, pinning me to the ground.

His blade glints in a ray of sunlight. I seize his arm, bucking and twitching to remove myself from beneath him. He merely smiles, a contemptuous toothless grin. Aware of Merek struggling to free himself from the other man's grasp, I recall the pair from the tavern, the previous day. My attacker prizes his arm free, thrusts the dagger, slicing my leather jerkin. The pain and shock, immediate and intense. He brandishes the red stained blade for me to see, grabs my jaw with his spare hand, leaning in close, his breath smells of rotten meat.

"There is a time for everything, and a season for every activity under the heavens: a time to be born and a time to die." Ecclesiastes 3: 1-8

There's a searing throb in my head from the fall. My right hand moving to the pulsating wound in my side, covering my fingers in warm blood, nausea washing over me. Vaguely aware of Merek lying face down in the grass, I can do nothing but watch, as the two men ride away. Caprice, my trusted horse, my companion. Sprawled on the ground, I am fading, in a cloak of pain.

Chapter 2

Wren

Settling into the high-backed chair, an opened book upon my lap. Father will be cross if he discovers I have snook it into the sewing room, but above the line of trees swaying gently in a light breeze, which mark the perimeter of the grounds like tall wooden soldiers, it is so much lighter up here. I count my blessings; grateful father has seen fit to allow myself, and my sister Alys, the opportunity to learn to read. Not everyone would agree it is fitting for a woman. Father's small library is mainly academia, and of little interest. Therefore, the First Folio of Shakespeare has become my favourite. The life and death of King John. The tragedy of Macbeth is compelling, but my preference lies among the comedies, one more captivating than any other. *As you like it.* A tale I return to frequently. Seeming never to tire of Rosalind, fleeing persecution and finding love in the Forest of Arden. Silently I read… No sooner met but they looked; no sooner looked but they loved…

An insistent ramming on the main door, followed by raised voices in the hall, piques my curiosity. Placing a strip of blue ribbon on the page and closing the book, I tentatively step onto the landing. Father, is at the foot of the stairs, issuing urgent instruction to the maids. "Prepare a room at once and hurry, the man is dripping more blood than a slaughtered sheep."

Peeping to the hall below, I am surprised to see a man bent over, his clothes blood stained, another man holding him upright. Alarmed. I descend the stairs. "May I be of help father?" The stooped man holds a shaking bloodied hand to his side, face etched in pain. He glances at me, for no more than a moment, that is all, but the meeting of our eyes flips my heart with a rush of joy.

"Go to your room, child," Father replies brusquely.

The afternoon passes in a blur of activity. The stable hand is sent to the home of my uncle, local physician John Jones, who arrives within the hour on a dappled mare. He is a slight man, with dark hair greying at the temples. We pass on the stairs.

"Good afternoon, Wren." His expressionless face bows politely. "I hope to find you well."

"Yes, uncle, thank you, I am well." He continues onto the landing, and although it is not my place, I call after him, "Please take excellent care of him."

He nods imperceptibly.

Arlet, a tiny middle-aged woman with jet black hair and a turn in her left eye, has been in service to the family for many years. I do not like her, and suspect the feeling is mutual, using her misfortune to stare, which unnerves me. Mother says she cannot help her affliction, but sometimes, I wonder. She does it now, giving me that look as she removes father's empty soup bowl. He wipes his mouth with a cloth.

"It appears," I turn my attention to him. "The two fellows were attacked by horse thieves."

Mother pales. "It is worrisome husband that such scoundrels are in the area."

"Indeed, my dear wife, but rest assured I have told the stable hand, most clearly, his responsibility for keeping the horses safe."

"You don't believe the men are so unabashed as to come into the grounds, do you? They wouldn't come into the house?"

"No, no, do not trouble yourself dearest, it is a mere precaution that is all. I can't imagine them so foolhardy to stay in the area, they will be eager to sell the horses on no doubt."

Arlet serves me a plate of trout. My stomach churns noisily. Arlet smirks at my unladylike grumblings, and the cold dead fisheye mocks me. Pushing the grey flesh around the plate, my mind elsewhere, on the man lying injured upstairs. "What of the injured gentlemen?" I enquire lightly. Father eyes me sceptically.

"The least injured will remain in the stables and leave at first light. Let us pray he does not lose the horse I have arranged, on his trek back to Tenby." He shakes his head. "As for the patient, we must ensure he has all he needs to aid his recovery." Father waves his fork. "Ensuring Emlyn sees us as respectful and kindly, will go in our favour."

"Father, I am confused. What association is Emlyn to the injured gentleman?" I tuck strands of hair into my cap.

Father frowns. "Our guest, Wren, is Sire Lockhart Edwards."

My heart leaps. "Oh, goodness." I push a fist against my lips, forcing it back to its rightful place within my chest.

Father casts me a disgruntled look. "I can understand your concern, Wren; you must not worry yourself."

Emlyn's brother. My head whirls with this unexpected news. No, it cannot be.

"This is delicious." Father chews a mouthful of fish, subject over.

The trout will not bring the nourishment I require, and a few meagre mouthfuls is all I manage. "May I be excused father; it has been an eventful day."

"As you wish." He waves me away without taking his eye from the plate of bone and tail.

All is quiet on the landing. I fight the urge to knock and ask over Lockhart's welfare, but the door opens unexpectedly and Gladys, a maid of similar age to myself, emerges from the room, cheeks flushed from the heat of the fire roaring in the grate. "Ooh Miss, you made me jump."

Caught in the act of my indulgence I am flustered, searching for something to say. "How is Sire Edwards?" I hope to sound polite rather than desperate for news.

"He will live Miss; just needs time to heal. The apothecary has tucked a square of moss under the bandage, instructing me to ensure it remains covering the wound." Obviously pleased to be chosen for the task, I too am grateful Gladys will be his main caregiver, she is a gentle, thoughtful girl.

"Then I am sure that will do the trick." Uncle prefers the old methods, passed through the generations, arguing it is in fact the scientific physicians, doling out poison with little notion of the harm they inflict, who are the charlatans. Gladys holds onto the door, obscuring my view, but I am drawn by golden rays of evening sun lighting the floor through the partially closed damask curtains. They beckon me, decorum and propriety fading with the sunset. I edge round the door; she can hardly refuse me. "I will just check on Sire Edwards before I retire."

The plum coverlet edged with gilt braid lies across his hips, resting beneath the bloodied bandage. My insides warm, and I feel giddy, for I have never seen a man undressed this closely before. Alys tells me her husband is covered in hair like a monkey, but Lockhart's chest hair is sparse, I surmise this a reflection of his youth. Several years younger than Emlyn, and quite different. A shadow of stubble, waves of dark hair, long lashes resting upon his cheek. I recall his eyes are light blue; imprinted from that first look, they reveal so much about a person. He is tall, for a Welshman, I will need to stand on tiptoe to kiss him. I bite my lip at such impropriety; we haven't even been formally introduced. Surely, if Lockhart were married, my heart tightens at the prospect, Emlyn would have mentioned it. What coin of fate has cast you into my circle at this point in life, Lockhart Edwards?

Late to rise, my sleep dream filled and restless, I hurry across the landing. A window in the far wall would have been preferable, enabling sunlight to flood the stairs for at least part of the day. Mother complains that without natural light it remains dismal and dark all year. Father, not a man open to the whims of women, dismissed her request when the house was built, has dismissed her every suggestion since. I meet Arlet, her arms a bundle of linen, halfway down the stairs. She steps aside to allow me passage, but in the shadows I am very aware she may stick out a foot and I could stumble and look foolish. It has happened before. A wider staircase would also have been preferred.

The shutters in the drawing room remain closed, a thin strip of sunlight creeping through a badly repaired slat falls across mother's glum face, a band around her forehead accentuating the deep furrowed lines. "Is something wrong Mother, Lockhart, he is improving?" I ask cautiously. Mother knits her hands. "You are what is wrong my dear." Pursed lips are a sign I know, repressed anger bubbling with the prospect of release.

"You have no right to involve yourself with Sire Lockhart." She has heard of my visit. "It is simply not right, entering the room of a common soldier, all be it one with connections. Your hedonistic attitude is beyond belief." It is true, my actions have been inappropriate, but to attempt an explanation when mother is agitated and cross is pointless, and how can I explain the need to see him, when unable to understand it myself? "You are a wilful child." Mother closes her eyes and kneads her forehead.

"Are you suffering another headache Mother? Would you like me to fetch your tonic?"

"Just promise you will leave the servants to care for our guest."

My heart flutters. "I believe offering help in his time of need is something I must do."

"So, you refuse?"

My silence speaks volumes.

"Very well, I have tried to reason with you, I will hand the situation over to your father. Now, I must lie down, this is all too much for me to bear." Mother rings the small bell on the table beside her. Arlet enters the room. I suspect she was listening at the door. "The hangings had better be drawn," Mother says.

Opening the shutters, I sink into the cushioned window seat, embroidered during the heat of a particularly warm summer, two years past, alphabet neatly sewn around the edges in red lettering. A reminder my carefree days are almost at an end. Now six and ten, I will be married before this summer is through. Against my will, I am betrothed to Governor Emlyn Edwards of Tenby castle. The prospect presses my chest with sadness. We have met briefly, and I find him difficult to read. His self-importance I do not find becoming. Bragging of his wealth may impress others, but I find the tendency irksome. However, father insisted the request for my hand be accepted. Blackbirds and sparrows peck in the garden, busy at this time of year building nests, and I wonder if I will be happy building a nest with Emlyn. He has proved himself polite and gracious, and yet, fondness towards him is not forthcoming.

Whilst out walking one day, I became overwhelmed by fatigue, a black shroud of despair, knowing this man would never be of my choosing. Turning for home, a hare ran across our path. Father brushed away what he called silly superstitions, but I am sure I witnessed a warning, a harbinger of bad luck. I shudder at the memory.

Collecting my black bonnet and woollen cloak from a peg in the hall, I step out into the chilly bright morning. Hyacinth of purple and pink prepare to bloom along the edge of the pathway leading to the arbour, my place of refuge, and I rest upon the stone pew. After resigning to the loveless marriage ahead, hopes and dreams which I had believed dead, in fact were merely hidden away. Reduced to ash as my inner flame reignited. I consider if there is such a thing as love at first sight, for this is how I feel. "What can I do to help Lockhart?" I whisper, my face turned to the sun's warmth peeping through the branches of apple trees. The fragrant blooms buzz with early bees, flitting amongst spring blossoms. Closing my eyes, breathing slowly and deeply, I smile. Mother will be cross if she sees me. Stay in the shade, she will say. A lady's skin must be pale if she is not to resemble a fishwife. I care not, and exhale a long sigh, dozing in the comforting heat when a thought appears with clarity. Grabbing my skirts, I run back across the lawn and into the house.

"I believe reading to Lockhart will be of benefit; it may stir him from sleep." I press the book tightly to my chest. "I will choose a light-hearted tale." I can see from her sideways look Gladys is unconvinced but places a stool beside the bed for me. Tucking stray hair into my coif, I fidget self-consciously, smoothing my skirts. There is always a positive to what appears to be a negative, no one will suspect my motives. "As you like it, by William

Shakespeare." I pause and begin, "As I remember, Adam, it was upon this fashion bequeathed me by will but poor a thousand crowns." My voice is a pitch too high, and I feel a little shy, stumbling over words, I force concentration. "And, as thou sayest, charged my brother on his blessing to breed me well; and there begins my sadness." My eye strays to Lockhart's face, a crease to his forehead, which wasn't there previously. My heart whips into a flurry of excitement. He mumbles words, I cannot grasp.

"Perhaps you should go Miss." Gladys suggests, as we stand by the bed, ogling him like a prized specimen.

I shake my head, unable to speak. He grimaces in pain, opened lips revealing a chip to a front tooth, I wonder the story behind it. He settles once more to sleep, and I release the breath I am unconsciously holding.

"There is blood on the bandage Miss, I need to change the dressing." I know Gladys wants me to leave.

"You will need warm water firstly, will you not?" I look at the empty jug on the small table.

"Yes, Miss, but I can get it quickly, I won't be gone long."

"What if he wakens again? I think it better I remain until you return." Gladys shifts foot to foot.

"Gladys," I sigh heavily. "He is injured and sleeping, I would barely consider him a threat." She can hardly throw me out, and the chance to be alone with him for a few minutes is too much for me to resist. "Go on then, hurry," I encourage. "The sooner you go, the sooner you are back."

Gladys slides out of the room, closing the door softly. I hear the creak at the top of the stairs, footsteps padding down. We are alone and I bite my lip, confused by my adoration, the instinctive connection, and familiarity to this man, for it makes no logical sense. A current of desire to physically touch him. This would be wrong, for many reasons, and yet I find my hand reaching. Fearful, I pull back. I reach again, fingertips brushing the warm skin of his muscled upper arm, and I gasp, not wanting or daring to move my hand away. Heartbeat thumps loudly in my chest, my body bubbling with joy. Stroking the soft hair on his forearm, I quote Shakespeare, "From henceforth I will, coz, and devise sports: let me see; what think of you of falling in love?"

I hear the latch click, and quickly withdraw my hand, embarrassed. "I have everything I need now, Miss." Gladys places the jug on the table, tipping warm water into the pewter bowl. I dip my head, hiding my blush. How I would love to stay, attend his wounds, but cannot.

"Very well, but you must fetch me if there is any change." Reluctantly I turn to the door.

"Oh, Miss, your father wishes to see you in the drawing room." I nod in acknowledgement, taking one last glance.

Mother sits rigid as an alabaster statue in the armchair, hands pressing on her lap, father remains standing. A light drizzle falls from an overcast sky, darkening the room. I straighten my dress, and tuck stray hair beneath my coif. "You wish to see me father?" Sensing the tension, I wait for father to speak. He is a short pale-faced man, long moustache speckled with grey, matching the few remaining hairs, on his almost bald head. A respected wool merchant, the arrangement of my betrothal to Emlyn, a means to an end. This marriage will open doors previously closed to him, negotiating deals he would not normally be party to. Emlyn is a man with connections.

"Your mother and I are concerned. Your attendance to Sire Lockhart is not in keeping." He furrows his brow. My heart sinks.

"I wish only to aid in his recovery," I protest.

"What of Emlyn, what would he think of you being so intimate with his own brother?" The tips of father's ears redden.

"I would hardly call sitting by his bedside and reading, intimate."

"Do not speak to me in that tone young lady, you need to watch that fiery tongue. Governor Edwards certainly will not accept such behaviour." His mind is working; I can tell by the moustache twitching. "Being on the right side of Governor Edwards is beyond doubt the best place to be. You must see that, Wren."

He doesn't even like Emlyn but somehow believes palming me off on him is his duty as a father, to see me provided for. That as a mere woman of such delicate disposition, I cannot possibly know what is best, decisions must be made on my behalf, and I should be grateful. My anger at such flippancy for my welfare sits in the pit of my stomach, growling.

Chapter 3

Lockhart

I awaken to find myself alone in a room far more splendid than my own at the castle. Heavy drapes at the window, a small table, and blazing fire. I wonder where I am. My eyes flick to the door as a maid enters with a weaved basket filled with small logs, which she places beside the hearth. "You are awake, Sire. How are you feeling?"

"A little better." My words are hoarse, and I cough, which hurts like hell. The maid straightens the coverlet around me. "How long have I been here?" I ask.

"This is the third day Sire." I gather my thoughts into a semblance of order.

"My comrade, Merek, is he injured?"

She explains, "he suffered no more than a sore head and bruising. We expect him back within the next few days, with a horse to take you home."

I rub the pain in my temples, imagining Emlyn's response. Stupid enough to be set upon is bad enough, but to renounce two horses as well. My gut wrenches, remembering Caprice has gone. "What is your name?" I ask the maid, a distraction from the lead weight of sadness.

"Gladys." She smiles warmly. "Luckily your friend realised after you were attacked, you were not far from here, so we have tended you best we can."

"Where exactly am I?" Unable to recall anyone I know in these parts.

"The Davis's residence Sire."

The weight in my stomach grows larger. "Cedrych Davis?"

"That's right Sire."

"The home of mistress Wren Davis?"

"Yes Sire, Miss visits and reads to you. Took it upon herself to take extra care of you, with you soon to become related."

I am no longer listening, her words tumbling around my head fall into place. The young woman soon to become my sister-in-law. A visceral pain seizes my heart, with dark foreboding.

I am sat in a cushioned chair by the fire, the coverlet tucked around my legs, when Wren enters with a shy smile, a dimple in her right cheek, causing my heart to flutter. She is most becoming in a simple green gown with white shawl collar, fastened at the centre by a red taffeta rosebud. Attractive without being too formal, nor flamboyant.

"You are feeling stronger?" she asks.

"Yes, thank you. Please, will you join me?" I indicate the chair opposite. She sits with hands cupped in her lap, alluring blue eyes flecked with gold, rimmed with dark lashes. I wonder if she is aware, of the effect she is having on me. I instigate conversation, "I understand we are to be related?" My heart constricts.

"Yes, that is correct, it will be very different living in a castle, I expect."

I sense her unease. "I am sure you will become accustomed to it, in time." Wisps of hair have slipped from her cap, and she teases them back into place. I imagine the dark tresses cascading her back, and my groin tingles. She is promised to Emlyn, stop thinking of her this way, it is hardly fitting.

"You live at the castle also?" she enquires.

"Yes, I have lived there most of my life."

She looks at me earnestly. "You have no living parents, I understand."

"No, unfortunately not, Mistress. I never knew my mother, and I was still a boy when father died."

"Emlyn said he had taken you in at a young age." I note a flicker of irritation which she covers with a further question, "Do you have family, other than Emlyn. A wife, perhaps?"

"No Mistress, I am not married. There is only Emlyn, I'm afraid."

"Do you not get along?" Her eyes question.

I huff nonchalantly. "Emlyn continues to employ me so…" the sentence left unfinished. What can I say, when she is to be married to the man?

"I miss my sister Alys, very much since she married."

I am grateful for the change of subject.

She sits in shadow, her back to the window. I note a rainbow of colours arc around her. Perhaps the fall caused head damage, affecting my eyesight, or the valerian prescribed by her uncle, known to cause hallucinations and visions. I glance around the room to test this theory, but everything else appears as expected. Is she a witch? The thought pops into my head uninvited. I have heard said their appearance can be changed, and an unsuspecting man can be tricked into believing they are fair maidens.

"You have become very pale," she remarks.

"I feel a little discomposed," I apologise. "Please excuse me, Mistress."

She stands. "I will leave, so you may rest."

The bright colours follow her to the door. She pauses, looks back at me, smiles, and inside a spark ignites. I grumble to myself, there is nothing untoward regarding Wren, quite the opposite, but having never bore witness to anything similar before, I consider if others are aware of the unusual light around her, or if it is just me.

The Davis's residence sits within a parcel of land between the villages of Llangadog and Llandovery. A detached stone dwelling, servants housed on the top floor, bedchambers and sewing room on the central landing. There is a drawing room with large leaded casement window to the ground floor, along with the study, and dining room. A long corridor separates the kitchen and pantry from the main house.

I meet Wren in the hall, and we follow a narrow path alongside the house sweeping past the kitchen garden bordered with hedgerow, sparrows darting between the branches fall silent as we pass. It is the first time I have been outside in over a week, and the world feels daunting, but Wren believes the air will benefit my recovery.

"The trees and bushes are budding; I love this time of year," she comments. My pace has notably slowed, strength and stamina not yet restored. Wren glances at me sideways. "Are you continuing with the valerian and turnip extract uncle recommended for the pain?"

"I am hoping to manage without it." Wishing now I had taken it.

"I understand, but if it helps…" She places a hand upon my arm, and my heart overflows from the warmth of her touch. "Come, we shall sit awhile."

She guides me to a secluded arbour with stone pew, strewn with a carpet of pink petals. I brush them to the floor, and we sit, thighs almost touching. It would be gentlemanly to create distance, but relishing the intimacy, I do not. A blackbird chirps sweetly at the tip of a Scots pine, looking to attract a mate. I envy his confidence. Not that it matters, I can do nothing when she is promised to another. Growing accustomed to the scintillating colours, deciding them too beautiful to be sinister, they draw me to her like a moth to light.

We sit in comfortable silence, but she will consider me impolite if I do not make conversation. "You have a beautiful home."

"Yes, it is lovely, I have never lived anywhere else. Have you lived elsewhere Sire, other than Wales?"

"No, Mistress, I have lived in Tenby all of my life."

"It's just…"

"Speak your thoughts."

"Lockhart, it is not a Welsh name."

"No, my mother was of Scottish descent. Before I was born, she made my father swear to give me her family name." I relate the tale told to me in childhood. "Father said it was lucky I was a boy, as otherwise he wouldn't have known what name to give me. He swore my mother knew, though how that could be, I cannot say."

"May I enquire how your mother came to be in Wales?"

"I am not sure, Mistress. I assume her family came to Wales at some point in history, but how far back the connection to Scotland goes, I do not know."

Once rested we leave the grounds and walk beside a meandering stream flowing as effortlessly as our conversation. Stories from my childhood make her laugh, the dimple in her right cheek adding to her attraction. I like to make her laugh. I speak of Enid, the nearest I had to a mother. How father spent most of his time working out on the boats, a sailor in his youth and later a fisherman. I have never spoken to anyone with such honesty and openness; it feels easy with Wren.

We stop by a small bridge and Wren speaks without reservation. "They say faeries live in the crevices under the arch." She dips her head. "You must think I am foolish, to believe such things."

Her rainbow of light sparkles in the sunshine and I ache to hold her, protect her. "There are many Welsh legends which suggest you could be correct, Mistress Wren, not everything is always, what it seems." I hope Emlyn does not oppress her endearing charm.

Beyond, sheep graze in the field, chewing the bounty of grass in enviable contentment. I lean against the bridge for support, overcome by light-headedness. I gaze at the distant trees, note a sparkling green haze. I focus more intently, but they become less distinct, leaves and branches melding into a green cloud. I turn my attention back to the sheep, pale shapes without definition, no longer solid. My head spins, everything merging in front of me. I slow my breathing to restore calm and close my eyes.

"Are you feeling unwell?"

I open my eyes. Wren looks concerned. I am grateful to see the sheep and trees appear normal again. “I am well, Mistress.” I lie. “Just need a moment more to rest.”

With an urge to connect with the ground I crouch on my haunches, placing a hand on the grass, feigning interest in a red dragonfly basking in the sun by a patch of small blue flowers. Impulsively taking the dagger at my belt, I dig them up, brushing off loose soil, and offer them to Wren.

“Forget-me-not.” She smiles, her mesmeric eyes holding me entranced. “Thank you, Lockhart.”

Unspoken words clutch my throat, my collar tight. I rake a hand through my hair, unsure of the appropriateness of conveying the messages of my heart but know, this is the only woman I will ever love. “I hope Mistress, Wren, I do not speak out of turn.” I kick the ground with the toe of my boot, reminding me of Edwin at the castle. The delicate blue flowers in her hand childish, and confidence deserts me. “I wish I could stay longer.” I fail to meet her eyes. “Despite the circumstances, it has been a pleasurable stay.”

The moment lost; a fate sealed.

Chapter 4

Lockhart

Dapples of sparkling sunshine filter through the summer leaves of Sycamore, Beech and Ash. Rustling whispers of a warm breeze drift in across the ocean. Searching in my mind through Shakespeare's Forest of Arden, for my damsel, Wren. I quote, "Can one desire too much of a good thing?" I remembered seeing the same book Wren read from in Emlyn's small library, and stole it, hiding it in my chest. The books are purchased simply for him to appear learned.

I am almost home after collecting taxes in Kilgetty. I enter Tenby's protective walls, with no intention of reporting back to Emlyn until I have quenched my thirst. Trotting through the town to the back of the Black Horse Tavern. I tether the fawn horse. She is temperamental, nothing like Caprice, tugging on the reins to free herself.

"For goodness's sake, you can tell you belong to Emlyn, you're as annoying as him."

I enter the dark gloom of woodsmoke and stale beer. Hazy rays of sunlight streak through the bubble glass window, and I sit alone with my thoughts and a tankard of ale, back resting against the rough stone wall. I find myself thinking of Niamh, Emlyn's second wife. A scrap of a girl, with an Irish brogue, farcical and annoying as a Jay's cry, but still. You would be blind not to notice the bruises, and deaf not to hear the rumours. At the time I chose to look away. Shame punches me in the stomach. Now I fear the same fate befalling Wren. Derision for my brother spreads like mould under my skin. It is equally possible, I argue with myself, that Wren's sunny disposition can relieve Emlyn's grief for Angharad. What does it matter? I sigh loudly. Emlyn is right, I have nothing to give a woman, especially one as refined as Wren. Without land or money, what could I offer her? It is pointless bemoaning the circumstances, I decide. Wren belongs to Emlyn; I must accept that. Though convincing my heart may take a little longer. Yet something about the upcoming wedding doesn't add up.

"Just get on with whatever is needed, but do not be too frivolous."

"Are you paying for the wedding? Is it not usual, for the bride's father to do so?"

"Must I again remind you of your station brother?" My mind replays our conversation.

It is warm in the tavern, orange flames blaze in the fireplace, and I unfasten my leather jerkin; Gladys did an excellent job repairing the damage. In the pocket I unexpectedly find a sprig of lavender. Recalling the old woman, I cannot fathom how she got it into my jerkin without me noticing. Guilt curdles in my belly. I shouldn't have been so harsh; she meant no harm. I sniff the dry stalk; a faint floral scent remains. Although I am not superstitious, it is said to bring luck, and I could certainly do with that. I shove it back in my pocket.

"Busy in here today. Mind if I join you?" A stout gentleman indicates to a vacant stool beside me.

"Yes, Sire, of course, excuse me I was within my own head." I offer as explanation for the blank stare.

"Mabon Price." The stranger extends his hand. "Visiting relatives." We shake, the doffing of hats now seen as subservient. "The wife's cousin," he continues. "We have travelled from Pontypool; a tiring trip, and a nice drop of the fair liquid is most needed." Raising his tankard, I follow the formality, exchanging polite conversation about the weather and state of the roads, relieved when he finally falls silent.

I return to contemplating the colours I observe around people. My previous assumption that they were unique to Wren is unfounded. I slowly ascertained that everyone has something similar. Not always clear, but if the sun catches a certain angle, or I concentrate without force, they are visible. It confuses and worries me. Wren's colours are brighter than any other and I consider if this is due to my attraction, if this affects what I see. I stroke my growing beard, which I have kept because Wren liked it. How am I feeling now? Distress, I pinpoint, but why? I glance at Mabon, noting a dark grey shadow swirling around his shoulders, laced with maroon, edged in lighter grey. Sadness, ill health. A cold slither of panic snakes up my spine. How could I know that? I swallow, my heart threatening to leap from my chest. My instinct is to flee, but I am thwarted by the paralysis of anxiety. Taking a large gulp of ale, I notice my hand shaking, my mouth dry as straw, and consider if alcohol is the cause of these delusions. Dismissing the idea, my mind whirls. You only surmise to understand the meaning of the colours, perchance you are wrong. Or maybe, going mad. Visions of life as a beggar, a lunatic, feared by those once considered friends, fill my head. Calm down Lock, use this opportunity to prove your mettle.

"Pardon me for being so forward, Sire." I run a trembling sweaty palm through my hair. "May I enquire the reason for your visit? Your wife's cousin, did you say?"

Mabon's jovial expression softens. "Not good reasons I can tell you that Sire. Between you and me," he looks around briefly, "she has only days left; wife is taking it badly; very close they are."

"I am sorry to hear that, Sire."

"Yes, a sorry situation indeed. Incredibly young, poor woman, a dreadful shame, and I am not a well man myself; the journey has taken its toll." He rubs a hand over his chest, where I note another shadow. A heart condition. "In fact," Mabon downs his ale, "I best get back."

A smoky grey trail follows him. I rub my eyes with the heels of my hands. This cannot be real. It is impossible. Seeing colours, I can put down to my eyes playing tricks. This development, sensing emotions, even ailments, is terrifying and intriguing, or perhaps merely a barb. My eyes rove the tavern, looking for candidates to conduct an experiment. Spotting a group of men standing by the bar, I mentally reach out to them. Bevan, the barrow boy is surrounded by a translucent cloud of greyish blue anxiety. Robert, who works down Sergeants Lane with the blacksmith, and walks with a limp after an accident many years ago, has a thick blob of red around his knee, and I sense pain and inflammation. Some men I cannot distinguish, hidden behind an impenetrable wall, but with others their feelings are clear. Amazed by this new skill my eyes land on the dark recess at the back of the tavern, where a group of French sailors docked in the harbour after unloading a shipment of wine and salt hunch over a table, smoking tobacco in clay pipes, speaking in their native tongue. Will language be a barrier? I concentrate. Deep red, like dried blood, mingled with black, a thick fog hanging above their heads, no separation between one man and another, a spiral of anger, frustration, and tension. It spreads around them, and across the floor, creeping up the legs of tables and chairs and feet of unsuspecting victims. What began as an investigation is slipping beyond my control, emotions and visions I cannot switch off. Fear clutches my throat and stomach. I need to get out. I weave unsteadily through the throng and tumble through the door. Leaning against the wall of the tavern, deeply breathing salty sea air to steady myself. I clamber into the saddle, blindly leading the mare through the town, out through the south gate, and canter down to the castle beach.

Tying the horse to a wizened bush bent by strong Atlantic winds, a crescendo of waves rumbles in my ears. I make my way to an opening in the rock of St. Catherine's Island. A sheltered spot, only visible at low tide. This is a place to hide from the world, where I have returned since childhood. I squat, drawing circles in the wet sand with my finger, the way I did as a boy. I lean back against the rock. The sky is awash with cloud, except for one circular gap like an opening to the heavens, brightening the distant hills with rays of sun. I barely notice these beautiful wonders, always too busy to stop, rest, and absorb the scene. Living in Tenby creates complacency. I easily forget how lucky I am to live here. Wales is magical, and all I have known. As a boy my tad captivated me with stories of foreign climates and strange lands. Of mountains covered with snow. Despite this, he often remarked that everywhere paled in comparison to Tenby. So why would I want to be anywhere else? I sigh, unanchored after the changes in me over which I have no control. Adrift, isolated, and alone. "I am a soldier trained for war, the hilt of a sword at my hip. I don't know anything else." Lately, it has lost its appeal. Is this due to the change in war? The skill of the sword becoming secondary since the introduction of muskets. After all, I reflect, a single gunshot can instantly kill. "Perhaps I am a coward. The blood of men on my hands not so enticing after all." But doubts about my vocation, only part of the problem. Seeing misty colours, sensing emotion is nothing short of terrifying. I run a hand through my hair. "What is wrong with me? I do not understand any of it." I close my eyes, breathing slowly and deeply, concentrating on the rise and fall of crashing waves, calming the eddy of thoughts. Slowly, I relax…

Hearing a voice I open my eyes, raising myself to standing. A shadowed face appears around the side of the rock and covering my eyes with a hand to see more clearly, I recognise the frail figure. Of indeterminate age, loose weathered skin on a skeletal frame. Grey wiry hair frames a long face. Often heard mumbling, he is known locally as a seer, who is sought for advice or predictions of the future and easily dismissed, if his answers do not fit. Thin tight lips and small smile reveal his few remaining teeth. Cocking his head on one side, his smile turns to a frown, and he looks perplexed, as if eyeing a creature never encountered before.

Uncomfortable under his gaze, embarrassed at being found in this space under the rock, I ask, "Are you alright Ranulf?"

He points a bony finger at me. "Sire Lockhart, are you not?"

"You know very well who I am." I scowl.

"I thought I did, but, well, this is a surprise." Ranulf grins. "Not what I expected, very unusual in fact." Ranulf is looking at something over my shoulder, and I twist my head, finding nothing but wet rock and sand.

"Unusual, how so?" I keep the conversation light. "Are you seeing things again Ranulf?"

"Seeing things, oh yes, and so are you." Ranulf sweeps a hand. "You see the mist, don't you?"

I laugh nervously. "I don't know what you mean."

"Colours, you see colours around people. It is not developed, you suppress it, fear it. You have them too, clearer than I have ever seen. How could I not have noticed before?" I swallow my rising apprehension. "Abilities also, use them wisely Sire Lockhart."

"I need to get back." I brush sand from my breeches, unnerved by the day's events, but he is stood in the opening and grabs my arm as I try to pass, his green eyes bright and alert against his grey pallor.

"You are in danger," he says, as though the touch reveals something hidden. "Take this." Ranulf places something within my palm, closing my hand around it. "Keep it with you, it will afford you protection."

I pull away from his grip, eager to escape his intense stare. "You are as crazy as they say Ranulf." Fearful thoughts run amok, and I make my way back across the sand.

Ranulf shouts after me, "Follow your heart on the night of the storm, for your past nor your future, is set in stone."

Chapter 5

Wren

The barbican towers of the north gate loom up ahead. I stare dispassionately beyond the curtained carriage at the menacing Goscar rock, erupting from the sand like a grim manifestation of my fears. A lone gull perched atop, takes flight, dipping low, then rising, sailing on a current of warm air. I envy its freedom. The horses are fidgety, awaiting the gate to open fully, eager to be on their way, and I want to scream, to turn and run, cry out at the injustice. I do none of these things and simply sit with my hands cupped on my lap in compliance. My eye is drawn to the castle on the hill, grey walls daunting and disconcerting. One section is little more than a ruin, large holes in the roof, slates missing. Why anyone would choose to live there, I cannot understand. Yet here I am, about to make it my home. Even on this bright August morning, it chills me. Entering the oppressive town walls, folk stand aside for the horses, stretching, hoping to be the first to view the new bride, and gossip, sharing comparisons to Emlyn's previous wives. I sit back out of view, and bite my lip, ordering the tears not to fall.

I am greeted by a scrawny man with bent legs. Emlyn's personal aid offers a hand to my elbow. Bile catches in my throat as I step from the carriage, onto the dry gritty soil of my new life. Gethin walks ahead. My eyes remain fixed forward, my dress brushing the walls of the narrow corridors, and curved stone steps that lead to the upper floor. Gethin indicates an open door with a hand movement, and I move into the centre of the room. My eye drawn to the bed, drapes tied to each post, revealing a heavily embroidered coverlet of a blue so dark, to be almost black. Adorned with golden flowers and pale green leaves, it is not to my taste. Across from the bed is an ornate fireplace in grey Welsh stone, cold and dreary without the warmth of a lit fire. There is a small leaded window, too high for me to see through. My eye flicks to a small round wooden knob, almost hidden within a panel beside the bed. Perhaps a connecting door, do Emlyn's chambers lie beyond? I am not a child; I know what happens between a man and woman, and the thought of doing such an act with Emlyn turns my stomach.

Gladys teases small white flowers into my black hair, chatting excitedly. "Isn't this wonderful Mistress. My mother has been telling everyone I am to assist your marriage preparations at the castle."

I offer a small smile but cannot help comparing these dismal surroundings to the majestic Pembroke castle, where I attended a summer gala four years past. "I am certainly glad you are here. It is good to have a familiar face." I shiver, despite the heat of the day.

"It will probably just be nerves," Gladys offers as explanation. "You will be fine once outside in the warmth again Miss, it is perfect weather for a wedding."

"I am sure you are right Gladys."

"Goodness," Mother exclaims, entering the room. "Just look at your face, what did I say to you about keeping out of the sun?" I raise my eyebrows, and Gladys stifles a grin. "More powder," Mother demands sternly.

The pale look is old fashioned. The modern style dictates a hint of redness to the cheeks and lips, but I say nothing. Once finally satisfied I am as white as the summer clouds, Gladys helps me to dress, the stays fastened so tight I can barely breathe. Stepping into the gown, it feels heavy on my small frame. Like my heart.

"Beautiful." Mother stands back to admire me. "Take a look." The pale blue taffeta skirt enhances the colour of my eyes. Tiny blue flowers embroidered into the white bodice nips my small waist, but the elegant woman in the mirror, I fail to recognise. The glass reflects a fictitious figure. Numbness seeps into my bones. A winter frost of resignation, hardening my resolve to get through this day.

Wearing a red feather hairpiece, and taffeta of golden brown trimmed with ivory lace, Alys bursts into the room. A mother hen parting the clouds of doom.

"Oh, what a beautiful bride! Enchanting, that's the word." She clucks, her enthusiasm cracking the protective shell around my heart, enough to bring a little warmth. Alys orders me to turn full circle, then embraces me.

"I will leave you two while I prepare." Mother kneads her forehead.

Alys holds my hands; my eyes filling with tears, unable to mask my feelings from my dear sister.

She whispers in my ear, "Wren, are you not happy to be wed today?"

I cannot lie. "Gladys, go and help mother."

Alys ushers her out of the room and returns her focus to me. Words pour out in a torrent of anguish; I cannot prevent them. "I do not want to be here; I do not wish to do this. I do not love him." Tears fall.

"You may, in time," Alys attempts to reassure me, patting my face with a handkerchief. "Often it comes later."

"No." I drop my gaze. "I will never love him."

Alys lifts my chin with a finger to study my face. "There is another?"

I bite my lip.

"Wren, who has stolen your heart?"

"You must not to tell." She pats her chest three times, the way we did as children, a secret promised to be kept. "It is Lockhart, I love Lockhart."

"Emlyn's brother?" Alys asks askance. I nod, covering my face, hiding my shame.

"Oh sister, I am sorry, I had no idea." Alys rubs my arms affectionately. "Is he younger, more attractive?"

"He is everything Emlyn is not."

Alys sighs sincerely. "I can understand your head being turned; you wouldn't be the first in such a position, but my dear Wren, it is going to be very difficult for you, especially living under the same roof."

I voice my frustration, "How am I to spend my life married to Emlyn, knowing my heart belongs elsewhere?"

"We all have our crosses to bear," Alys sympathises. "Rhys is a good husband, but there is no great romance, he is a very practical man. However, I have taken my vows to honour him, as you must to Emlyn."

I shake my head. "I just don't understand why father decided Emlyn is the best suitor for me. Emlyn is, is… a lubber wort." Alys frowns at my description. "Do you think father does not care for me because I have been outspoken? Is he punishing me?"

Alys considers thoughtfully, "I cannot say why father has chosen this for you, but now he has, what choice do you have?"

"But it is unfair, I know my own mind."

"What can we do though dear Wren, only make the best of it."

"I could refuse."

"You know you cannot. To do so would bring embarrassment to father. He would have every right to exile you for the humiliation, and Emlyn, imagine how he would react. He would ensure you were never wed. Spread rumours of you being other than chaste, such would be his anger."

"So, I am to go ahead just to save face, to ensure the men are not put in an awkward position?"

"At least this way," Alys offers, "you will be able to see Lockhart."

Chapter 6

Lockhart

In breeches of the darkest green, best hose and off-white linen shirt, I add a sage brocade doublet and wide collar, fiddling clumsily to fasten the ties and straighten the tassels. Rummaging in my chest for the small hand mirror, I move the leather jerkin to one side and notice Angharad's book. *The Man in the Moone*. Years tumble away. I had been sent by Emlyn to his wife's chambers, for some reason I can no longer recall, but spying the book on Angharad's trestle, the temptation was too hard to resist.

She found me flicking through the pages and asked, "Do you read?"

Unsure if I was embarrassed at being unable to read, or being caught, I shook my head. I had been ten and seven. Angharad was not beautiful, in the conventional way. Her nose a little too long, her lips a little thin, but she was dignified, and I admired her greatly.

"Would you like to learn?" she had offered, instructing me every Tuesday evening thereafter, helping me to piece the words.

It is said the work is fictional, but I like to believe there is some truth in the tale. That a man can travel to the moon on the trail of swans. Angharad said the earth having a magnetic pull, as documented in the book, held scientific proof. The story still holds a deep fascination for me, and I have tried to continue learning the written word. Any free moment I stare at the letters, comparing them against Shakespeare's work, but mostly it makes little sense. Words I cannot pronounce or understand the meaning. Without help it is a struggle. Yet sometimes something leaps from the page, and I have found myself wondering if Angharad is aiding me from on high. "Why are you thinking of Angharad, today of all days?" I scold myself, replacing the book and finding the mirror. Its heavy wooden frame passed onto me when Angharad purchased a decorative replacement. She was particular on the importance of appearance, and often reprimanded me, in a light-hearted manner, on my state of attire. "How do you expect to turn a girl's eye looking dishevelled?" I miss her. In the glass a familiar face looks back, and I lift my top lip to reveal the chipped front tooth, replaying the ricochet of my jaw at the impact of Jarin Evans fist. I run my tongue across the indent, considering if Wren minds. Frowning at my reflection, I recite the section of Shakespeare which I have mastered. "Then shall you know the wounds invisible. That loves keen arrows make."

A knock, and Gethin's voice through the door. "Are you ready Sire? Governor Edwards is asking where you are, we need to get to the church."

Inhaling deeply to steady my nerves, I open the door. "Well, I am here now. Shall we go?"

Streaks of sunlight shine through the large stained-glass window, illuminating the altar and chancel steps, in shades of yellow. The only indication of the heat of the day, beyond the cold stone walls of St. Mary's church. A scattering of people, mainly dignitaries and castle staff, are chatting in hushed voices. Vacant pews indicate that the people of Tenby, are making their feelings known. Wren's mother is fiddling with her gloves. A gangly woman, taller than her husband by a good two inches, and round shouldered, reminding me of a cowering dog. Wren is more like her father in build. Her sister, Alys, is sat with husband Rhys, the pair, of equal stature, fit together well. Having been wed over two years, no children have yet come forth. There's still time. Glancing over my shoulder, the bands of colour around the congregation, something I have become accustomed to seeing, appear brighter than usual, though insignificant compared to Wren's iridescent shimmering light, which holds a depth of hue unlike any other. A small smile creeps upon my lips, and I consider again, whether emotion affects what I see. I shake the image from my head. What am I doing, thinking of Wren, in a church, on her wedding day? But the longing refuses to depart. Thinking of her with Emlyn pains me in a way I have never experienced. Am I just jealous? Sitting beside Emlyn, our thighs touch in the narrow pew, and I try to move away a little.

"Stop fidgeting," Emlyn hisses.

Maybe Emlyn and Wren will not have children, I scoff, but retract the thought, fearing what may happen to Wren if she does not produce a son. I stare disdainfully at Emlyn, note an absence of colour, merely a misty grey. Sadness, health issues? No, this is darker than I saw around Mabon. Cold, deep as an ocean, hiding what lurks beneath. I rake a hand through my hair and Emlyn glares.

Whispers settle into a hush; the way birdsong is silenced by a circling buzzard. Emlyn and I make our way to the front of the nave. She is here, and others are turning to look, but I cannot. I envision pushing Emlyn out of the way and marrying Wren myself. The uproar that would cause. She reaches Emlyn's side, and I cannot help but glance. Her black hair pinned in a fashionable bun, her arc of rainbow shimmering in the sunlight.

I distract myself from the proceedings, admiring the arched wooden ceiling structures. Carvings of mermaid, fish, and beasts decorate each join, believed to be seventy-five, in all. I study the reflections on the wall, cast by the candle to my right, flickering shadows. My lower back aches, and realising the stiffness of my posture, the tension in my rigid jaw, I adjust position. I focus my attention on the minister, a gaudy man with a hooked nose and pointed chin.

Cloud covers the sun, the church darkens.

"I now pronounce you, husband and wife."

The door to my heart slams shut.

Sat to Emlyn's right at the head table, the feast of pheasant and game does not appeal, and I push the food around my plate.

"Cromwell is a fool, believing he has any chance of overthrowing the king," Emlyn scoffs.

I am only half listening, unable to quell the nagging feeling I have just made a dreadful mistake. The serving maid appears beside me and curtsies. "Yes, what is it?" I snap.

She blushes, and I regret the harshness of my tone. "Cook asked me to enquire if the food is to your satisfaction Sire."

I glance at the full plate. "Tell her the food is exquisite; I just do not have much appetite today." She scuttles away. Emlyn beckons with a furtive eye movement, and I lean in closer to hear above the reverberating voices in the hall. "What is wrong with you?" Emlyn jibes. Flushed red cheeks clash with his breeches and doublet of Ruby velvet. "Your demeanour is more fitting for a funeral than a wedding."

I rub my beard. "A little too much ale last night brother," I prevaricate. Emlyn furrows his brow.

"Well make some effort man." He turns his back to me, bragging of his latest purchase. "A black stallion of good breed, will make a good stud, earn me plenty of coin."

Wren doesn't appear to be eating much either, and I consider if she is overwhelmed with the day, or fearful what the night will bring? Revulsion crawls across my skin like lice in a bed, thinking of her with Emlyn. This is crazy, I rub my temples. She is but a woman, there are plenty more. I may not be the most handsome man in Wales, but I have never had any trouble catching a girl's eye, there are plenty willing. I down a full glass of wine, hastily refilled by the maid, I down that too.

A travelling troupe of actors perform a humorous play, followed by music. Lute, harpsichord and violin. Emlyn guides Wren onto the floor, parading her around the circumference of guests like a prized mare. Her strained smile doesn't fit the easy carefree radiance I recall from our time together; her opalescent rainbow appears somewhat distorted, jagged. I swear Emlyn is leaching the colours.

I am introduced to Alys and her husband, Captain Rhys Llewelyn. We speak at length on the Pequot war in America, with the ease of old friends. "Of course, the English were the victors." Rhys concludes, "The native tribes I understand, fought amongst themselves."

Spotting a fellow captain, he excuses himself, and I find myself alone with Alys. "Are you settled in Hawarden castle?" I instigate conversation.

"It is a fine building," Alys replies courteously. "Much larger than Tenby. Have you travelled there?"

"I haven't, though I once escorted Emlyn to Conwy, that's not far from you, is it?"

"It is some distance, but I can guarantee it will have been a damp visit."

I laugh. "I believe it was. Does it rain there even more than here?"

"Oh yes, much more." I feel she is appraising me. "You are not yet betrothed Sire?"

I am taken aback by such a bold question. "I have not so far had the pleasure of finding a lady to take as my own."

"Is that so?" She frowns, checks over her shoulder, and beckons me closer. "You must promise to take care of Wren."

I am flummoxed. "May I ask why? Do you believe she needs my care?"

"She trusts you," Alys whispers.

I reply with caution, "Of course, I will do what I can, but I am sure Emlyn will ensure her needs are met."

"You don't believe that any more than I do." Alys scowls.

"Continue to enjoy the remainder of the evening." Our eyes fall on Emlyn, and realising Wren is missing, my heart sinks.

"I cannot keep my new wife waiting any longer." He leaves the hall amongst a barrage of lewd comments.

"Make sure she bleeds, Sire," men shout. And women giggle, whispering behind their hands. I down more Madeira, grateful for not being invited to escort Emlyn to the bedchamber, as I had been for his previous marriages.

Chapter 7

Wren

I grip the coverlet tightly to my chest as Emlyn staggers around the room, removing stockings and breeches. Finally slumping on the edge of the bed wearing only his shirt, he belches, and I shudder, sick with loathing, but there is no escape. My former life already blurring.

Without turning to look at me, he asks, "Are you a virgin bride?"

I'm shocked, concerned he has found the hidden pot of blood Alys passed to me, just in case. "A husband expects blood. It is not always forthcoming regardless of your previous conduct." Her words repeat in my head. "Of course, husband." I am irritated he thinks so little of me.

"I will know." He turns and stares at me, asking in conversational tone, "So, what did you and my brother do together when he was injured, and you were alone?"

My heart flips over and over. "I helped care for your brother Emlyn, I felt it was my duty." My cautious reply.

"Humph, I am not blind woman, I saw the way you looked at him today. Do you take me for a fool?" Emlyn climbs onto the bed, drawing the hangings. Trapped in oppressive darkness, he straddles me, and I stiffen, unable to move under his weight, he pulls the coverlet brusquely from my hands. "Am I the first to touch you?" He strokes my face with rough fingers. Every part of me recoils from his touch. Emlyn whispers in my ear, stale alcohol lingering on his breath. "I asked you a question wife."

"You are the first," my voice quivers.

"That better be the truth, but think on this, dear wife. If I ever find you in his bed, I will kill you both."

Emlyn lunges, his tongue forcing its way into my mouth, I struggle not to gag, his hands grope me roughly. Fear is threatening to overwhelm me, but I must not succumb, must distance myself from the impending ordeal. My sense of self, I feel, is reliant on this. He is knelt between my legs, my heart racing with horror. I feel sick, swear I will vomit, when I make the decision to silently quote Shakespeare. A distraction, a separation of mind from body, a way to disparage Emlyn. Macbeth feels most fitting. Present fears are less than horrible imaginings. I quickly recite another. False face must hide what the false heart doth know.

"Do you wish it were Lockhart taking you? Oh dear, poor Wren, you got the rotten apple, but knowing I am hurting you, and him, is double the pleasure for me."

I bite my lip as he forces himself into me. Pinned beneath him, barely able to breathe, I pray: for it to end, for him to stop. My mind searches for a further quote. Things bad begun make story themselves by ill. Finally, a groan leaves his throat, and he slumps, crushing my lungs. Heavy breathing in my ear slowly settles, and he moves away without a word, turning his back. I lie still, fearing any movement will disturb him and it will begin again, until grunting snores echo around the confined space. Slipping my hand beneath the pillow, the contents of the jar spill onto the crisp linen. "Blood will have blood." I whisper Macbeth. "What's done cannot be undone." Swallowing the bile in my throat, I hiss resolutely. "You will not break me Emlyn Edwards. You may be my first, but you will not be my last. Love will find me."

The days have grown short and dark. My initial hope of finding at least contentment, if not happiness, has slipped away with the autumn leaves. Silent surrender, under Emlyn's increasing bitterness. He spends a great deal of the day occupied with business, but I am afforded little privacy and wonder daily how I will possibly be able to live a whole lifetime this way. Escorted wherever I go by two female guardians, appointed by my husband. Attired in black, they hover at each shoulder. Crows awaiting meaty titbits, to regurgitate for Emlyn. My every movement and expression is recorded in their dark eyes. Daydreams have become my only means of escape. Behind closed eyes, I imagine a more equal society, without pomp and ceremony. As my true self, I tend plants and flowers, soil trickling through my fingers. Within the confines of my bed, hangings drawn against the light of day, I can almost smell the sweet aroma of honeysuckle, feel the soft apple blossom caught in my hand, plucked by the breeze, showering the land in pink petals, such is the clarity of my imagining. Sometimes I dare to add Lockhart to the scene. He is always attentive and kisses me tenderly, love radiating in his blue eyes. This is the one thing Emlyn can never give me, and I crave most of all. The look, which passes between those truly in love. Others would believe me foolish. What can be more important, they may say, than fine furnishings and jewels? Romance does not put food in your stomach, nor a roof over your head. Today I am out of sorts, nips of guilt. After all, Emlyn doesn't physically beat me, just treats me roughly, and as my husband this is his right. I do not believe this is how it should be, but it is the way. I rub the bruises on my arm. I never expected Emlyn to be a doting husband, but during our brief meetings before marriage, I had thought to have the measure of him. A bully, but he had shown kindness towards me. Jealousy. You cannot force someone to love you, and Emlyn knows that. Unable to disguise my feelings for Lockhart, he makes me suffer. I wonder if Lockhart is aware of my unhappiness. I saw him yesterday. My heart plummeted, and I averted my eyes, afraid my guardians would see the longing in me, to touch him, to speak of my love, of my sadness. He observed the bruising on my wrists, I am sure, his eyes narrowed, questioning, and instinctively I pulled the lace of my sleeves lower, for what could he say, when I am Emlyn's wife, Emlyn's property?

I have found that if I drag my chest beneath the window, I can see a beach beyond the castle. My guardians always remove it, and I always put it back. I stand here now on tiptoe, watching the fiery orange sun slipping into the horizon, spreading shimmering light across the water. "What should I do?" I whisper to the ocean, pulled by a retreating tide, leaving small shells upon the shore, and I would love to be out there collecting them, examining each one. Maybe I would find a jewel and grasp it in my hand and make a wish, to follow the setting sun to a new place, a new beginning. The jewel would buy my passage on a fine ship. I imagine offering it to the captain. I sigh, returning to reality. Perhaps if I speak to Lockhart, explain my plight, beg him to find a way for me to escape? Or maybe escape together. No, I dare not hope, it would be unfair to put Lockhart in such a situation. Why would he go against his brother for me? Yet I long to converse privately with him, the way we did when he was injured. I quote *Romeo and Juliet* in a murmur, "Under loves heavy burden do I sink."

I return to my bed and curl my feet under my gown like a child, making myself small, for the night-time I fear the most. I gain no pleasure, but Emlyn is insistent I provide a son. I am hopeful he will then leave me alone. A physical pain has lodged within my heart. "Lockhart," I breathe wistfully. "I don't understand how I care so deeply for you, it is foolish, but my heart insists." I hold to my chest the posy of forget-me-knots, saved between a folded piece of parchment. Remembering how our hands brushed, lightning fire shooting through me, taking my breath away. Praying he may utter all I longed to hear. That he cared deeply, and we would run away together, far from here, from Emlyn. But he did not, and I am left to consider if the feelings are not mutual, as I hoped, or if circumstances are all that prevent his acknowledgement.

Glistening tears blur my vision.

"Why am I unable to choose who I love, who I marry?"

I thump my pillow, a half-remembered poem, written over a hundred years ago by the female Welsh poet, Alis Wen, comes to mind. I and Alys often recited it as young girls, the similarity to our two names, and the dream of romance, had spoken to us. "Beautiful, accomplished, splendid, if he can be had, and brave, to strike where there need be; a youth in age, wall strong, and a man of the finest body to be had."

I swallow the lump welling in my throat. "My father told me this, that best for me is to love a repulsive man, yet the heart asks for a lad pure, lovely, and light of its own." Just as Alis Wen held a view of marriage quite different to that of her family, I too value qualities other than the status and security provided by an older man, and my role, to be a dutiful wife and provide an heir. A deep dark pit of despair festers in my stomach.

"I wish you were dead Emlyn Edwards," I whisper, unable to prevent a low guttural groan. Hiding my face in the pillow to muffle the sound, salty tears streak my face, slipping under my chin and into my ears.

Chapter 8

Lockhart

In the Black Horse Tavern, Aelwen edges through the men huddled around the golden firelight, cocooned from the first frost of autumn, glistening beyond the four walls. "I will get these," I offer, emptying coins from my pouch. A smooth black stone sits amongst them. "What do you think this is?" I hand it to Merek.

Turning it over in his palm, he shrugs. "Where did you get it?"

Aelwen places the tankards of ale on the table.

"Ranulf gave it to me." Aelwen snatches the stone, holding it up in the dim light. "Did Ranulf say anything to you?"

"No," I bluff. "Why?"

"Because I think it is black onyx, which is said to offer protection. Perhaps he has instilled it with magic," she gibes.

I snatch it back. "Don't talk rubbish Aelwen. I doubt it's anything other than what it appears, a pebble from the beach." Even so, I shove it in my pocket, deciding no harm can come of it.

Perched on the stool in my room, rubbing the shiny black stone between my fingers, I add the last log to the fire. Why would Ranulf think I need protection? And from what, or whom? He said I have a light around me, as I see around others. I rummage in my chest for the mirror, but with only a faint glow from the firelight, it merely reflects shadow. What had Ranulf meant, that I have abilities? Am I some sort of wizard? Is that why I see colours? Does the stone hold magic as Aelwen suggests? My mind flits to Ranulf's talk of a storm, but nothing makes sense. "I guess I will have to keep an eye on the weather and be extra vigilant when a storm is brewing." A loud knock on my door at this late hour makes me jump.

"Sire, Governor Edwards wishes your attendance immediately." Gethin sounds distressed.

Opening the door, I scan the corridor. "A problem?"

Gethin stands awkwardly in his nightgown, bulbous blue veins on pale spindly legs. "Please hurry."

Entering Emlyn's private chambers, Gethin retreats, closing the door. Shadowed in the darkened room, Emlyn is stood with his back to the fire, atmosphere thick as tar. "Is something wrong Emlyn?" He is guzzling the contents of a tankard, wiping his mouth on his sleeve.

"Good of you to join me, brother." He hurls the pewter cup in my direction.

I dodge, the remaining contents splashing my face and clothing. It slams against the wall with a thud, clattering onto the stone floor. "What was that for?" I exclaim, wiping my face.

He staggers drunkenly. "You honestly think I cannot see Lock? You undermine me at every turn, and after everything I have done for you."

I step forward. "You are making no sense brother."

Emlyn draws his sword, and I halt abruptly, hand instinctively moving to the hilt at my hip. Emlyn waves his sword indiscriminately. "You were little more than a child when father died," he laments. "His last wish, the request I take you in. Have I not provided you with a home, shelter from the world? Trained you as a soldier, to ensure a wage?" he is shouting. "A room of your own, to retreat and be alone. A horse, which you then forfeit." His fist is clenched around the sword. "Nothing is enough for you; you throw it back in my face." Emlyn shakes his head, laughs dryly, lowers his sword and pours another drink, spilling most of the contents, swaying unsteadily to the seat by the fire.

Hunched over in the darkness, the resemblance to our father is striking. He sits in silence, and I consider my reply with care, a wrong turn of phrase may instigate further aggrievance. "Do you believe me ungrateful?"

"The deceit Lockhart, that is the worst of it," he replies without taking his eye from the flames.

"I haven't deceived you brother, what makes you think so? Oh wait, let me guess. Tom Griffiths, what nonsense has he put in your mind? I wouldn't trust him, sly as a fox he is. He will try anything to get what he wants."

"Shut up," Emlyn snaps. "I don't need Tom Griffiths to express your short comings, I am well aware, oh, so very aware of your lies." Emlyn raises his sword, examining the blade, the steel glints in the firelight. My hand returns to the cold hilt by my side, warming in my sweaty palm. "My wife." The raw emotion in Emlyn's voice surprises me, and my heart tightens. "You knew how much I loved her." I try to organise my thoughts.

"I am confused, brother."

Emlyn turns to me, eyes alight with anger. "Every Tuesday evening, for the last two years of her life, you met, alone. Why was that?"

The implication clicks, and I shake my head vehemently. "Angharad, do you mean, are you suggesting? You cannot seriously think we were, that we were…"

"The gift of a mirror. That was not to ensure you were presentable, before you, attended her," Emlyn growls.

If I say the wrong thing now, I am spent. He will come at me, and we will fight, and regardless of our verbal spats, we have never, come to blows. It's the last thing I want.

"Tell me, dear brother, did she make you a man?" Emlyn spits into the fire, expelling the words.

"I swear there was nothing between me and Angharad, on my life I swear. For goodness's sake, man, she was teaching me to read." Emlyn meets me with silence, and a hardened stare. I hurry on. "Is that why you despise me? Because you believe I slept with your wife?"

"What I need to know Lock; is why you take every woman I love? First mother, then Angharad, who knows, maybe Niamh, and now, Wren."

I am scrabbling for the right words. "There was nothing between me and Angharad, nor Niamh, and as for Wren," I falter. "I have never, touched her."

Silence stretches, every heartbeat widening the chasm between us. "Do you love her?" The catch in Emlyn's tone grips my heart in a vice, and desperately I search for a bridge to cross, a way to reach out to him. "Emlyn, I…"

"Don't." Emlyn glowers. "Don't lie to me, just, go. Vacate this castle by dawn." I remain rooted, a heavy weight sinking into the depths of my stomach, words fail me. "Get out Lock." Emlyn sighs wearily, his head drooping forward.

"Emlyn, I swear…" I begin weakly.

Emlyn turns, his eyes dark. "I said, get out."

Closing the door softly, I thump the heel of my hand against my forehead. I didn't handle that well. Stomach churning with anxiety, I reexamine the conversation. Emlyn obviously didn't believe me. Perhaps I should have lied, to protect Wren. Maybe I should go back and explain. Explain what, I chastise. That I am very sorry but have unfortunately fallen in love with his wife.

I pace my room, a barrage of thoughts flit around my head like annoying summer flies. Where can I go? Will I even make it through the night or be dragged from my bed? Hung, shot. I gulp. What about Wren, what will he do to Wren? I cannot allow her to be used as a bartering tool between us, but how do I get her away from Emlyn? I stare into the flames, wisps transformed from gold and orange, to puffs of grey smoke, stretching to the coolness of the chimney, to their death. A memory flickers into awareness. I was aged seven or eight, in the copse up a tree. On a branch, three small speckled blue eggs lay in a nest, just beyond reach. The next thing I recall, a bright light filled my vision which I slowly ascertained contained a woman encased within. She smiled warmly and I felt no fear as she reached out her hand to me. With no recollection of what happened next, when I opened my eyes, she was gone, and I was on the floor beneath the tree, twigs and leaves in my hair. I must have fallen. The sun was almost set, and I was fearful of the consequences of being away so long. I remember standing easily, surprised to feel no pain, not even a scratch. I never told anyone. Who would believe me? I thought of her often for a long time after, believed she was an angel who came to help me, but haven't thought of her for years. So why now? Are angels real, can they be called upon to do our bidding? Would it be worth trying, for Wren? Not sure I am deserving of divine intervention, but deciding anything is worth a try, I fall to my knees, holding my hands in prayer. "If there are angels, please present a way to help Wren, show me what to do."

I open one eye, having fallen asleep clothed. The half-light of dawn encapsulates my room in a pale-yellow glow. I hear raised voices and hastily pull on my boots, grabbing my sword, tying it at my hip. Opening the door, a little, to assess the situation, fearing there are soldiers coming for me.

The door to Emlyn and Wren's chamber is open and from within I hear a man shout, "Get out of bed."

Fearing Wren victim of rough treatment, I run. Reaching the open door, I see Emlyn on his knees, a man pulling his hair, forcing his head back, a dagger pressed to his throat. Wren holds the bed coverlet tightly against her, face frozen in terror, but appears unhurt.

"Lock," Emlyn begs in a small voice, "save me."

Drawing my blade, I cautiously step into the room. A man lies in wait behind the door and grabs me from behind twisting my arm painfully. My sword crashes to the floor. I am forced backwards by the hulk, veins protruding on his neck and muscled arms. My head is between his hands, and he slams it hard against the rough stone wall, over, and over. The crashing of my skull reverberates through my whole body. When he releases me, I slip, dazed, to the floor. Emlyn cries out as the man yanks harder on his hair.

"You think you are above everyone, that you can do as you wish without consequence." Emlyn's face distorts with pain. The man turns, smiling, a toothless grin.

My attacker on the road to Llandovery. I am at a loss to understand what is happening, or the reasons, and endeavour to scramble to my feet, but I cannot. My chest feels heavy, compressed, like a weight is pushing against it. I try again to drag myself from the floor, but every attempt intensifies the feeling. My lungs are burning, on fire, crushed by an unseen source. Heartbeat thudding in my ears, pressure building in my head, my breathing shallow and painful. I wonder if I am having a seizure of the heart, and screw my eyes shut. Opening them I find the room sheathed in a dreamy haze, interspersed with pinpricks of flashing light, connecting strands fine as spider webs. I feel part of it, enmeshed within. I blink several times to focus, my eye locking on Emlyn. A wave of compassion ripples through me, the bridge connecting us as brothers abruptly reawakens, the chasm receding. Determination to save Emlyn impels my anger against the force on my chest. Whatever this is, get off me. I feel a shift, and realise the more will I have, the more resolute to be free, the less hold it has. In my right ear a women's voice whispers, "Lockhart, do not interfere, allow fate to take its course." I twist my head to the side, but no one is there.

"Aargh." Emlyn's stark anguished cry pierces the air. I jerk my head back, see the dagger tracing a bloodied line across his throat, spurting as the jugular is torn, reddening my shirt with his blood. The man releases Emlyn, his body crumpling like a discarded rag.

"Come, we are done here." He kicks Emlyn and turns to the door.

"What about him?" The burly man motions to me.

The toothless attacker squats by my side, wiping the blooded dagger on my sleeve, his breath of rotten meat. "In fact, the law requires that nearly everything be cleansed with blood, and without the shedding of blood there is no forgiveness. Hebrews 9:22" He smirks, replacing the dagger in his belt.

It must be a dream, for I sit in surreal silence, transfixed at the horror. The sparkling mesh of lights remain, the mesmerising beauty incongruent with the violent act. A glowing white orb has appeared from the invisible, but I have no fear. Something resembling grey dust motes, as perceived when caught in sunlight, begins rising, from Emlyn's lifeless body, swirling upwards into a column of mist, moving towards the ball of light.

Spellbound I watch them mingle, become vapour.

"Lockhart!" Merek hurtles into the room taking in the scene.

"I'm alright," I reply, "but Emlyn."

Merek sits on his haunches and places a hand upon Emlyn's chest. "His heart is still," he whispers, closing the lids of his unseeing eyes. "May you rest in peace." Noticing Wren, Merek moves to the bed. "Mistress, Wren." He shakes her shoulders. "We must leave." Wrapping a cloak around her shoulders, he helps her into soft slippers, averting her eyes from Emlyn.

"Lockhart!" She kneels beside me, her eyes questioning.

"It is not my blood." I reassure. She touches my arm, and the crushing sensation in my chest subsides. I let out a long sigh, my lungs filling with air. Breathing has never felt so good, the room returning to its normal solidity.

"This is not the time to be resting, Lock." Merek remarks sarcastically, holding out a hand to me. He steps into the corridor, beckons. "Come."

"Where are we going?" I ask as we head down the steps.

"The smugglers passage," he grabs a lantern and indicates for us to follow.

"Should we not stay, protect the castle?" I argue. Leaving is cowardly. Merek dismisses my concern.

"Our soldiers must have been hijacked in the hall whilst they slept. We couldn't defend the castle by ourselves, and we don't want Mistress Wren's life to be put at risk."

We run through the derelict section of the castle. At one time it held criminals awaiting to hang from gallows tree hill. Some say they remain, permeating the stone, trapped behind unseen doors, chained to a distant past. Soft green moss grows on crumbling walls, dark stillness and shadowed forms clinging to every crevice. We enter a section where the walls remain reasonably intact, though part of the roof has collapsed. Merek hangs his lantern on a metal hook, shoving aside a warped wooden panel. It scrapes the floor, revealing a black door of equal height and width. Pulling back the bar holding it shut, he drags it open. It makes a loud creaking. Beyond, a tunnel carved through rock. Merek looks around the chamber briefly before stooping and stepping inside, a brisk nod his signal to follow. Closing the door behind us, aware if someone lies in wait within, there is no way back.

The passageway is dank, even with lanterns, visibility no more than a few feet. Along the cold stone, down many steps, we take a sharp turn to the right. The passage narrows, the floor slanting down, steep in places, the smell of damp hangs in the freezing air. In the gloom of shadowed darkness, it is difficult to see. I cling to Wren's cold hand; afraid she will fall. Ahead, a faint glow becomes visible in the distance. We make our way towards it, coming out into the cave. We know there is a boat hidden, having used it numerous times to row out to a ship and smuggle contraband into the castle. We drag it across the north beach, the town walls behind us. Clouds race across the sky, forced along by the easterly wind, intermittently blocking the watery sun, but I am relieved to see daylight.

We battle with the oars, the small vessel rocking in the rising surf. I am fearful the boat will overturn, or we will drift off course and be swept out to sea. Merek shouts to be heard over the crash of waves. "We will head to Wills Mark."

"Caldey island is closer," I shout back. Wren is shivering and I wish to see her back on solid ground.

"We will be safer with Branwen," Merek reassures.

The island of Wills Mark comes into view, a lone figure on the headland. Several years have passed since I last saw Merek's paternal grandmother, but I know it is her. Rarely venturing into Tenby after being shunned by the family for marrying a man from the island, albeit years hence, from her first husband's death. The news met with a verbal disapproval by Merek's mother, in language I never believed a woman knew, let alone would repeat. Wills Mark is known locally as Gwrach Ynys. Witch Island. Stories of human sacrifice, babies hung by their ankles over a spit. How much is rumour, how much truth I can only guess. When you see an islander in Tenby you look away, for it is told they can steal your soul just by looking into your eyes. That said, many secretly travel across the water, sometimes in the dead of night, to buy tinctures and potions.

We pull the boat onto the shore, and Branwen greets us. The passing years have lined her face, her mane of dark hair flecked with grey. "It has been too long," she reproaches, folding her arms and addressing us with a frown. Merek averts his eye.

Offering Wren a hand to step from the boat, I introduce her, "We are in need of your help, Branwen."

She merely nods, hooking her arm through Wren's. "Come my dear, you will be safe with me."

She wraps Wren in a large shawl and sits her by the fire. "I must prepare a brew." Branwen wanders to the back of the room. We sit in silence until she returns with a cup, adding hot water from a jug by the fire. She hands it to Wren, who holds it in shaking hands.

I sit beside her. "Branwen only uses herbs, like your uncle, it will do you good."

"I guarantee there is nothing which will cause harm," Branwen says. "Mint to calm and soothe, and lavender to aid sleep, that is all."

Wren sips slowly and the drink soon takes effect, her head drooping onto my shoulder. I ache to put an arm of protection around her, to draw her closer.

Branwen serves Merek and I with warm ale. "Who do you believe is behind it?" she asks after we relay details of the events.

"I don't know. Any insight, Merek?"

"Mystified as you." He shrugs.

"Where were our men?" I continue. "Nowhere in sight, it is strange they did not try to alert us, even if they were being held as you suspect."

Merek nods. "The men were not in uniform, their sword skills amateurish, Emlyn it seems, their aim."

"I agree, but the man who murdered Emlyn was the same who attacked me on the road to Llandovery, the other, the one who attacked you. So why not take the opportunity to finish the job, when they had the chance? I do not understand it."

"Nothing about it seems right." Merek shakes his head. "No one tried to stop us leaving."

We pause to reflect.

"How many soldiers has Emlyn disbanded over the last few weeks?" Merek asks.

I shrug. "I'm not sure, why?"

"Certainly, enough to leave the castle vulnerable to attack."

"Are you suggesting he may have known?" I'm shocked. "But he was killed."

"Or double crossed," Merek argues.

I rub my temples, the excruciating pain in my head from being slammed against the wall making it hard to think. Could Merek be right? Did Emlyn know the castle would be sieged? Why would he allow that? He was certainly tired of his responsibilities as governor, and without doubt had coins hidden. With pockets of land in various parts of West Wales, including the acres pledged in the dowry, he wasn't short of options, but why did he not simply step down? I think back to a recent argument with my brother regarding the soldiers, expressing that I believed his decision foolhardy when rumours circulated of an imminent war. He wouldn't listen, never did, believing he always knew better. A trait that ensured his downfall. Was he double crossed as Merek suggested?

"I am sorry, Lockhart." Merek cuts into my thoughts. "I know he was your brother, but the townspeople were struggling to pay the high rents and taxes, whilst he blatantly afforded himself great luxury by comparison."

"Are you suggesting someone we know is behind it, from Tenby? surely not." I feel hollow, spent. "He was the only blood kin I had."

"I'm worried about Aelwen, I must go back." Merek takes up the oars.

"Try to find out about Emlyn for me. Where they have taken him," I plead.

Merek nods, and I push the boat out into the choppy waters. It rises and falls with the waves, reflecting my turbulent mood. An overcast sky, grey as my thoughts. Sombrely I reflect on the passing of time as the boat moves further away, becoming a speck on the ocean. Some days father's death seems weeks ago. The dark stuffy room with closed shutters blocking out the sunlight, like stepping into another world. Father still and silent on the narrow cot, Emlyn weeping beside him. I had never seen Emlyn cry before, nor since. The scene replays. Will Emlyn's death be another memory, forever close as an unwelcome visitor, relived over and over in my mind? His cry, life ebbing away. Yet I did nothing. I did not save him. Guilt lodges in my brain. Yet I swear I was unable, the force of my head hitting the wall must have caused the deception of what I saw, what I heard. I rub the sore lump on my skull and wince. What else could it have been?

I walk closer to the shore, bending to grab a small flat smooth stone. I flick it out to sea, and it skims the surf, one, two, three times. The wind tugs at my hair, blowing it into my face, irritably I tuck it back inside my hat. It reminds me of Wren, the way she tucks stray hair into her coif. A small smile spreads across my lips, and I head back to the shack.

Branwen is stood at the door; hair covered with a woollen shawl. "We need to talk." I glance at the door. "Wren is sleeping."

Following her to a wooden outbuilding, she motions for me to sit on a pile of straw. Dry stalks stick into my breeches, pricking my legs, and I wriggle uncomfortably. Branwen remains standing, her arms folded, eyes narrowed, staring past me, the way Ranulf had. Local gossip suggests Branwen knows things about people, secrets, and predicts the future. Once warning a crew of sailors not to board their ship but wait until the following day. Debris and bodies washed up on the shore a few days later.

"Tell me what you can see." Her face softens, kindly, but my heart hammers, pounded by an inner blacksmith, reshaping, moulding, preparing me. For just maybe, she is my best hope of gaining answers.

"Colours, I see colours around people," I confess.

"Can you see them around me?"

I nod. "Yes, I see blue and purple, violet. What are they Branwen, what do they mean?"

She sits beside me. "I knew you were coming," she says excitedly. "I was told; I just didn't know it would be you."

I am perplexed. "What do you mean?"

Branwen ignores my question. "To think I have known you all your life but was unaware of what you held within."

"Within me?"

"Prowess, to foretell and heal, waiting to be released."

I frown. "Ranulf said I have abilities, is that what he meant?"

Her eyes are animated. "Did he say anything else?" she prompts. I think back.

"He said to follow my heart on the night of the storm, for past nor future is set in stone."

Branwen gasps, covering her mouth. "Do you not see what that means, Lockhart?"

With clarity, I do. "The storm!" I exclaim. "I thought Ranulf meant the weather, but he was referring to the castle being stormed, wasn't he? But… but that means I had the capacity to thwart the attack." A whirlpool of thoughts circle. "I could have prevented Emlyn's death." My heart sinks.

Branwen cocks her head. "We cannot control everything, some events are destined, do not chastise yourself."

"But…" I begin, broken by this revelation.

"No," she reprimands taking my face in her warm hands. "Tell me more." Her eyes lock onto mine, and instantly I am shrouded in a blanket of calm. "What else do you see? Do you see anything around Wren?"

Grateful for the opportunity to unburden, I explain the colourful arc I observe, which faded when she was with Emlyn. Once I start, it pours out like molten lead. How I sense people's emotions, and the way I see the world has changed. "I do not understand any of it."

Her eyes remain focused on mine. "Tell me what happened with Emlyn. Did you see anything when he died?"

I see it clearly, lodged in my mind. "It looked like particles of dust rising from his body. A column of mist."

Branwen nods. "His soul leaving."

My logical brain steps back from this notion. "I do not hold your beliefs of a continual soul; it is madness to think in such a way." A rising panic sickens my stomach. "You are talking rubbish Branwen." Forcing my eyes from her gaze, I stand swiftly. "I have listened to enough of your nonsense." My head is still pounding, and I head to the door.

"Lockhart, wait."

"Leave me alone." I stride briskly back to the shack.

Branwen calls. "When you are ready for the answers, I will be here waiting."

Chapter 9

Wren

Having taken an interest in the shelf of herbs, Branwen is explaining, "Dandelion can be made into a tonic to aid the liver."

From the small window we see Merek pull the boat onto the shore, and hover, chewing his fingernails. My stomach rolls with anxiety.

"Merek is back." Branwen addresses Lockhart, pacing like a caged animal. He turns on his heel to meet Merek at the door, tension creasing his forehead.

"What is happening at the castle? where is Emlyn's body?"

"Let me get in first, I am freezing."

Lockhart drags a stool closer to the fire and Branwen hands Merek a cup of mead. I remain at the back of the room and listen; this is men's business. Nervously tucking stray locks of hair into my coif, I wonder what the people of Tenby are saying of our departure. My unspoken fear is accusations by my guardians of planning Emlyn's demise. Out of spite they would gladly see me hung from a noose on gallows tree hill. Lockhart hunches, elbows on his knees, eager to hear the tale.

Merek shifts uneasily. "Tom Griffiths is the new governor of the castle." Lockhart's mouth falls open. "He reassures me you have nothing to fear in returning to Tenby, neither you nor Wren." He glances at me briefly and hurries on. "On condition you ask no questions." Lockhart's shoulders stiffen, hands balling.

"Tom Griffiths, why does that not surprise me? His intent to overturn Emlyn has been clear since becoming a town councillor." He rakes a hand through his hair. I have noted he does this when nervous or stressed. I find it endearing. "So, I am to pretend nothing is amiss. That my brother was not murdered before my own eyes, and we did not flee from the castle in fear of our lives." He is on his feet, pacing again. "What of Wren, did she not witness her husband taken from her in such a horrific way?"

Emlyn's final gurgling cry is never far from my mind. Nightmares replay all I saw and heard. I did not love him, but for his life to end in such a horrific way, I would never choose. Feeling off kilter by the relived memories I sit on the bench. Branwen sits beside me, rubs my back for comfort. Her empathy astounds me, and I am most grateful.

"Like it or not, this is how it stands, what choice do you have but to accept the situation?" They fall into an uncomfortable silence until Merek pipes up, "There's something else."

"Go on," Lockhart encourages.

"Does she have to be here?" Merek indicates to me. Lockhart frowns.

"She needs to hear the truth, so yes, she does." My heart expands at Lockhart's sensitivity towards my feelings. Merek strokes his beard and sighs loudly.

"There are rumours circulating in Tenby, which suggest Emlyn planned for the castle to be sieged."

Lockhart folds his arms across his chest. "Rubbish, utter rubbish."

"No, it's true, the soldiers were given the night off, told not to return until morning. The staff warned to stay behind closed doors, regardless of what they heard."

"Where you aware of these plans?" Lockhart cocks his head.

"No, of course not." Merek does not meet his eye, and a seed of doubt, plants in my head. Merek presses, "From what I can gather, Emlyn refused to pay the agreed amount, and the men took matters into their own hands."

"No!" Lockhart throws up his hands. "He would not do that, why would he?"

"I know this must be hard for you Lock," Merek sympathises, "but he must have been aware of the unrest amongst the people of Tenby. Townsfolk had been hatching a plan to upsurge him, and no doubt someone informed him of their intention."

"Like Tom Griffiths," Lockhart mumbles.

"Mark my words," Merek continues. "He would not have gotten far. Once the truth of his underhand dealings came to light, he would have been arrested and left to rot in gaol whilst awaiting trial, at least this way…" Merek leaves the sentence unfinished.

"You are telling me to forget what happened, that Emlyn is better off dead?"

My head is spinning, shocked. Emlyn spoke highly of Tom Griffiths, but certainly tired of the castle, the insurmountable repairs were a bone of contention. Emlyn admired the Merchants houses, spoke of acquiring a fine home of his own. The role of custodian for Tenby castle, a means to an end. Was it possible Emlyn had gotten in over his head and struck a deal with Tom? Perhaps the idea was to disappear into the night, taking his wrongdoings with him, allowing Tom to take over. As his wife, I expect he would have taken me, but where? Another town, another country? Away from my family and all I have ever known. Separated from Lockhart. I swallow the bile amassing in my throat, contemplating the fate which may have awaited me, of which I knew nothing, had no say or control over. Women, lower than their husbands in every way, treated as prized jewels or pieces of furniture, without feeling, and with utter contempt.

I notice Merek rummaging in his pocket, coughing to gain Lockhart's attention, leaning forward, whispering so I cannot hear, discreetly dropping something into his hand. Lockhart examines the item covertly, slipping it into his own pocket.

He looks at me, a little embarrassed. "Do you feel able to return to Tenby?"

Unaccustomed to my opinion being sought, yet pleased Lockhart thought to do so, I tuck loose hair into my coif. "Well, I feel the most important thing right now is to go back and bury my husband."

Merek hisses under his breath, albeit loud enough for me to hear. "What do you think you are doing?" Lockhart looks at him blankly. "Asking a woman, have you gone soft man?"

"Emlyn was her husband."

"Yes, and your brother, and as such, you should take control of the situation."

"I am. We are returning to Tenby to bury Emlyn, which is the right thing to do, is it not?"

Merek nods imperceptibly, throws me a look of scorn which shocks me.

"Then let that be the end of it." Lockhart bristles.

Biting frost sparkles in low morning Sun. In the church of St. Mary's, where three months earlier I had been married. Father on my left, Lockhart to my right, rigid as a statue. Most of the pews remain vacant, the people of Tenby failing to come to pay their last respects.

"I am surprised the locals are not lining the streets to cheer," Lockhart comments aggressively.

His usual light blue eyes are as stormy as a grey Welsh sky. His warm breath wisps in the freezing church, and images of a fire breathing dragon come to mind. In truth, I am the dragon, a monster, praying to be free of

Emlyn, I got what I wished for, but at what cost? Never considering the effect losing his brother would have on Lockhart. Without home, work, or family, he merely shrugged when I asked of his plans. I fear he can see through me, to the evil within. The coffin is lowered into the cold dark ground. The minister places a handful of soil into my palm. Offering his last prayers, I sprinkle the grains through my fingers, they make a pitter-patter against the wood. "I'm sorry," I whisper. Heart, numb as my hands and feet, rigid with cold, I can barely walk. Father holds my arm as we depart, guiding me blindly to the awaiting carriage. Stepping inside my heart sinks. Arlet is sat upon the hard wooden bench, shawl wrapped tightly around her. Why had father chosen her? He would know I would prefer Gladys to accompany me home. Perhaps that is why. She gives me that look as I settle beside her. Father is talking to a gentleman outside, and from what I can muster, he has connections to Tom Griffiths.

"I hope Governor Griffiths will see that my family have been left in an unfortunate predicament. I would be extremely grateful Sire, if you would see fit to inform him, I bare no malice, in fact, I am happy to see him in such an eminent position. Nothing more than he deserves."

I hate to think of him kowtowing to Tom, especially knowing the way Lockhart and Merek spoke of their suspicions regarding the castle siege. I wish father would hurry, I would like to be on my way, put it all behind me.

"Mistress." Arlet speaks in a hushed voice.

"Yes, what is it?" I am in no mood for conversation.

"I didn't know you had interest in the black arts." I look at her with a puzzled expression.

"I hear you went to the witch island."

I stiffen. "We had to escape to safety, is there a problem with that?"

"I know now what you are Mistress, and I can help you."

"In what way can you help me?"

Father clambers in. "I think that went well; all things considered."

His smug smile ignites my anger. "Are you referring to the funeral of my husband, or your conversation with the gentleman?"

"Well, erm, both, I suppose. You know this is very inconvenient for me Wren."

He knocks on the carriage and the horses move through the narrow streets and out of the north gate. I don't look back.

It is an odd feeling to be home in my own room, something I never expected. You would think it a relief, yet I cannot settle. Father has already made eligible men aware of my availability. Just thinking of such a thing makes me sickly and wonder how long I can delay. I have expressed to father that it is surely distasteful when Emlyn is barely cold. "Well, you can't stay here indefinitely, we must ensure you are suited whilst still in your prime."

I am sat brushing my hair when there is a knock at my door. "Come in." I am surprised to see Arlet. "What do you want, Arlet." I say wearily.

"I told you I can help you, Miss, and I am here to do just that."

"In what way?" I ask guardedly.

She moves over to the fire and sits on the floor. I am aghast she has done such a thing uninvited. "Come on." She beckons. "You can't see from over there."

As I tentatively move closer, she begins shuffling cards, retrieved from the folds of her skirt. I have seen father with other gentlemen play a card game, but they are four numbered suits, whereas these are pictured, and I fail to understand. "I don't know what this is, but I think you should leave." I try to sound forceful.

"Don't you want to see what your future holds, Miss?" Her mouth is curled.

"I do not believe that you can do such a thing." I fold my arms.

"The cards read your fortune; you only have to choose." She lays them out on the floor. They smell fusty and I guess she keeps them hidden somewhere, under the floorboards in her room perhaps. "Come on Mistress, sit beside me and I will help you."

"Why would you help me?" I am suspicious.

"You stayed with the witch, she may have tainted you, don't you want to find out?"

"If you are referring to Branwen, I found her very agreeable."

Arlet shrugs. "Birds of a feather."

"What are you implying?"

"Did she have dead animals hanging in her house?" Arlet asks in a strangely excitable tone. I am unnerved, skin prickling with warning.

"Of course not, don't be ridiculous."

"They use them as sacrifice, you know."

I move to the door and open it. "I would like you to go now."

She collects the cards and shrugs again. "As you wish."

I am in a forest, trees heavy with foliage, overhanging branches blocking light, crouched, fearful, breathless. I hear voices, horses, dogs barking. I run, roots trip me, stones dig into my bare feet, I hold my heavy skirts up to free my legs, and sprint faster and faster. I find myself at the top of a cliff, teetering on the edge. Footsteps approaching, closer and closer. Do I leap into the abyss? I am grabbed from behind, pulled around to face Emlyn.

Waking with a jolt, perspiring, heartbeat drumming in my chest. I pull open the drapes around the bed, needing light, craving air. Since Emlyn, I no longer feel safe when they are fully drawn. The fire still casts an orange glow, I cannot have slept long. Noticing something on the floor but unable to make out what, I tiptoe across the cold flagged floor. A card from Arlet's deck, face down. I reach to turn it over, and gasp. A baby, blood spilling from its stomach. A horned figure grinning sadistically, wielding a forked prong. The devil.

Chapter 10

Lockhart

In the Black Horse Tavern, Dilys is cleaning tables with a dirty rag. The only one who doesn't avert their eyes when I enter. I am treated with indifference by the locals since Emlyn's murder. It's a hard cross to bear. "Sit over here Sire." She beckons. "Dafydd, pour Sire Lockhart a drink."

The pair, as round as they are tall, run the tavern. She hovers by the table, and I rummage in my pouch for coins. "This one's on us." Dafydd puts the tankard down.

"Thank you, that is most generous." I am surprised by their gracious token.

Dilys nudges Dafydd with an elbow. "Go on, ask him." I look from one to the other.

"All right woman, stop your fussing." Dafydd leans in. "If you need a place to stay, you can bed down in the cellar. It isn't much but it's dry."

"I have a spare blanket, and you will be fed," Dilys whispers with a smile.

I am baffled. "Why would you do that for me?"

"One good turn deserves another," Dilys says resolutely.

"What have I ever done for you other than drink your ale?" I am no mood for riddles.

Dafydd explains, "If it wasn't for your mother's skill our daughter Rhia wouldn't still be with us."

"Skill! I wasn't aware my mother had any skill?"

"She was a healer," Dilys murmurs. "A good one."

Stretching my long legs, bones ache, numb with cold; the thin blanket offering little protection from the stone floor of the cellar. The aroma of baking bread forces my frozen feet up the wooden steps to the kitchen.

"Almost ready." Dilys' cheeks red as apples.

My fingers and toes tingle, soaking the warmth and I pull a stool closer to the bread oven.

"I can't get the loaves out whilst you are sat in front of the door," she complains light-heartedly. Reluctantly I move over a little, allowing her room to shovel the golden-brown mounds onto the table. "Will be hot a while yet, Lockhart, why not go wash up first and prepare."

"Wash, on a Saturday!" I exclaim.

Dilys brushes a stray curl from her face with the back of her hand. "Lockhart! It is Merek and Aelwen's big day."

I stare blankly.

"The wedding." She tuts.

The congregation of guests fill the church. Sat beside Merek on the front row, I cannot help but compare to Emlyn and Wren taking their vows only a few months earlier. Whenever my thoughts turn to her, as they do so often, a sharp blade twists in my heart. Feeling a tap on my back, glancing over my shoulder, it takes me a moment to recognise Nerys. She has undoubtedly matured in the two years she has been away from Tenby, into an extremely attractive woman, surrounded by a glow of red and orange.

"Hello Lockhart." She smiles sweetly.

"Oh, hello Nerys, how are you?" Bombarded by a rush of emotions from the assembly, their voices reverberate in my head.

"I was sorry to hear of Emlyn's passing." Her doleful eyes shine like jewels. "If you are in need of company, please do not hesitate, I will be most willing to visit you." Her lips curl into a seductive smile. Sparks of orange fly towards me, and I cannot escape them, hit by a burning poker of desire. The bride's arrival quietens the congregation, and offering Nerys a small nod, I shake the conflicting thoughts of her and Wren from my head and follow Merek to the front of the church, pivoting to admire Aelwen gliding down the aisle.

"Why am I scared?" Merek asks through clenched teeth.

"Just nerves my friend, wait until you see her, she's radiant." A light pink mist swirls around the couple taking their vows, and a stab of yearning, of unrequited love, brings a lump to my throat.

Guests move freely between the row of houses. Merek's extended family louder and more raucous with each passing hour. A welcome respite from my gloom, I remain in good spirits, despite Branwen's eyes boring into the back of my head. There are questions undoubtedly only she can answer, but today I intend to forget my troubles.

Finally catching Merek alone, I pat him on the back. "Congratulations."

He grabs my sleeve. "Lockhart, I need to speak with you, privately." He pulls me out of earshot from the others. "I have been trying to find a moment all day to tell you, Lock," he whispers, "before I burst."

"Go on."

"Aelwen is with child," Merek confides. "We realised before the wedding, so you understand the need for discretion on this matter, I trust?"

"Wonderful news." I am sworn to secrecy.

"There you are, what are you two being so secretive about?" Nerys makes her way to us.

"I will leave you to it." Merek winks.

"Come and sit with me, Lockhart." She hooks my arm inviting me to squeeze into a small gap between her and Uncle Aeron.

"Sorry about Emlyn," Aeron passes me a tankard of Ale.

"You're the only one in Tenby then, other than me." I take a large gulp. "Well, death is generally hardest on the closest family members I find." Aeron reasons.

Nerys buts in, "It is a wedding; we don't want to get all maudlin. I want to have fun." She smiles and bites her lip, light brown eyes creasing with mischief. "Do you like my gown Lockhart?" She pushes against me. "I am in service to a family in Swansea, and my mistress kindly offered me the dress for the occasion. It needed a few nips and tucks, and repair to a rip down one side but I'm a good seamstress. Does it suit me?"

The smooth fabric and cut is luxurious compared to the rough attire I remember her wearing. The red sateen gown, shiny as her black hair, worn high to reveal the delicate pale skin of her neck and chest. It fits like a glove. "Yes, it is as lovely as you."

By late afternoon a blanket of darkness has fallen, and my tankard has been filled many times. "Oh, Lockhart, you are so brave, tracking down cattle rustlers," Nerys compliments. "It would be wonderful to know I had a man who could protect me from the evils of the world." Her eyes are sultry.

"Well," I agree boastfully. "It is the duty of a soldier to do such things." The alcohol causing my tongue to loosen, my manner to become pretentious. "You are very beautiful Nerys," I squeeze her leg. "But right now, I need to go outside." I move unsteadily to the door. The December air is chilly, the ground dusted with a sprinkling of hailstone from a recent shower. My hand against the wall, relieving myself, I spot Nerys in my peripheral vision. She has followed and watches.

"Looking to see what I have, are you?" I tease.

Nerys giggles, twisting a lock of hair between her fingers. "What I need to know Lockhart, is are you able?" Moonlight lights her face and she glances up from lowered lashes.

"Asking for it are we?" My arm slips around her waist.

"Depends on what you are offering."

"Perhaps I should just show you." Heartbeat increasing, pumping blood to my groin, slipping a hand up her skirts I fondle her soft buttocks, breeches tightening against the strain, a tingling warmth of excitement. I pull her closer, kiss her roughly, closing my eyes, and freeze, pulling away with a jerk.

"What's wrong Lockhart?" Nerys moves her mouth towards mine. "Kiss me again." Half-heartedly I press my lips against hers, but passion has subsided, as quickly as it began. Nerys is pretty but she isn't Wren.

"No, I do not want this." I turn on my heel.

"Wait, Lockhart, we can try again." She grabs my sleeve. "Maybe somewhere warmer, more private."

Shaking my arm free, angry with myself, angry with her, with life. "I said no!"

Ducking to avoid trout dangling from hooks, I wander aimlessly around the market. Pigs' trotters with yellow nails hang on skewers by the butchers, and tripping over the broom of a man selling his wares, I curse under my breath. Moving to the glovers' stall, a delicate lace pair catches my eye. Wren would like these. Her name a branding iron across my heart, a festering sore of longing reopening like a picked scab, every time I think of her. I attempt distraction with the scullery ware. Perhaps a Christmas gift for Dafydd and Dilys. Who else is there to buy for? Salivating at the mince pies by the dairy stall, I consider the few coins in the leather pouch slung around my hip. My meagre savings stretched tight as muslin over a jam pot. I need a job. Returning to the tavern empty handed, I sit with my back to the fire looking towards the town square through the bubble glass window. St. Mary's overseeing proceedings like a protective mother. A church has stood on the same sight since Norman times. The sky is grey with hints of gold from the setting sun, stall holders loading unsold goods onto traps and carts led by mule or cob, dispersing into the fading light to wives and home. The market dates to 1290 and I have been visiting all my life yet now feel a detachment. A loose cog on the wheel of life, no longer an integral part. I hadn't realised how important Emlyn was to my sense of self, and of belonging in Tenby. An invisible wall separates me from the world. I miss him more than I thought I would. The realisation pains me. Last night I dreamt of him lying in the cold ground, his eyes open, staring. In his crossed arms the cheap metal pin I had placed there, had pierced his heart, dried blood congealed around the wound. The pin was found in his pocket, and I knew it to be Angharad's favourite, despite its lack of value. I wonder if I did the right thing, if burying it with him was what he would have wanted.

After a warming cawl supper I force myself from the stool, through the warmth of the tavern to the cellar steps, heat fading with every footfall. Lifting the thin blanket, a rush mat lies beneath. A gift from my two unlikely friends. Gratitude for Dafydd and Dilys fills my heart, the mat affording some respite from the cold stone floor, I curl into a tight ball and hope for sleep. My mind has other plans, churning over events. Conversations with Wren whilst recovering from my injury. Her shy smile when accepting the forget-me-nots. How beautiful she had looked in her wedding gown. Poisoned arrows of jealousy stab into the happy memories. I should have found a way to prevent her marriage to Emlyn, I chastise. My heart recognised her unhappiness, yet I continued to be the dutiful brother I have always been. I turn onto my side, dragging the blanket with me, tucking it around myself irritably. I saw the dulling of her colours but was not man enough to do what my heart told me. If I had, she would not have been put through all this, and Emlyn might still be alive. Images of Emlyn's lifeless body impress on my mind and thumping the heel of my hand against my forehead I exhale loudly, becoming ambivalent. Come on Lockhart, face it, Wren deserves better than you and you know it. Just because you speak amiably, does not mean she considers you other than a charming acquaintance. Her feelings were clear after the funeral; she couldn't bear to look at you. Forget her, move on. My heart anchored in the depths of the ocean, stuck, unable to move forward nor back. "This is pointless," I say aloud to the darkness. "Going over this causes nothing but torment." Yet thoughts continue. "Damn it," I scold. "I know I have made mistakes, but from a comfortable life in Tenby castle, to this. How far can a man fall?" The last thing I expect is an answer, but a woman's voice expresses clearly.

“On reaching the bottom, the only way is up.”

Scrambling upright, I stare wildly into the inky darkness. “Who is there?” I ask tentatively, straining, but other than the thumping of my heartbeat, silence prevails. The hatch above and to my right, secured from the inside, opens onto the street. Barrels of ale brought on a cart pulled by horses, arrive every other Wednesday. I help with the unloading, gaining a few coins for shifting the heavy caskets onto the planks, to be rolled down to Dafydd in the cellar, but it is Friday evening, it couldn’t be that. A glimmer of moonlight seeps around the edges of the hatch. Mumbled voices from revellers still at the bar. Perhaps someone is playing the fool, my fear a source of amusement, but surely there would be whispers, or sniggers, something, I argue with myself. I am often woken by a footstep thumping across the wood, but there would be some sound in the distance if that were so, I reason, and there isn’t. I must have imagined it, I determine, the mind playing tricks on the cusp of sleep.

Chapter 11

Lockhart

Waves grey as pewter, slap against the shore of Will's Mark. Red squirrels and hedgehogs, cosy in their winter hibernation, sleep through the cold damp days of winter. Human inhabitants, adding further layers of clothing before venturing out.

"You will be at Aelwen's beck and call from now on. Yes Aelwen, no Aelwen, that is all I will get from you in future." I laugh, dragging the rowing boat onto the sand.

"Take that back." Merek pulls a face.

"Oh Aelwen, my love." I clutch my chest, avoiding the retaliating punch in the arm. Merek tries to grab me, but I'm too quick, turning and running off. Merek gives chase.

"I will not change to suit any woman, mark my words." He shakes his fist with mock defiance. Innocent fun, a reminder of youth and playful days. Hedgerows of gorse trail along the path, small yellow flowers interspersed in thorny bush, adding a spark of colour amongst the bare withered plant life. "I will take my dagger and cut out your tongue." Merek's cheeks reddening with the exertion.

"You will never catch me; you are too heavy." A pheasant takes flight in a state of panic, as we rush by. We fall headlong through Branwen's door.

"Greetings, it is good of you both to come." She smiles. "Today of all days."

Having fixed the paddock fencing, I stroke the light brown horse. "You will be safe again now," I reassure the mare.

Merek smirks. "Talking to horses, whatever next. It's a dumb animal; it doesn't understand Lock."

"Animals are far more intelligent than most men you come across," I retort.

Merek shrugs, returning the hammer to the wooden box. "Well, are you coming, or staying here to converse with your new friend?" He looks at the darkening sky. Daylight fading, clinging to the edges of cloud in waning hues of blue and grey. "We need to get moving, else we will be rowing back to Tenby with nothing but a crescent moon to light our way."

"Need to get back to Aelwen, do you?" I wink.

"Only because I want to, not because I have to." Merek huffs.

"I think I will stay awhile, if that is alright with you, Branwen?" After considering this visit for days, I see Branwen as the only possibility of gaining insight into what is happening to me. I admit, I am afraid of what I will learn, but what choice do I have.

"Certainly." She smiles, tying the gate closed with rope. "Aeron can collect you tomorrow after the day's fishing."

Burning wood crackles in the fire, and I stare absently into the flames. "You never gave me an answer; about the colours I see Branwen." I rake a hand through my hair.

Branwen sits beside me. "Everyone has an array of colours around them. If you know how to read the various depths and shades, you can read the person. What ails them, what they fear, and how they feel."

I recollect my experience with Mabon and the French sailors in the tavern. "I think I am able to do this Branwen, but how, why, when others cannot?"

"It is available to all, but most remain unaware."

"I don't recall always having this ability though. Was it the attack? I hit my head, could that have been the cause?"

"I don't know, Lockhart, but it is a gift, a blessing, which has awakened within you. I see the colours too, so you are not unique."

"Well, I am pleased to hear that." My tense shoulders relax a little.

"You have the brightest colours I have ever seen," she remarks matter-of-factly.

"Me! Are you sure about that?"

"Oh yes, Lockhart, most certainly," she insists. "There is forest green, the mark of a natural healer, and violet, as you say you see in me also."

I nod, acknowledging shades of purple swirling around her like a cloud of morning sunlight.

"That means your visions are of a higher level," she pauses. "Mainly you have gold, very rare Lockhart, to see gold. You are being guided, protected by a special spirit."

"Guided!" I gasp incredulously.

"Everyone has a guide which stands beside them, always, but your guide stands behind you, so close, she is walking in your footsteps."

"She? should it not be a man?"

Branwen laughs. "It is most definitely a female energy, that is all I can tell you."

"Could it be my mother? Dafydd said she was a healer."

Branwen shrugs. "I don't know, but you are very blessed to have your guardian so close she is able to influence your life and decisions. Not entirely mind, you still have free will."

"Is it bad, or evil?"

"Hush, Lockhart, healing is a gift, how can it be evil?"

"I am not sure about any of this Branwen; your beliefs are not the way I see the world. Witches have been hung in England you know."

Branwen laughs again. "We are not witches; we are simply aware that there is more than we have been told. We help people, not hurt them. You are looking at the world as you have been taught to see it, like a horse wearing blinkers, observing a very narrow vision, a limited reality. That does not make it right, or true."

"Have we not progressed though, from the old ways?" I rake a hand through my hair.

"People in the past believed in a world different to the way it is perceived now, that is true. Each century brings new discoveries; every era believing they are making progress from what is seen as the ignorance of those who have long since passed. We now find ourselves living largely within a harsh doctrine. A God who watches and punishes according to our sins." She shakes her head. "Yet fear suppresses the spirit, it doesn't make sense, why would any god want that?" She opens her hands in a questioning way. "Our connection to nature, connection to all, has been revered for as long as can be remembered, and I believe this is the right way."

I stroke my beard, considering. Branwen resumes, "Only in recent history has it been questioned, considered other than normal, other than truth, but denying the existence of a spiritual presence around everything. Man, animal, nature, is ignorance, not progress."

My brow creases. "Progress is a good thing though, surely. Man has made such giant strides. Trading in foreign lands, improvements in architecture."

"Has any of this helped the majority? Has it brought improvements to the locals in Tenby?"

I consider the poverty within the town. Children gaunt. Tall Merchants houses built by the fathers of those children, working long days, for little coin. Never enough to nourish their offspring, nor break the chains from a life of toil. Progress, I acknowledge perhaps for the first time, is generally beneficial, only for the rich.

Branwen sighs. "All I am trying to say, Lockhart, is there is always more than one way of looking at any situation, and on Wills Mark, we see life differently. Now enough questions, it is getting late, and we need to prepare."

"Prepare for what?"

"You will see." Branwen moves to the shelf of herbs and tinctures.

"One more question." I watch her carefully measuring an assortment of ingredients into a tankard. "The rainbow colours around Wren, what do they mean?"

"I believe she may be a faerie," Branwen replies casually, still concentrating on the brew she is concocting.

"Are you serious?" I say a little too loudly, and she turns to gauge me, looking past me at something unseen, making my stomach jittery.

"Your golden radiance is smooth," she says, almost to herself. "Which indicates you are perhaps more open to the suggestion than you show." She returns to the brew, adding a strong-smelling liquid, conversing as she works, "Long before the Christian religion was established in Wales, communication with faeries was common. I can't say I have seen any myself, but from what I understand, they appear remarkably like us but come from the Otherworld. Often referred to as shining ones, or shining people, because they have soft shimmering colours around their head and shoulders, I believe Wren may be one of them."

I find this suggestion incredulous. "Do you believe she is aware of this?"

"No, I shouldn't think so."

"But…" I begin.

"No more questions." Branwen mixes the ingredients, handing it to me.

"What is it?" I smell a trace of cinnamon, but the aroma is foul, and I screw up my face.

"Down in one," she advises.

I am unsure; she senses my qualms. "I am not going to poison you Lockhart, it will help you relax that is all."

"Why do I need to be relaxed?" I ask cautiously.

"Trust me, Lockhart." I examine the liquid, hold my nose closed between thumb and finger and drink, fast as I can. Hot and spicy, I feel the burn as it slips down my throat, coming to rest in my stomach like a hot potato. Branwen moves to the door, fastens her cloak with a pin and pulls up the hood.

"You had better bring yours, it will be cold."

She takes it from the peg, and I wrap it around my shoulders. Taking a lantern from the hook, I follow her out into the cold dark night. "Where are we going?" I ask, breath feathering in the biting December air.

"Yuletide, a time to celebrate the return of light. Rebirth," she calls over her shoulder. A trickle of fear knots my stomach.

A canvas of stars shimmer in silent observation against an ink black sky. The crescent moon threads a narrow trail of light through a thicket of trees. Bare skeletal arms of winter branches reach out in stillness, fallen leaves sparkling with frost, crisp underfoot. The eyes of a creature glow in the darkness, my skin prickling with warning. I think of Merek, curled beside Aelwen in the warmth. "What is the purpose of this Branwen?" I ask with trepidation.

"You have nothing to fear." Branwen continues, deeper into the woodland. The path widens, and we reach a clearing, a small fire burning brightly in the centre, plumes of grey smoke billowing into the night. Around us, a circumference of shadowy trees.

"What is this place?"

"Just do what is asked of you." Branwen looks back through the trees.

"Why, what's going to happen?" I hear the uncertainty in my question.

"I told you, there is nothing to fear." Branwen points. Flickers of light move closer, people holding lanterns. "It is just time, that is all."

"How did they know we were here?" Panic squeezes my heart tightly.

"Just do what is asked of you." Her eyes are focused on the direction of glimmering lights. The leader wears a golden cloak, hood low over their face. Stars and moons embroidered into the fabric dance with the swinging lanterns. Something about that walk is familiar. The figure stands before me, and long wrinkled fingers pull down the hood, Ranulf. I swallow the wave of nausea.

"I don't understand, what are you doing here?" My mind reels with visions of wizards and witches, and rituals. The remaining group, I now realise, are all women, but none wears a cap or bonnet. I gawp, their attire, simple white gowns, shoulders draped in animal fur, barely decent. Branwen indicates to the ground.

"Kneel, Lockhart." Is this a sacrifice. Am I tonight's offering? "Kneel," she repeats.

My mind urges me to run for my life, but my legs refuse to cooperate, shakily sinking into the damp earth, cold seeping through the fabric of my breeches. Branwen sits with the women, forming a circle around Ranulf and myself.

"What are you going to do to me?" I feel woozy, light-headed, and consider if I have been hexed. What had been in that brew?

Ranulf speaks with supremacy, "You are within a sacred circle; you are quite safe."

"A sacred circle, what does that mean?" I attempt to scramble to my feet, but Ranulf pushes me back down authoritatively.

"Whatever ridiculous rumours you have heard, are false, we are here to help you." He turns to Branwen. "Did you add mandrake; he is very anxious."

"Of course. Perhaps I should have put in more, but we don't want him comatose, do we?" I look from one to the other.

"Never mind, we will manage." Ranulf returns his attention to me. "Do you have the onyx?" Initially puzzled, I remember the stone, and with trembling hands, fumble in the soft leather pouch, handing the black stone to Ranulf. "You must trust us," Ranulf speaks in kindlier tone, taking the stone and clutching it in his palm. "We are gathered in honour, to awaken the dormant fire within. Firstly, you must take the oath. To swear your power will be used for good, to help and heal. Do you agree to this?"

My mind a fog of uncertainty and doubt, I wet my lips; mouth dry as sand on a summer beach and shake my head. "I do not understand."

Ranulf furrows his brow. "Agree to the words."

My eyes flit around the group of women, resting on Branwen. "Agree," she urges assertively.

I find myself nodding. "Alright, I agree." Anything for this to be at an end. "Can I go now?"

"You must speak the words aloud," Ranulf says. "Repeat them after me." Ranulf's poetic tone rolls off his tongue like a mother singing a lullaby to her babe. "The power I hold within me, I swear to use for good, to heal the inner spirit. I manifest, with love." I repeat, my reprise unusually melodic in tone. Ranulf stretches his arms skyward. "I call upon the great mother of the earth. To Arianrhod goddess of the moon and stars, to the great father of the sky. To Bran, and Nudd of the sea and sun. I call upon the spirits from the north, east, south and west to protect and guide our druid son, as we welcome him into the fold, on this auspicious night."

Druid! What does he mean? There have been no druids in Wales for hundreds of years. Ranulf sweeps a pointed finger around the seated women, and each reach for the hand beside them, forming a link. "Now you have protection, Lockhart, you must swear to live alongside the cycles of life, not to force or rule nature, but to show respect and honour, in the knowing that you are connected to all. The following words must, therefore, be spoken from your heart; feel their truth and they will show you your power. They will show us all, what you are."

I begin with reluctance, reciting after Ranulf. "I am a man pure of heart, from my power and wisdom, I am never apart. I vow from this day to honour my soul. To serve the gods and goddesses of Wales, for the good of all." A movement stirs deep within me, an awakening of, I know not what, but it feels light, yet strong, a completeness of all I am. Ranulf continues. "The onyx will protect you; you have shown great wisdom keeping it close. It will be returned; you will have need of it in the future but now we must see what it can show us."

He speaks an incantation over the stone, in an unknown language, and turns, throwing it into the fire. Flames leap, crackling like a hog, turning on a spit. A low murmur, whispered by the women, increasing in volume, chanting. Derwydd, derwydd, druid, druid, accompanied by a slow thudding drum from an unseen source, reverberating around the clearing. I feel the vibration in my chest, breathing slowing to the rhythm. Ranulf stands behind me holding my head in his hands. "Look into the fire Lockhart, what do you see?" I concentrate on the dancing flames. Sparks shoot, and instinctively I jump. Ranulf presses his thumbs into the centre of my skull, index fingers firmly in the middle of my forehead, whispering in my ear. "Look, Lockhart, open your mind and your heart." Slowly, swirling patterns and balls of coloured light arise within the fire. Yellow, blue, green, moving together and then separating, over and over. Mesmerised, my logical brain unable to make sense of it. Slowly, a face forms from the coloured lights. Emlyn, eyes, and mouth agape. I try to look away, but Ranulf holds me tightly. "Do not be afraid, look." The face fades, overtaken with an image of a field, bloodied men, strewn across the grass. I am choked with terror, instinctively trying to back away, but Ranulf refuses to free me, and the image changes again, bodies wrapped in shrouds, lifeless within a large muddy hole. Not one, or two, but many. This must be the work of the devil, I have been tricked, used to conjure the dead, punishment for Emlyn's death. I am to be consumed by the fires of hell. My mind races in chaos and confusion. The images billow into the dark sky, replaced with an awareness, that a creature lies curled at the base of the fire. Slowly it unravels. Red scales and a long tail. Heat from the fire is burning my face, but I remain spellbound by the creature which continues to expand. "No, no." I hear myself cry out in fear, realising what is before me. Is this my time to die, will my life end like this? My heart thuds wildly in my chest. I swallow hard, I cannot breathe. The creature's width diminishes the fire, heat emanating from the beast, which turns to face me.

The women chant. "Ddriag, Ddriag, Ddriag." Dragon. My heart pounds in my ears. It's hot breath rising in the freezing night air, so close, almost touching my face. Sick with fear, my whole body begins shaking. The dragon cocks its head to one side, observing me with yellow slanted eyes. I try to move away, but Ranulf prevents me. Its long-forked tongue, flicking in and out, touches my cheek, hot and prickly on my skin. It is so unexpected I incongruously want to laugh. Can I believe my own eyes?

Branwen kneels beside me, turning my face to look at her. "The Welsh dragon is a very powerful symbol, Lockhart." She smiles. "It is the protector of Wales and its people. It is incredibly wise, knows when to use its strength and dominion. The dragon is feared by those who do not understand it, but you have been blessed with its protection. You can call upon its acumen and vigour to help you; it will speak to you as a fire within. When you feel its heat, you will know your choice is the right one. Learn to listen to it and act upon it. The dragon represents change and transformation, the time has come for you to accept and use your faculty and insight, Lockhart. The dragon will help you."

The fire is warm against my back, and light against my closed lids tells me it is morning. Opening my eyes, I find myself on the floor of Branwen's shack, wrapped in my cloak. With no recollection of returning here last night, memories drop like pebbles, rippling in my mind. The ceremony, the dragon, did that really happen? The latch on the door clicks open. "Ah, you are finally awake." Branwen enters, bringing a gust of cold air into the room. "A good day Lockhart, even the hens have given us a gift." Two brown eggs sit in the palm of her hand.

I scramble to my feet. "I need air." Stumbling out of the door, a biting wind sweeps across the island, watering my eyes with cold. Resting my hand against a tree for balance, I wretch, but am unable to expel the contents lurching in my stomach, burning with heat. Breathless, I lean my back against the rough bark. White waves crash against the shore, the wind howling and whistling like a mythical creature, pressing against my ears, freezing my hands and feet and face. Everything looks the same, I reassure myself, I haven't fallen off the edge into a different world. I wander to the track, staring deeply through the trees, trying to convince myself it had been a dream, vivid, but a dream, nonetheless. Or perhaps an hallucination, brought on by the drink Branwen had prepared. It begins to rain, and I head back indoors.

We eat in silence, scooping the last of the egg from its shell.

Branwen asks tentatively, "So, how do you feel today, Lockhart?"

I glare sternly. "How do you think I feel?"

"Well, I do not know, different maybe?" she offers.

"Different, you think I should feel different after your poison," I snap like an angry dog. "I trusted you Branwen and you poisoned me, why did you do that? Tell me what happened last night because nothing makes any sense."

Branwen is equally roused. "How dare you suggest such a thing, Lockhart? Poison! Why do you think I would do that?"

"I have no idea, Branwen," I yell back. "I no longer know what is real and what is not."

Branwen indignantly stands with hands on her hips. "Reality is but an illusion Lockhart."

"More riddles, Branwen, really. Why can you never give me a straight answer?"

She sighs heavily and sits by the fire. "I understand your confusion." She is speaking in that voice again. The soft gentle tone which soothes. "But I reassure you, the golden light around you is shimmering brighter than before. Seated close to your physical form and sheathed within a delicate celestial female energy, dispelling any separation, appearing as one with you. I am in awe Lockhart, at the depth of connection, the likes of which I have never encountered before." Her magic is working, my anger dissipating. "Reality is different for everyone, each sees from their own point of view; therefore, nothing is real, only an interpretation. What you saw last night, Lockhart, what happened, was for a reason, of which I do not fully understand, I have not been shown. I am simply following the guidance I am given, that is all we can ever do."

"I am finding it all very unorthodox," I admit.

Branwen smiles. "All that is happening is hard for you to comprehend, you have nothing to base these changes on. No previous experience of this type, at least, none of which we are aware, but believe me, Lockhart, I was told many months ago to expect someone special. That morning, when I saw you out on the boat with Merek and Wren, I knew this was who I had been waiting for. Even under the grey sky, I could see the bright light shining around you. I wish you could see it Lockhart, it is so beautiful. When you came ashore and I saw it was you, I could hardly believe my eyes. As a child I had never been aware of you having any special abilities. You did not appear to have the sight; there was nothing which told me you had a calling. It is so unusual; I have never witnessed it before. It would normally be seen in childhood, even if it were repressed and yet, you seem to have, I don't know, developed it. I am not sure how to explain it, but I was given the privilege of helping you unlock your power last night. Remember though, you always have a choice, Lockhart, free will. If you choose to believe what you saw, then it is real."

"I am struggling to make sense of it all Branwen. Why me, why have I been chosen?"

She laughs. "Why any of us? We cannot always see the bigger picture Lock. Life is but a cycle, no beginning, no end, all we can do is live as best we can, making decisions on what we feel to be right, day by day." Branwen pokes the fire back into life and continues. "Moving onto the island to be with my beloved Gerwyn was a life changing decision for me. Knowing the wrath, I would encounter from my first husband's family, and the locals of Tenby. It was not taken lightly, but in the end, I was called and knew I must take heed. Gerwyn acknowledged my visions and herbal treatments, encouraging me to develop the skills I had suppressed for so long. He was a good man, and a good husband. Gone three years now, but I feel him close, every day." She sighs sadly. "Now it is my turn to help you develop. Repay Gerwyn and the druids for all they have done for me."

"So, what am I to do now? I do not feel any different, should I not feel different?" I rake a hand through my hair.

"Sometimes we are forced to change through the events in our lives, but more often, change happens slowly, creeps up on us, and only when we look back, can we see how far we've come. Maybe your changes will happen swiftly, maybe slowly, but happen they will. Nothing and no one remains unchanged by life. You can choose to go with the tide, or fight against it, but in the end the tide will win. I find acceptance has always been the best policy for me." Unconsciously I rub my stomach. "Do you have a burning sensation?" she asks.

"Yes, deep inside."

"That's good." Branwen smiles.

"Is it?"

"Yes, it is the dragon making its presence known, it will settle."

I don't believe her but decide against saying this out loud. Instead, I ask about Wren. "I care deeply for her Branwen, but I am unsure what I should do."

"Ah, yes, Wren, you must go to her."

"Why, is she in danger?" My eyes widen with concern.

"No, she is not in danger, but you are meant to be together, I have seen it."

"But she does not care for me," I mumble.

"What does your heart tell you?" Branwen asks. "Do you love her Lockhart?" I nod fiercely. "Then fight for her, know you can achieve anything you believe in. She too has power, which is hidden, together your power is doubled." She glances out of the window. "Look." She points and I stretch to see what she is observing.

"All I can see is a robin, pecking at the ground." It stops and looks at us, as if aware of our gaze.

"It a sign, Lockhart, Gerwyn is close by." I wonder if she is indeed mad, but again, keep this opinion. "Do you realise that everything, including birds, have a meaning?" She looks back at me. "The wren is a powerful druid symbol."

"The wren is just a small, feathered creature Branwen, seen in the hedgerows." I grin.

"It is far more than that, Lockhart," she piques. "The wren is associated with freshness, open to new insights, of a sunny disposition. A natural care giver and calm in a storm, resourceful and seeks balance in life. I would say that describes the Wren we know, perfectly, wouldn't you?"

"Yes," I agree thoughtfully. "I guess it does, but that doesn't mean she wishes to be with me, and even if she feels, as I feel for her, I cannot bring her back to Tenby. I have barely enough means, even to support myself."

"Not Tenby, no, here, to the island, this is where she belongs," Branwen says firmly.

"She is used to servants, finery. I'm sorry Branwen, I know this is your home, but I could not bring her here, to a shack."

"You must Lockhart, trust what your heart tells you."

Chapter 12

Lockhart

The sea is calm and looking back to Will's Mark fading into the distance, the undulating hills basked in a flood of sunlight, offer a magical appearance. I never imagined druids to live there. It just shows how little you can know about the area you live in. I'm not sure how they differ from witches but according to Branwen and Ranulf, I am a druid. I admit to being sceptical, previously never giving the island much thought, just part of the scenery. The islanders mocked by the locals of Tenby for behaviour viewed as dissident. That's as much as I was aware of. After my odd encounter, I recognise the appeal of druidism and wonder if I could spend my life there with Wren. I touch my chest, the onyx beneath my shirt now sporting a hole and thin strip of leather. "Wear it always. Not only does it offer protection but will reinforce your understanding of the circle of birth, death, and rebirth, and Lockhart." Branwen added. "Remember the fire of the dragon."

I am pleased to report the burning in my stomach has eased, but a dragon! The idea is beyond ridiculous. Uncle Aeron stands at the wheel of the boat, hardened from fishing the waters of Tenby coast all his life, unaffected by the nipping Atlantic air. I wipe sea spray from my face, returning the hand to my armpit. The day cloudless and icy.

"Have you heard about Gar?" Aeron's muscled arms ripple with tales, of shipwrecks and treasure, mermaids, and pirates.

"No." I shake my head.

"Broke a leg, clumsy oaf. Mind, the harbour steps can be treacherous." Wiry white hair rests on wide shoulders. "He'll be no use to me for a while, that's a fact." Aeron wipes his bulbous nose on a dirty rag.

"I guess not." My teeth rattle.

"How would you like coming out on the boat a while, you're in need of work I hear?" Aeron surveys me. "Pay will not be great, and it is hard, backbreaking, not what you are used to."

I accept without hesitation. "Yes, I would like to take your offer, Aeron, thank you."

"Aye well, you might not be thanking me after a few days bending over the side of the boat and you can no longer stand upright." Aeron laughs. "Let's hope you have sea legs like your father."

I feel a tug in my heart. "You were friends with my tad, you knew him well, didn't you?

"Aye, I did son."

"What was he like? I cannot really remember him."

Aeron sighs in reminiscence. "When Ifan and I were young strapping men, we made bets, on who would catch the most fish. Always was one for gambling your father, and the ale. Emlyn was a lot like him, in ways and looks. You are more like your mother."

"Am I?"

"Aye, a good-looking woman. Tall, like yourself. A good woman, kind, had her work cut out with your father, but he loved her." Aeron returns his gaze to the water. "They lost a fair few children along the way you know, Emlyn the only one who survived, until you. They let him get away with far too much, in my opinion, turned a blind eye, when they should have held him to task." Aeron shakes his head. "Does a lad no good to be spoilt, they need a firm hand. Your mother's death broke Ifan's heart, and Emlyn went off the rails, too old for a beating to make any difference. There were many arguments I can tell you, Emlyn determined to better himself by fair or foul means, in the end your father despaired." Beneath bushy eyebrows, round dark eyes wrinkle at the edges, softening Aeron's stern look. "As for you. Well, Ifan was lost, barely sure which end of a baby was up. So, he did what he thought best and paid our Enid to watch over you while he was working."

I listen quietly, sadly, always feeling a burden to everyone, yet father made Emlyn promise to take me in when he died. Why would he do so, unless he cared? Emlyn could have refused but kept me close. I swallow the lump in my throat. Love is often hidden, especially between men. Unable to show affection openly, deeds become their unspoken words. Guilt for failing Emlyn, gnaws like a rat feasting on my heart.

Aeron teaches me where to place the nets, how to set the sail, and secures me a room close by. The invisible threads of connection to Tenby, rerooted.

He drops a few coins into my hand. "You have earned it lad."

I follow the crowd of fishermen up the steep incline to the ship inn, treating myself to warm stew, and a hunk of bread. Gathered around the fire thawing out our bones, I am a little too close to Osian, nicknamed drewllyd, due to his sour odour, covering my nose to avoid the stench.

"Tell us a tale Aeron." Osian scratches his matted beard, which I am sure is full of lice.

Aeron stretches his legs to the fire, hands behind his head. "Let's see now, which shall I tell?" After a moment's thought he begins, "A beautiful girl she was, a faerie, from the waters of Llyn y Fan Fach. Sat, combing her hair in the sunshine. Gwyn, a handsome young farmer, was tending his cattle when he saw her, falling in love, just like that." Aeron clicks his fingers for emphasis. Osian moves to a stool closer to Aeron. He's hard of hearing, not surprising with the amount of hair covering his ears, but I am grateful to breathe freely again. "Now, at first the girl would have none of it, but eventually he persuaded her to marry him, but with a warning. Should he strike her three times she would vanish forever." Aeron stops for a swig of ale, and I lean a little closer with interest, elbows resting on my knees. "Now, the girl's father gave a dowry of faerie sheep, cattle, and horses, and the faerie wife bore three sons, but she dreamt often of the beautiful lake from where she came. One day the farmer, seeing her with distant eyes, tapped her on the shoulder to arouse her from her reverie." Aeron shakes his head. "That was the first strike. Unintentional, but marked all the same. Some months later, they attended a wedding, and the wife cries. Gwyn patted her shoulder, asking why she wept. I weep because the young couples' troubles are just beginning and so are ours, for you have just struck me for the second time." Aeron folds his arms across his chest. "From then on, the farmer tried hard not to strike her again, until they attended a funeral, and the wife laughs. He tapped her arm, telling her to stop. She turned to him, saying. When mortals die their troubles end, and now so too must our marriage, for that was the third blow. With that she vanished, returning to the lake, taking the faerie animals with her. Gwyn never saw his faerie wife again."

Mumblings of how truthful the tale, gather amongst the fishermen. Aeron pipes up, "That's not the end of the story." The muttering ceases.

"So, how does it end?" I ask eagerly.

Aeron looks me in the eye. "From time to time she would appear to her sons, instructing them on the use of herbal remedies. All three became respected physicians. So, you see, the story does not have an ending, it continues, within the faerie children."

My stomach has warmed, liquid fire spreading through my torso, odd, but not uncomfortable. Dragon breath, the realisation sparks a light. Branwen said it was a sign to be aware, but of what? I run a hand through my hair. The tale, is that it? Am I like farmer Gwyn, in love with a faerie? Has a spell been cast upon me? Dragons, faeries! I argue with myself. I thought you weren't superstitious. I touch my chest where the onyx lies beneath my shirt. In my pocket, the sprig of lavender, wrapped in a scrap of cloth. A spindle of thoughts weaves a tapestry. Wren's family live between Llangadog and Llandovery, which is close to Myddfai. Isn't that the location of Llyn y fan fach? The heat of dragon breath radiates into my back. The physician who aided me after my injury used strange herbal remedies, hadn't Wren said he was her uncle? Discombobulated and needing to formulate these ideas, I can't do that here; I must be alone. I down my ale.

"I don't know about you but I'm ready for my bed." Faking a yawn, I squeeze Aeron's shoulder as I pass.

"Come on Lock the night is young," Osian urges me to sit back down.

"I will see you tomorrow." I continue heading for the door.

"Bright and early," Aeron shouts after me.

I lift a hand in acknowledgement. Reaching the door, a gust of cold air and a man in uniform sweep into the room, spidery red veins on his nose, and cheeks. Castle guards do not frequent an Inn, such as this. All chattering ceases. "Lockhart Edwards?" He looks me up and down, already aware who I am. "You are to attend a meeting on the morrow, with Governor Thomas Griffiths."

"Is that a request, or an order?" I eye him suspiciously.

"You will be expected as soon as you dock." Huddling deeper into his buff coat he turns on his heel, retreating into the chilly night.

Shadows flicking across the walls of my tiny abode are ominous tonight. The summons to the castle curdling my blood. I mull over Aeron's story, deciding it's a coincidence. The rushlight fizzes and smells strong as Osian, but I must disperse the oppressive darkness. I turn the piece of birch, found on my way home, over in my hands. Branwen spoke of tree symbology, birch, one of the most sacred, known for protection and new beginnings, she had said, "I could certainly do with both." The silver-grey bark feels smooth, and an idea forms in my head. By the faint glow, my knife shapes a hollow scoop, its edges heart shaped. A twisted stem representing togetherness, the carving distracting me from my worries. On the back of the love spoon I etch the word, Cariad. Druids believe engraving words into an object gives them power. Feeling for any rough edges, I visualise offering it to Wren, her eyes alight with love. Branwen said conversing as if Wren were beside me, would bring us closer. My whispered words drift into the night.

Drips of water plop onto the table, pooling in a circle, sliding down the legs of the stool, pitted with woodworm, forming a puddle on the floor. With one eye open, involuntarily shivering, muscles I hadn't even been aware of having, ache. Fishing is harder than I anticipated. Rubbing my fist along the length of my arms, twisted in a bowline knot of tightness. The room is dark without a window, but a speck of daylight trickles in through the far corner. That shouldn't be there. Stiffly forcing myself from the pallet, kneading my shoulders. A clump of turf sits on the table as though waiting to be served. I wedge it back into the space it came from hopeful it will prevent the rain coming in. Not ideal, but it will have to do for now, I'm running late. Holding onto my hat, I sprint the short distance.

"Come on Lock, get a move on," Aeron shouts as I jump aboard. "We haven't got all day; we need to get some fishing done before the storm comes in. A gust catches the sail, lurching the boat into open water, and I will my stomach to hold on. Clumps of daisies cling to the sloping hillside where the castle sits like an ominous shadow. Merely months since I lived there, and yet, it seems so long ago. Time has a way of bending, stretching and shrinking. Around St. Catherines Island the surf carries us south, into pelting rain. The horizontal downpour pricking our faces with needlepoints.

"We will go around the other side of Caldey and try Will's Mark." Aeron is accustomed to the weather in these parts. "The waters are always warmer in that stretch; the fish will congregate there if anywhere."

Aeron is right, the weather calming considerably as the island of grassy hills and woodland rises in the distance. The rain blows out to sea, and we throw out the nets, the sun making an appearance, all is not lost.

By mid-afternoon slate grey skies rumble in the distance. "We need to head back whilst we can." Aeron points at heavy clouds gathering over Tenby. Heading back the weather moves in quickly, wind picking up, boat rocking precariously, crashing through waves, spraying over the bow and onto the deck, battling the elements. The storm gathers pace, dark clouds racing overhead. With numb fingers we tie ourselves to the boat with rope.

Aeron veers around Caldey island, trees bowing in reverence to the mighty gusts. Reaching Tenby, wrestling with the rope to secure the boat, gusts thundering around the harbour, almost pulling me off my feet.

"Lockhart Edwards?" I look up in surprise to see a messenger on horse.

"I am he."

"For you Sire." The man shouts to be heard above the roaring wind, presenting me with a damp letter. Recognising the seal to be that of Wren's father, I hurry back to my lodgings. Tom can wait. Peeling off my wet coat, my mind racing with questions. Will the letter be from Sire Davis or Wren? Why would either of them write to me? The door rattles in the wind, the rushlight is damp and will not light, adding to my irritation. It takes hold and a faint light swims across the table. Carefully tearing open the seal, a small sprig of delicate blue flowers falls to the floor. I take no heed, eager to read the message, holding the letter up in the dim light, following the words with a finger.

Dearest Lockhart,

I hope to find you well.

I write with deep sadness, for my dear mother has passed away after a short illness.

As Emlyn's brother, I felt it respectful to inform you of my father's arrangement for my betrothal, after a respectful period of mourning, to Sire Harold Roberts, who you may be aware is a merchant of good standing. My father believes this would be for the best.

Yours Sincerely,

Wren.

Married, no, how could I have been so foolish? Adrenalin pumps through my veins, my chest tightens, the walls of my room closing. I need to get out, clear my head. I grab my damp coat and half run half march towards the north beach, billowing sand sticking to my face. I rub the grit from my eyes, watering with cold, running faster along rippled sand, collapsing against Goscar rock, wiping my nose on the sleeve of my coat, a metallic taste in my mouth from the exertion. Breathing in the salty sea air, I allow my breathing time to steady. Waves rise and crash in the turbulent sea. The hills beyond, shadowy forms, barely indistinguishable from the heavy skies. The power of the water calms me, and I reconsider the letter. Why had she written? She had been under no obligation to do so. Had it been simply an act of courtesy? Losing her mother would hurt deeply. "My dear Wren, I am so sorry." On top of that, the impending betrothal. Her father's wish, but what of Wren's feelings? With little choice, she must do as her father sees fit. I stroke my beard in consideration. Normally I would be out all day and miss the messenger. If it hadn't been for the weather… Synchronicity, Branwen would say, and you should always take note, when it occurs. An idea worms into my consciousness. "Read between the lines Lockhart, what if she wrote so you have time to prevent it? What if she wants you too? Perhaps she feels equally, as you do for her." I remember the blue flowers. "Forget-me-not. You fool." I laugh joyously, turning my face skywards, shouting into the wind. "Thank you." With a glow of hope in my heart, I am ready to face Tom.

Flanked by two soldiers, I am escorted to Emlyn's study, instinctively straightening my back before entering. Tom Griffiths is sat upon Emlyn's chair, behind Emlyn's desk. The picture on the wall has been changed, portraying Tom sitting atop a brown horse.

"Sit, Sire." Tom points to a chair. Emlyn never invited me to sit, and I wrestle with indecision. "Sit down man, for goodness' sake." Tom tuts.

The chair wobbles, and to keep it steady I raise my right heel off the floor. Tom is of medium height, clean shaven bar a thin moustache, which curls at the ends. Wearing a cheap wig made of wool, a bigwig as it were. His heavily embroidered doublet is well-made, and he wears a cambric shirt. "No point in pleasantries, let us get straight down to business." Tom smirks, aware of my predicament with the chair. "Your brother, how shall we put it, enjoyed his extravagances, it seems." Tom leans back into the chair. "However, there appears to be a shortfall in coinage." He twiddles the edges of his moustache. "So, tell me Sire, where are the coins? Where did Emlyn hide them?"

"I am not sure what coins you are referring too, Governor." The word sticks in my throat.

"Come, come now, do not play dumb with me. We have found many hidden treasures, but so far, no sign of the coins." Tom remains composed. "The money Lockhart, where is the money?"

Having become astute at reading the mist around others, Tom's pallid colours come as no surprise. A blob of mud brown around his abdomen instinctively tells me he is prone to greed, not necessarily food, but wealth. Knowing not to trust him, sensing any coins will land straight in the man's own pockets. Coming from a family of landed gentry, as far back as can be remembered, neither short of money nor power in the town, but as the youngest of four sons, Tom has been forced to make his own way, prove his worth to his father.

"I know of no coins." I reply.

"What about his land, he owned acres at Kilgetty I believe, and on Caldey, plus that pledged in his wife's dowry. Did he hide the coins there?" Tom questions.

"There are tenant farmers out at Kilgetty, and on Caldey, and I have never seen the land pledged in the dowry, therefore I cannot say." I answer honestly, wondering if Tom believes me. Tom moves from the chair and perches on the edge of the desk.

"You have the audacity to claim no knowledge of the coinage. Do you also deny any involvement in the smuggling taking place, right under your nose?" Tom raises his eyebrows, and I swallow. A wrong turn of phrase will see my ankles in shackles and my head in a noose on gallows tree hill. If it could be proven I played any part in the smuggling activities, I will never see Wren again. Tom will lose no sleep over my demise, any more than he has over Emlyn's.

"A number of us had our, suspicions, but Emlyn was not one for sharing information, kept his cards close to his chest."

Tom frowns. "Not even placing trust in his own brother, that I find hard to believe. I would have expected him to confide in you above all others."

"We didn't get on; we were never equals."

Tom keeps his eyes firmly fixed on me; it is rather unnerving. "In days of old a castle would be inherited, I understand you may feel somewhat deprived since your brother's death, but in these modern times this is no longer the case. After all, Emlyn was not royalty," he scoffs.

"I never believed I would have any right to the castle," I answer passively. "Money is what buys position in this town, is it not?"

"Very well deduced, Lockhart."

I look out of the window, the way I would when Emlyn was riling me. Tom folds his arms, remains silent. The purpose, to make me uneasy, is working. He cocks his head and changes tack.

"Do you think I had your brother killed?"

My body tenses, but I recognise Tom's bate, hoping for a response, I will not rise to that. "I do not know," I grit my teeth. "Did you?" I cannot look him in the eye, if I see the truth there, I may well lunge at him with my sword and be done with it.

Tom laughs humourlessly. "There was no need." He stands and looks out of the small window, his back to me. "The townspeople had already decided it was time for him to go. In fact, I hear they were rather upset, denied the pleasure of seeing him hang. Things, from what I understand, how should I say, got a little out of hand." Tom turns to gauge my response. I remain perfectly still, determined not to show Tom the flames of anger burning in my chest. My leg is numb, holding it in one place, and silently I curse the chair, and Tom.

"I have no answers for you," I growl. "May I go now?"

Tom returns to sit behind the desk. "No, I have other matters of which I need to speak with you." His wig has slipped to one side almost covering one eye, it looks ridiculous. "You are no doubt aware the threat of a civil war looms over us, and I need good men in my infantry. I am led to believe you are skilful with sword and horse." He pauses, readjusts his wig, allowing me time to adapt to the change in tempo. This is the conversation I had been expecting. "I can offer you a warm room, food in your belly every night, and coin, if you are as good as they say."

Thoughts of a warm bed and nourishing food is indeed tempting, my room by the harbour, damp, freezing. I think of the damaged turf roof, that will need proper repair, and some days I eat naught but scraps. Yet, I am sure this man instigated Emlyn's death. I sigh deeply, silently. "I am unable to accept your offer," I answer pertinently.

Tom revises his proposal, "What if I were to proffer a promotion, shall we say, Captain. Yes, Captain Lockhart Edwards. Sounds very regal, does it not?"

Tom awaits my response. I have always dreamt of being a captain and mull over the advantages. I will be in a better position, have status, maybe Wren will see me in a better light. I can offer her the refined life she deserves, but what of my conscience? If the King, or parliament, declares civil war, there will be little choice but to fight, however, I surmise, until that time, the choices are my own.

"I am unable to accept your offer," I repeat.

"Ah, pride, I admire that. However, if we are at war, you will fight for the King? You are not foolish enough to be swayed by the ridiculous pledges of the parliamentarians, I trust?" Tom smooths his moustache.

"If Tenby and its people are at risk, then yes, I will fight for the King" I reply.

"Good man." Tom appears satisfied with the answer.

"I do not believe we have anything further to discuss." I stand abruptly, relieving my leg of the forced position, prickling with pins and needles, I desperately wish to rub it.

"Sit, Lockhart," Tom demands. "I will tell you when you are free to leave."

I remain standing.

"As you wish." Tom waves a hand, and I feel it a small victory, though thinking on it later, perhaps that had been Tom's plan. "Before you leave, I have a gift for you, Sire." Tom bends to a small chest beside him, producing a grey metallic goblet. "I believe it is a family heirloom of your mother's." Tom hands me a chalice. "As a mark of our understanding, I am returning it to you."

Tom raises his eyebrows. It is a bribe. The old Welsh law sees murder as an offence against the family and dealt with by payment of a fine to the victim's kin. Once accepted, the family are legally bound to forgo vengeance. English law now overrules the Welsh, and Tom knows that. He is being clever, for by offering a gift of inheritance, rather than money, he is covering his back. Beyond the tarnish, I am sure the goblet is solid silver, I recall now father speaking of it, and although the price has decreased substantially since the opening of the Spanish silver mines, it is worth more than I have ever had. Unsure if Tom realises the value, I accept the goblet, for what is my choice. Tom will ensure I never find Emlyn's murderer.

"So, the matter is settled?" Tom raises his eyebrows.

Reluctantly I nod.

"Good." Tom smiles smugly. "Now, you may go."

Leaving the castle, I notice a man in the shadows, who turns, pulling the brim of his hat low over his face.

Chapter 13

Wren

The clip clop of hooves on the driveway flutters my heart with hope, and leaving my embroidery, I cross to the window. Having agonised over the letter at length, my carefully considered choice of words sealed with a kiss and silent prayer that Lockhart will understand the hidden meaning. Perhaps, after Emlyn, he believes me a bad omen. Mother's death following so closely afterwards, calls me to question, if indeed I am being punished by a vengeful God. Even so, I felt powerless to resist the urge to reach out to him. "My goodness!" I exclaim, hand flying to my mouth. Lockhart, alighting from a fine chestnut stallion, walks to the front door. I watch him covertly from the upper window. Removing his hat, running a hand through his dark hair. Tantalising heat warms my womb. Be calm, be calm, there are reasons he might call. A business matter regarding Emlyn's estate perhaps. It will not be me he comes for, I am second-hand goods, and men wed virgins, don't they? Father is greeting him, muffled voices in the drawing room directly beneath the sewing room. Lockhart's unmistakable Welsh tone waking my every pore with recognition. My cotton gown, dyed the colour of Welsh gold, enhances the flecks in my eyes. I smooth the creases with shaking hands. A light knock on the door.

"Come in."

Gladys enters. I have pinched my cheeks to redden them, just in time. "Your father requests your attendance in the drawing room Miss."

Lockhart bows as I enter and my heart somersaults. His hair grown longer, tied back with a thin strip of leather. "Please accept my condolences mistress Wren, at the passing of your mother." His empathic blue eyes hold me in their gaze.

"Thank you Sire." I dip my head.

"Sire Edwards has asked to speak with you privately over some matter," Father remarks sternly. "I would prefer another to be present, Arlet will accompany you."

"No," I say a little too quickly. "I am quite comfortable being alone with Sire Edwards."

Father assesses him. "If you are sure."

"I am sure, father."

"Very well, I will be in the study."

My head swims; I take a seat on the cushioned bench. "Would you care to sit beside me?" I pat the heavy damask, surprising myself. Lockhart almost trips as he joins me, and I stifle a grin.

He speaks cordially of Tenby. "Merek and Aelwen have a son."

"Is the child well, surely he has arrived early, they have not been wed six months?"

"He is a big strapping lad like his father."

I can guess the reason but say nothing, and we fall silent. It has started to rain, droplets pressing against the window. Lockhart is skirting round the reason for his visit, straightening his doublet, staring at the floor, as though searching for words in the dust.

The silence stretches and I say, "It is a handsome horse you arrived on."

He grins, face full of mischief. "It isn't mine; I borrowed it."

"Oh, to whom does it belong?" I enquire.

"A squire, Mistress. Let's just say his card skills where not as good as he expected." Reminded of the devil card, I tuck loose hair into my cap. Perhaps sensing my disquiet, Lockhart becomes serious.

"Mistress, Wren, may I ask of your forthcoming marriage to Sire Roberts, do you care for him?"

Raindrops slide down the glass in bleak resignation. "Father believes it to be for the best," my forlorn reply.

"Wren, please look at me." His eyes reflect my sadness. "You may see me as a pretentious fool, and aware I may be met by a slap across my face, and instant dismissal."

Is the news he brings so awful it would cause such a reaction? I image pointing a finger at the door, him leaving with eyes downcast, like a dog with its tail between its legs. "Please express your thoughts, Sire," I say uneasily.

"I cannot seem to," he pauses, looking deeply into my eyes. "My heart calls to you." His words come quickly, "I think of you constantly, and always hoped, you cared for me." He lets out a long breath. I sense he has been holding onto the speech for a long time.

I should act demure, shocked, but cannot stop a smile spreading across my face. "You care, for me?" I touch my chest, my heart threatening to explode into a million bright stars of happiness.

"Yes, I have always cared for you. I understand you are worthy of much more than I can offer." He shrugs. "If you wish me to leave." He fumbles with the ties of his collar.

I cock my head. "I don't want you to leave, Lockhart. My heart speaks in the same manner, about you."

He mirrors my smile with his own. "Wren, your answer brings much happiness to my heart." Reaching for my hand, running his thumb along my skin tenderly, I am overcome. "I have nothing but myself to offer, no riches, nor land, but I will work hard, Wren."

"Oh Lockhart, I want only you."

A band of tension I hadn't consciously been aware of lifts from my shoulders. He fumbles in the pocket of his doublet, extracting a wooden object.

"It is a love spoon, will you accept it, cariad?" Understanding the significance of such a gift, I nod eagerly.

"Lockhart it is beautiful, did you make it yourself?"

"Yes, I know it's not worth anything but…"

"I shall treasure it."

"For now, I suggest we keep this secret. I must find us suitable accommodation, or your father will never agree."

"I will wait Lockhart, but father," I falter, and my heart plummets. "He will not hear of it, Lockhart, will deny us, bring forward the wedding to Harold, if he knows of such."

"We will find a way, Wren, I feel the truth of it." Lockhart helps me from the seat. Slipping an arm around my waist, bringing me closer, his touch infuses my spine with cascading warmth. Resting my head on his chest, his heart strong and clear beats against my ear. My own singing with joy. "Wren, may I be bold and ask if I might kiss you?"

I have no fear of this man; raising my head, gently, tenderly, our lips meet.

I write to Lockhart as often as I am able without arousing suspicion. It is mackerel season, he replies, says his face turned brown beneath the sun. Tells me Branwen has offered land on Wills Mark which comes complete with a building, although currently little more than rubble. He writes there are enough stones on the island to make a modest house. Selling his mother's goblet to thatch the roof. I understand it will be different to all I am accustomed to, but preferable to a life with Harold, who is the grand old age of forty-five. I shudder. When father questions my incoming mail, I tell him Branwen and I have become friends, how it is rare to find a literate woman. This small lie, I feel, worth the risk. He does not approve but allows me to continue. In the drawer of the small table in my room, I find the last piece of Velum. I must remind father to purchase more, he forgets everything I ask, perhaps deliberately to prevent my correspondence. *Dearest Lockhart,* I write. Gladys knocks and enters. "Your father wishes to see you in the drawing room, Miss." I slip the letter beneath my book, away from prying eyes.

"Sit, Wren," father points to the chair before I have barely entered the room. He shifts foot to foot. "We are moving to Cardiff," he says bluntly. "We will be leaving within the next few days so ensure you have packed what you need."

This unexpected news holds me in its grasp, and I await explanation. When none is forthcoming, I ask, "How long will we be away?"

He looks at me sternly. "You misunderstand Wren, we will not be returning, ever." He paces. "If you had married Harold when I requested you to, you would have been out of the way living in comfort by now, but no, you chose to defy me. Claiming you needed more time to grieve your mother. So, it is your own fault we find ourselves in this predicament. Harold will most likely renege on our arrangement when he hears about this, you think of only yourself, Wren."

Returning to my room, dazed and confused, deeply hurt by his words, the velum waits where I left it just a short while ago, yet my whole world has changed. I write to Lockhart with the utmost urgency.

Over the following days, men arrive, taking furniture, paintings, even personal belongings, indiscriminately pouring mother's jewellery into a sack. It is money to them, but to me, so much more, a value without price. Sadness becomes my companion. The servants are dismissed. Father remains in his study as they collect their belongings, but I cannot allow Gladys to leave without saying goodbye and wait by the front door. She carries her sack down the stairs, her usual bright demeanour packed away with her cap and apron.

"I am dreadfully sorry; I am sure you will find alternative employment. Father has written a glowing reference."

"None of this is your fault Miss," Gladys says kindly.

Arlet trudges behind her. "I think it is, actually, all your fault," she addresses me angrily, wagging a finger in my face. "Conversing with that sorceress. I've seen where you send your letters. Has she been sending you spells?" I am taken aback. "Funny, isn't it, how your husband died soon after you were wed, and where did you go, to that witch island."

Gladys pulls on her arm. "Think what you are saying Arlet."

She shrugs her off. "Then your mother dies," she growls. "Now we are all homeless after all these years of service."

Father appears from his study. "What is this commotion?" he demands.

I cannot speak, shaking after such a vicious attack. Arlet changes quick as flicking a finger. "We were just saying our goodbyes, Sire."

"Well, be on your way, you are not needed here anymore."

Our few remaining belongings are loaded onto the cart. Another chapter in the page of life ending. The weather is hot and sticky, reminding me of the day I married Emlyn. Was that only a year ago? So much has happened, so much has changed. I wonder if I am in fact to blame, bad luck follows wherever I go. The house, I surmise, sold to pay off father's gambling debts, but does our plight lie with me? Maybe I am being punished, for loving Emlyn's brother and that is wrong? Can loving someone be wrong? When asked were in Cardiff we will be staying, father has avoided giving me an answer, and I wonder if he even knows himself. It will be hard for Lockhart to find me with no address, no way of knowing where I am. All I can hope for, is he will not give up until he finds me.

Roads baked by the sun, clouds of billowing grey dust, irritating my eyes. We have come many miles, and I am parched and hungry. Father books us into an Inn, but I do not sleep, fearful of the noises drifting under the door. Laughter, shouting. A woman screams. I cover my ears but hear it still. Scuffles, banging doors.

The following day my rear is sore from bouncing along on the cart. I wish Cardiff would appear and we could stop, yet equally I fear it. By midday we have reached Merthyr Tydfil. Father purchases two small loaves from the baker's and I welcome the chance to stretch my legs. Bringing water to the horse, I gaze back along the road we have travelled while she drinks. Home, Tenby, Wills Mark, all seem so far. A farmer is moving his sheep, guiding them across the main street to a field beyond. There is a man on a horse, held up by the event, who looks, no, it cannot be. My heart pounds, I squint, cover my eyes with a hand to see more clearly. The sheep accounted for, the man on the horse sets off with a gallop. I watch him come closer, disbelieving, he seems not to have noticed me and is almost past before I shout. "Lockhart, Lockhart." The horse halts, he turns in the saddle. Lockhart dismounts, hurries back to me. "You came." My lip quivers with emotion.

"Wren, I feared I would not find you."

Father approaches, waving his arms. "What is the meaning of this!" He steps between us. "What are you doing here?" he addresses Lockhart.

"I am here to take Wren back to Tenby."

"Absurd, who do you think you are?" Father snaps.

"I believe Sire, with all respect, Wren wishes to come with me."

"You have no right." Father glares at Lockhart. "Come along Wren we must be on our way." Father grabs my arm pulling me towards the cart.

"Father, no, I wish to go with Lockhart." I shake my arm free.

Father stops, looks stunned. "Do not be ridiculous child, I will not hear of it. You cannot leave with this man; he is naught but a soldier. Correction, from what I hear, he is naught but a fisherman." Father attempts to push me onto the cart but Lockhart blocks his way. "We have had enough of your family Sire, now please leave." Father sneers.

Lockhart straightens to his full height and crosses his arms tight across his chest. "I am not leaving without Wren."

"My daughter deserves better than you, you have never been more than a puppet for your brother, and now he has gone. God rest his soul, you are nothing." Father scoffs. "Now get out of my way."

A man with wide shoulders, wearing a blood-spattered apron appears in the doorway of the butcher's shop. "What is the meaning of this ruckus?" He rushes towards us.

Father looks him up and down. "I see it as none of your business, Sire, what I require is a man of the Law. Do you have such a person in this town?"

The man narrows his eyes, forehead lined with deep wrinkles. "That will be me, Sire."

Lockhart steps forward. "May I be so bold to enquire the correct term to address you by, Sire?"

"Ifor Tudor, constable for Merthyr, have been for almost twenty years, and I don't like trouble in this town, so, explain, what seems to be the problem here?"

"This man," Father points at Lockhart, "is attempting to abduct my daughter, I insist you arrest him immediately. I assume you have the power of arrest?" He assess Ifor.

"I do not like your tone, or lack of respect, Sire." The constable frowns and they eye each other. He turns to Lockhart. "Is this true Sire?"

"No, of course not, I am, err, I am taking my wife back to Tenby." Lockhart using the man's dislike of father to his advantage, but wife?

Father folds his arms in defiance. "She is not his wife; I can assure you, and as her father, I am her guardian, and she comes with me."

"Constable," Lockhart speaks with a confident air. "I may call you constable?" Ifor nods. "My name is Sire Lockhart Edwards. Why not ask the lady her name?"

Ifor clears his throat. "Mistress, would you mind?"

Realising Lockhart's aim, I smile sweetly, cupping my shaking hands within the fabric of my skirts. "Yes of course constable, my name is Wren Edwards."

This is the truth, Lockhart and father both know it.

"But she is not his wife." Father splutters.

"I am sorry, Sire," Ifor looks apologetic. "The lady has told me she has his name, and by all accounts, that makes her his wife and his possession."

"Wren," Father implores.

"I am sorry father, but I am to go with Lockhart, please send word when you are settled in Cardiff."

"You are sure this is what you want?" Father asks quietly.

"It is," I reply.

"Very well." Father climbs onto the cart, addressing Lockhart sourly, "I pray your intention is to make an honest woman of her?"

"You have my word Sire,"

"And you will look after her better than your brother did? I will come looking for you if I hear otherwise," he warns.

"I promise."

Father clutches the reins, staring ahead. "Do not think you have my blessing."

"Until you are married you will stay with me," Branwen insists.

"How can we marry? Father will not give his blessing." I protest.

Branwen smiles. "Ranulf can do it."

I glance at Lockhart, who appears as perplexed as I, asking Branwen, "Ranulf, how?"

"Oh, Lockhart, he is a druid. He may be unable to perform a Christian ceremony, but he can perform a druid wedding. If we draw up a spousal, it will be perfectly legal."

I know nothing of these people and their beliefs. Until my arrival on Wills Mark, druids were a people and place I had never heard spoke of. Old Welsh customs I had deemed myth and legend, belonging to a distant past. Certainly, no longer practiced.

"I do not really know anything about the druid religion." I am anxious, and tuck stray hair into my cap.

"Druidism isn't a religion, it is a way of life, honours all life," Branwen explains. "Since Christianity became the approved way, we have become isolated, but still very much a part of Wales and Welsh tradition and will always remain so."

"Can you tell us more, about what you do?" Fearful of the rumoured association with the occult.

"Druids are aware of all nature can reveal," Branwen begins. "The sky, sun, stars, the cycles of the moon, cloud movements, the rise and fall of the tides. The cycles of seasons, animal, and human. To understand our place within the world, not to control, but to live beside it, in harmony." Lockhart is sitting forward, elbows on his knees. "Our culture is based on truth, in word, thought and deed, making the land fruitful and everyone worthy."

"What about rituals, ceremonies?" Lockhart asks.

"Yes, we have ceremonies and celebrate the coming seasons. It is our way of giving thanks for the bounty we receive. Some druids are also blessed with the ability to journey to the Otherworld; it is not so far away as you have been led to believe."

Lockhart strokes his beard. I have noticed this habit when collecting his thoughts. "What do you think, Wren?" He turns to me.

Branwen cuts in. "See, he is already a druid, he just hasn't realised it yet, accepting all as equal. The elements, the animals, man, and woman."

"I am not sure," I reply. "It sounds right to honour all things equally, but I have been raised a Christian, I must admit I am a little concerned Branwen. Do you believe God would punish us, for such a transgression from the Christian faith?"

"Why would he penalise you for honouring all things?" Branwen looks a little confused.

I drop my gaze to my hands cupped in my lap. "It just appears our love for each other is being punished."

"I am uncertain why you would think this way, Wren," Branwen says quietly.

My lip quivers: I look to Lockhart for support, and he takes my hand, a simple act which would be frowned upon in Tenby, in fact anywhere but here. "It's just," I dab a tear at the corner of my eye. "Emlyn dying, then mother, father losing the house, it feels like we are being dealt the wrath of God."

Branwen sits beside us on the bench, tenderly tucking another lock of hair back inside my cap. A simple gesture that makes me feel acknowledged, heard, for what may well be the first time in my life, and I wonder, maybe, if this could be where I belong. "My child, God does not punish. Regardless of your past teachings, I assure you, neither the Christian God, nor the druid god's and goddesses wish for anything other than your peace and happiness. They may send learning, things to overcome, but never for punishment, always to show you something, although understanding what it is, may not always be easy." Branwen kisses my forehead, the way a mother does to her beloved child, something my own mother failed to do, even once. I feel cared for by this woman I barely know. It warms my heart, feels, right. "You deserve love as much as anyone; you and Lockhart are meant to be. If you choose to see recent events differently, with awareness, you may realise all that transpired, ensured you were brought together. Divine guidance, angels watching over you. Call it what you will, it matters not, but understand, jointly your power is doubled. Your love reaches out to touch others."

I bite my lip apprehensively.

"I sense your unease." Branwen looks thoughtful. "It is perfectly understandable, there is a lot to take in, but let me choose a different tack." She smiles covertly. "There are stories that suggest Jesus came to Wales, before moving on to Glastonbury, where he received lessons from the druids."

"That cannot be true, surely?" Lockhart frowns disbelievingly.

"Well," Branwen considers. "The druids of Glastonbury were established long before Christianity, therefore, would certainly have been there in that era."

His eyes widen.

"All I am trying to point out, is that the beliefs of Christians and druids are possibly based on the same ideals."

Mulling over what I am being told, it is both farfetched, yet somehow believable. Lockhart eagerly asks more questions, "This island, has it always been inhabited by druids?"

"Probably the people here originally would not have identified themselves with that name as such, but it has always been a spiritual and mystical place."

"So why is the island called Will's Mark? That doesn't sound very mystical, or even Welsh."

"There is a story about this also." Branwen grins conspiratorially. "Will is short for William, which means resolute protector, and Mark, denotes to identify, symbolise as it were, the importance of the place."

"Why is it important?" Lockhart asks thoughtfully.

"Well," Branwen continues eagerly. "Have you heard the suggestion that Taliesin himself was born in Tenby, or here about?"

Lockhart shakes his head.

"He obviously held the place close to his heart, even writing a poem. One part goes; There is a fair fort on the coast; pleasantly, each is given his share. I know in Tenby, pure white the seagull, the host of Bleiddudd, lord of the fort."

"A fort," Lockhart chips in. "Would that be where the castle is now?"

Branwen nods. "I believe so."

"That's Tenby though, not here."

"Ah," Branwen continues. "We must consider, Caldey island was once connected to Tenby, but tides and time tore it from the shores. So, the fact is, at one time this island would also have been joined to Tenby."

"I guess that makes sense." He strokes his beard again. "That still doesn't tell me why it is a place of importance."

"Oh, but it does. Wills Mark, resolute protector for a place of importance."

We both look at her blankly. "Lockhart, it is a portal for Annwn, the Otherworld. I told you it was close."

Lockhart scoffs. "Annwn is just a myth, isn't it?"

"Taliesin spoke of it, and it has been suggested, he travelled there, maybe even received guidance from the Lords of the underworld, and if Taliesin did in fact come from this area, then it makes sense that this is the place he came to gain insight."

I consider this revelation and find my voice. "I have heard it said Annwn is a mirror image of this world, with castles and kings and green pastures, but I have never heard any suggestion of it being located anywhere near Tenby."

"What folk fail to understand, is there are a number of locations where you can enter, Annwn is everywhere." Branwen smiles broadly. "There are portals located in various parts of Wales, and in England. Glastonbury is just one of many, and as I previously mentioned, a place of druids, and possibly visited by Jesus. The name of this island suggests, one of those gateways is here." Branwen's eyes rest on mine. "It is home to the faeries Wren, and I believe Taliesin knew this."

A shiver snakes up my spine. "There is no suggestion of any of this bearing any truth though, is there?"

"If you have been taking notice." Branwen sighs. "You will be aware that everything has a meaning, you just need to search it out."

Lockhart scratches his head. "You speak in riddles Branwen."

"This island," she spreads her arms, "as I said, was once part of Tenby, therefore made from the same properties, mainly limestone."

"So," Lockhart frowns. "Why does it matter what it is made from?"

"Limestone is an assisting stone. It grounds and centres you, encouraging purification and positive thought. It enhances healing."

"It can do all that!" Lockhart shakes his head.

"Yes, it can." Branwen points a finger at him. "Mark my words this is why people like us are here, in this specific location, to aid what needs to be done."

"Which is?"

"To hear the echoes from Annwn, Lockhart, and transform what has been before."

I feel great unease; I am eager to change the subject. "Can you tell me about the marriage ceremony, what would that be like?"

Branwen turns her attention to me. "Well let's see, in Druidism there are ten degrees of marriage, I think the first degree would be the most appropriate. A union between a man and woman of equal rank and property. The way things stand, I believe this to be correct, would you agree?"

Lockhart smiles at me, love evident in his eyes. "We agree," Lockhart replies for us both, but behind my smile, anxiety and concern trickle through my blood.

Chapter 14

Lockhart

The embroidered green doublet complements dark green breeches. "It seems to be my wedding outfit. I wore it for Merek's and…" Wren and Emlyn taking their vows impresses on my mind's eye.

"Till death do us part. The past is over, let it go." Ranulf offers a crooked smile and nods admiringly. "The green man, how apt."

The small congregation gather on the headland. Merek, Aelwen and baby Bevan, along with my adopted mother, Enid. A second wedding working its magic of putting any grievance towards Branwen aside. Both look guarded but stand together. Aneira, our closest neighbour on the island, her son Halwyn and daughter Ffion also in attendance, alongside the women in white gowns, who I now understand to be a sisterhood of druids. They circle the congregation. A rippling sea gently slaps the shore below, bright yellow sun dipping in and out of fluffy white clouds, blowing lazily across the autumn sky. September is an auspicious month for marriage, Branwen says. A time for harvest, gathering the fruits of your labour, a time to give thanks to the land for sharing its bounty.

Wren arrives on a pony led by Aneira's husband, Geraint, in the pale green grown she wore the first time I saw her. Embroidered emerald leaves added to the central rosebud, and lace to the plain collar and cuffs, complimenting the lace gloves, a gift from myself. Her dark hair crowned with a headdress of wheat and corn leaves. In similar coloured outfits, we fit perfectly.

Throughout the ceremony, a lump sits in my throat. My heartfelt words are spoken with a smile. "I ask for the blessing of our union, from father of the sky and mother of the land." It feels surreal, that I am an actor in a play, barely believing my wishes have come true.

Wren's words, precise and thoughtful, "I promise to love, respect and honour you."

Ranulf instructs us to hold hands, Branwen tying white ribbon around our wrists.

"Your union has been blessed." Ranulf smiles at each of us. "You are now husband and wife."

Merek pours grain over our heads, some finding its way down my collar. I grab Wren's hand and actively pursued by the others we run downhill to Geraint's farm, laughter carried on the breeze drifts into the trees and settles on the ground. Every footfall feeding the land with joy.

We enjoy a fine feast of apples and pork, washed with wine. "Did you know," Geraint informs, "Norman rulers changed the words of meat. Their Lords ate pork, not swine, beef, not cow, and mutton, not sheep."

"Who cares," Merek pipes up, munching a chicken leg. "Call it what you will as long as its edible."

We laugh, and he shrugs licking his fingers. Music follows. Geraint on the drum, Halwyn playing the flute. My footwork is far from refined, and I try not to embarrass Wren, bowing at the end of the tune. "Let's get a drink." I lead her to a bench. Handing her a cup of wine she drinks thirstily, and I take the opportunity to speak what prays on my mind. "Are you concerned that we did not marry in church?"

She replies honestly, "I admit I am unsure, of what this new life will bring. It will take some getting used to, for it is very different to how I lived before." My brow creases, and she touches my face. "Slowly I am coming to realise the value of the druid life. Just look around you Lockhart, look at the happiness here amongst these people. We do not need a church, we have all we need right here, I am sure God has given us his blessing."

Hand in hand through the starry night, music and singing drifting across the island, we head to our home. "I must carry you over the threshold, it is Welsh tradition." I lift her easily and we fall headlong through the door. A rushlight glows faintly beside the bed and we stand in awkward silence. Until the marriage is consummated, her father has the right to demand her back. I brush her lips tenderly with mine. "Are you happy Wren?"

She nods.

"Do you wish me to leave, until you have retired?"

"I feel a little shy," she confesses. "Perhaps if you just look away?"

I wait, a pep talk running through my head, about taking it slow, and being gentle.

"Lock, I am ready."

I turn to find the woman I love, lying in my bed. Instantly hard with longing I quickly undress, grain falling from my shirt which makes us laugh, lightening the tension. Wren fiddles with the ties on her shift, and I slide in beside her lifting her chin with a finger, looking deeply into her eyes. "Wren, you need have no fear of me, I will not hurt you. I do not want you to dread me coming to bed at night. I do not wish it to be like that for us, so if I do anything you do not like, tell me." I search her face for approval.

"I trust you Lock." Leaning forward she kisses me, her warm lips pressing against mine.

Wrapping my arms around her I stroke her back, my need increasingly urgent. Slow down, I remind myself, slipping the simple undergown from her shoulders, cupping her breast and planting small kisses on her soft skin. She gasps, her hand pressing on the back of my head, keeping me there, which excites me further. My hand slips between her legs, and she moves slightly, inviting my touch. Slowing to increase her pleasure, but it will be too late if I don't act. Positioning myself between her, the sensation of her warmth and softness wrapped around me, something I imagined many times, threatens my control. I move, slowly, and steal a glance; her eyes are closed, responding to my movements. Sensations build, my movements quicken, beyond the point of return. A catch in my breath, the pleasured moan… Breathless, I rise onto my elbows to look at her. She bites her lip, looks coy, and says, "Lock, I did not know it could be so nice."

Wood is stacked into a tower on the headland. Skulls of dead animals and large stones placed around the circumference in preparation for the celebration of Samhain. I ask Branwen the significance of the festival.

"It is a time when our world and the Otherworld move closer, so dress in your darkest clothing."

"Why do we need to do that?"

"To avert evil and ensure only helpful spirits are around us."

With no intention of taking chances, I dress in black. The setting Sun draws the druids from their homes, and we sit in silent reverence, observing the sky alight in fiery orange and red. Overcome by the beauty, I vow to take time to notice the world around me, to feel my connection to nature. The final band of golden light sits like a mantel across the horizon. Stars appearing, as the world grows dark. The bonfire is lit, smoke billowing to the hunter's moon, which casts a rippling white glow across the sea. Cadfan Owen, who sells meat in Tenby on market days, and Loan Pritchard, supplier of eggs and vegetables to the castle are here on the island. More druids in the area it appears, than I previously realised.

"Who are the women in white sat in a circle?" Wren asks, remembering they had been guests at our wedding.

"They are a sisterhood of nine, performing healing work, they live in the woodland," I explain.

She is about to ask more, but Ranulf has moved to the fire, and silence falls on the gathering. Raising his hands to the sky, his embroidered cloak twinkles in the firelight. "On this night of Samhain, spirits are set free to roam and we must protect ourselves from the evil ones, remain concealed, ensure the demons are given no opportunity," Ranulf sweeps his hands, "to take our souls." He clutches his heart and dips his head.

Geraint beats the drum, a slow rhythmic thud, thud, thud.

"We call for protection, protection for our spirits, guidance for our souls." Ranulf circles the bonfire, chanting, "Spirits protect and guide our souls; spirits protect and guide our souls."

A gust blows in across the ocean, seemingly in response to his words, golden flames pulled higher. Branwen joins the chanting, instigating others to follow, clapping in time to the drumming, building the energy that reverberates around the island, rising into the night sky. "Spirits protect and guide our souls; spirits protect and guide our souls."

Ranulf falls to his knees, hands in prayer, the chanting and drumming ceases. "We ask the God's and Goddesses of Annwn, to honour the departed ones from the last year. Our loved ones, now residing in the Otherworld. We give thanks, for our harvest and our health and pray, we will be blessed in the coming year with abundant crops. Bless the animals preparing for hibernation, that they sleep safely through the dark days of winter."

A lighter atmosphere resumes. Friendly chatter, food, and games. I emerge from a barrel of water, hair stuck to my forehead, an apple in my mouth. Wren laughs heartily. "You remind me of a wild boar's head, on the dinner table of Kings."

A bowl encased in a woven sleeve, embroidered with a design of mistletoe, is placed in the centre of a small table, and filled with water. Ranulf sits on a stool, hands held over the bowl, whispering an incantation. He calls Geraint to come forward and sit opposite. "Stir the water." Ranulf instructs him. Geraint dips in a finger, swishing it around.

"What is he doing?" Wren whispers to Aneira, sat beside her.

"Telling fortunes, he calls it scrying."

I am surprised and intrigued.

"Your crops will grow well next year, and Aneira will bring you another son."

Ranulf pats him on the arm. Aneira whispers to Wren, but I overhear. "He is correct, I am with child, but no one knows, it is early days, I haven't even told Geraint." She sniggers. "He will know now."

Wren is called next, but despite my urging and prompting she shakes her head.

Ranulf shouts over, "No need mistress Wren, you will have a babe in your arms by next Samhain, I can see that without you coming any closer." Everyone laughs and Wren's cheek dimples, I think the prediction pleases her.

"Lockhart, your turn, let us see what you have to show us." Ranulf beckons. I sit precariously on the stool, stirring the water. Ranulf gazes intently into the pool of clear liquid for a long time, a questioning expression on his face.

Mumbles begin amongst the crowd and feeling uneasy, I ask, "What do you see?"

Ranulf looks up. "I do not understand what I see. It is showing me two lives interlinked, some elements the same, some not." He frowns in confusion. "Give me your hands." Ranulf's hands are small and warm. Closing his eyes, forehead tense with concentration, they fly open, wide with awe. "Your reason for being earth bound is… A second chance." An intense heat warms my stomach. Dragon fire within? Leaning forward, Ranulf whispers, "Bifurcation, that is what I see, come and find me tomorrow, alone." His demeanour lightens. "Lockhart is indeed a druid, with the gift of second sight. Who is next?"

As the night draws late, the islanders settle by the fire, drawn to the remaining warmth. Ranulf takes on the role of bard, reciting poems from the time of Taliesin, "I am old, I am young, I am Gwion, I am universal, I am gifted with a perceptive spirit. I remember the ancient wisdom of the Gwyddylffitchi, defenders of the cauldron's fire." I reason that if Taliesin had been a druid, it must be part of the Welsh blood. With the moon at its highest, we hold hands around the dying bonfire, bowing to the souls of departed loved ones. Thoughts of Emlyn amass in my throat. The air has grown damp and chill, the celebration at a close, slowly the islanders disperse to their beds. Ranulf remains by the fire absorbing the remaining heat. Branwen has joined him, and they glance in my direction. Certain I am the topic of their conversation, sensing something is about to unfold which I cannot stop. It is time to tell Wren everything.

Snuggled in bed, Wren rests her head on my chest. I silently ask for the right words, and a warmth returns to my stomach. "Wren," I begin nervously. "There is something I need to tell you. I am not sure how to explain it, because I do not fully understand myself."

"Go on," she says sleepily.

"I appear to be different Wren; I do not know why. It has begun only recently, as I do not remember being this way always. However," I falter. "I see things others cannot."

"What sort of things?" She yawns.

"Well, colours around people. Yours are beautiful Wren, like a rainbow."

She pulls away, frowning. "I do not understand Lock; I don't have rainbow colours."

"Oh, but you do Wren, Branwen believes it is because you are a faerie."

"A what?" She sits bolt upright. "A faerie, I think I would know. I am just an ordinary Welsh girl, nothing special."

"Yes, you are." I smile. "You are special to me."

She laughs dryly. "Well, that may be so, but a faerie!" She cocks her head. "Is being amongst the druid community the reason you think this way, faeries and spirits; indeed, all manner of entities are seen as fact here."

I contemplate her question. "They may have had some influence, but I realised before we came to the island, that nothing is quite as it appears."

"So, is there anything else you wish to tell me?" she asks tentatively, and I rake a hand through my hair.

"I sense how people are feeling or if they ail."

"Are you telling me you can read minds, can you read mine?" she asks cautiously.

"Oh no, not mind reading Wren, you misunderstand. I just sense if they are troubled, or angry, or hiding something."

"Is that why you have always suspected Tom Griffiths of wrongdoing?"

"I guess so, yes, it is an intuitive feeling."

"Is this why you brought me to Wills Mark?"

"It seems destiny brought us to the druid community; do you not feel that?"

"I am happy here, with you, although I do find some of the customs a little strange. As a Christian these new ideas are not what I am used to, they do appear somewhat, dare I say, primitive."

I pull myself up, piqued by her reply. "The ways of these people are as old as Wales, Wren; do you not feel it within you?"

"Lockhart, I feel much confusion," she answers honestly. "Some days I savour the simple druid life, the warmth of the people. Other days my past follows me like a dog snapping at my ankles, tripping me. I say the wrong thing, I judge people, though I do not mean to." Tears well. "Every forward step in acceptance of this new life is pursued closely with a doubt." My heart constricts. Wrapped in my own doubts and fears, I failed to fully acknowledge how difficult these changes are for Wren. She dabs her eyes. "What did Ranulf see in you tonight, Lockhart? He said you were on earth for a second chance, what does that mean?"

"I do not know Wren; he wishes to speak with me tomorrow. What I do know, is there is a growing awareness inside of me, which I cannot ignore and need to understand. Branwen tells me I have a dragon within me, and a guardian standing behind. You, my faerie, stand before me." I kiss her forehead. "Branwen believes you also have healing powers; we can help each other." I scan her rainbow to gauge her feelings.

"Does it scare you?" She asks quietly. "Seeing things."

"I am a soldier trained for war, Wren." I say bravely. "But yes, I am a little scared. In battle you can see the enemy, this is something I cannot see but equally know I must face."

"Do you see it as an enemy?"

"I guess that depends on what Ranulf has to say."

"Sit, Lockhart." Branwen scolds with a sigh. "All this pacing, you're wearing a hole in the floor." Dust scatters in rays of sunlight filtering through the open door, Branwen brushing the offending dirt outside, only for most of it to return back indoors. "The spring equinox is a good night for your journey, a time for new growth, new beginnings." She rests the broom against the wall and wipes her hands on a grubby cloth. "We believe you are ready."

Since Samhain, instructions in the form of learning, initiations, and practice of the druid way, have become central to my life. In the still of night, when only the hoot of an owl or cry of a fox disturbs the blanket of silence, my mind travels often to Ranulf's words, the day following the scrying. "I believe you are guided for a specific purpose. One which you failed to achieve in a past life." When questioned, Ranulf said he knew not the objective, only the importance of its fruition. The words stitching into the fabric of my being. Yet months later, I am no further in knowing what, or why.

Ranulf reiterates, "The dragon has been neglected long enough, but take heed, for it can be a perilous journey to Annwn, one not to be rushed. We are being honoured, our souls offered a leap in progress, if successful." Branwen turns to me.

"Today, offers an opportunity to move closer to the Otherworld, maybe not enter it, that may take longer. We shall have to wait and see, you can never be sure, what will happen."

I drum my fingers against my breeches. "Is it dangerous?"

Branwen's eyes flit to Ranulf. "You will be safe," he replies. "Now I must leave you to it."

"You are not coming with me?" I look pleadingly at Ranulf.

"There is no need for me to be there." He grins widely, revealing the gaps between his teeth. I look at him sideways.

"They are all women; you can't expect me to be alone with all of them."

Ranulf laughs, pressing a hand into my shoulder. "Don't be scared Lockhart, they won't make you do anything you don't want to." He winks mischievously.

Leaves of bright spring green shimmer in a gentle breeze. Accompanied by Branwen, we traipse through woodland undergrowth to the dwelling of the nine sisters. A circular wooden structure. Sitting east of the island, offering views across the vast expanse of water, and the welcoming light of dawn each new day. A turf roof bright with yellow dandelions billows with grey smoke from an opening in the centre. A shiver of uncertainty races through my veins. Witches around a cauldron come to mind, and I wonder if they have plans to boil my bones, or brain. I have listened to too many of Aeron's stories.

"Don't look so worried." Branwen urges me through the door. Skulls of sheep and goat hang on the walls. A heady aroma of sage mixed with woodsmoke, basking the room in a foggy haze.

Two sisters hook each of my arms. "Come Lockhart, you are most welcome."

I glance over my shoulder to Branwen, but she does not look my way. A white sheet draped over a thin branch and fastened to the wall with twine acts as a curtain and is opened by an older woman with black hair and pale wrinkled skin. We duck inside, where a small dark room is lit with candles, bird feathers and coloured stones are placed strategically upon small boulders.

"Sit, Lockhart." Glenda indicates a small stool in the centre of the room. She is tall and willowy, a long plait of fair hair braided with white ribbon, resting against her back. Sian is shorter, with straight, dark brown hair, and deep brown eyes. Both of similar age to myself. Sian pulls off my boots, unbuttons my doublet, and removes my shirt. The older woman stands guard by the entrance, staring. Her hair is twisted into a tight bun and piled on top of her head like an adder waiting to strike.

"Is this strictly necessary?" I whisper to Sian; this is not what I expected.

"We must cleanse you, remove the darkness," she explains, pouring rosewater into her palm from a small pot, massaging it into my chest, the sweet aroma a pleasure. Glenda stands behind me and presses her thumbs on each vertebra from the base of my spine up to the soft indent of my skull, then circles just above the bridge of my nose with her third finger, splaying her hands upwards into my hair, exerting force at the point of the fontanelle. I relax into the soothing movements and close my eyes, feeling the imprint of their hands.

Sian breaks my trance. "Wear this Lockhart, colours affect your mood, and we need you as pure as possible, come through when you are ready."

Opening my eyes sleepily, she hands me a white robe, and they leave. Alone, I consider the option of sneaking out, but other than the way I have come, I see no exit. Aware of warmth in my stomach, I sigh. "You wish me to stay dragon, don't you?" I push a hand through my hair. "Be brave Lockhart, what is the worst that can happen?" Pulling the robe over my head before I can change my mind, I step beyond the curtain. Dried rushes prick the soles of my bare feet, and Glenda invites me to lie upon a long table covered in white muslin, handing me a sprig of dried mistletoe.

"Offer this to the guardians of the Otherworld. It is revered, marks the ending of darkness, and the coming of light and growth." She moves behind me, hands remarkably hot upon my head. Sian marks a symbol on my abdomen with fingertips, which tickles, and places her palms lightly over it. The older sister looks on, saying nothing, merely observing, her lips downturned, eyes so dark I cannot distinguish the pupils. The remaining sisters sit in a circle on the floor, holding hands. "Be at peace." Glenda blows warm breath over my face, and I close my eyelids. Telling myself I must be truly crazy to have agreed to this, that I should just make my apologies and leave. Soon, the tension in my shoulders and jaw subside, my breathing deepens and slows, heat from their hands seeping through my skin. In time, though I have no idea how long, I become aware of a tingling sensation creeping up my spine, and coloured lights, which dance behind my eyelids. Fascinated, I watch, remembering as a child, I would push fists against my eyes at night, and see coloured stars, much the same as this. Realising now, the colours are not stars, but spirals drifting away then coming closer, my body tingling. I'm aware of the women's hands, aware I am lying on the table, yet I feel absent. A brilliant white light appears, fading the spiral colours, filling my vision, wrapping around me in loving embrace, followed by a sensation of floating, moving towards the light, which feels natural, blissful. Remembering the mistletoe, I visualise handing it to the light, which whispers to me. What is it saying? I strain.

"The answers lie within Lockhart."

That voice, I have heard it before.

"Lockhart, awaken." Wren, I hear Wren. "Lockhart," her tone more urgent. Forcing my eyes open, I find I am home in bed; how did I get here? "Are you alright?" Wren is asking.

"Yes, I think so."

Branwen appears beside me. "What happened, can you remember?"

Leaving out being washed by the sisters, I don't want Wren getting the wrong idea, I relay what took place. "Coloured stars and swirls, spirals." I explain wide eyed. Branwen and Wren look at me intently. I rub my forehead. "A bright light, serene, beautiful, what could it have been?"

"Did you not ask?" Branwen queries.

"No, but it spoke. That is ridiculous though," I shake my head disbelievingly. "I mean how could it speak?"

"What did it say?" Branwen prompts, and I think for a moment.

"She told me the answers lie within."

Branwen claps her hands gleefully. "Wonderful, wonderful. Anything else?"

"I am not sure, I feel she did tell me things, but I cannot remember them."

"Excellent." Branwen smiles. "You did well Lockhart, that was immensely powerful. You cannot remember because she is working at a deeper level, behind your conscious awareness. What is inside must always change first before it is seen on the outside. She, you did say she, didn't you?"

I consider. "It sounded like a woman's voice."

"See, I told you it was a feminine energy, wait until I tell Ranulf." With that she picks up her skirts and is gone.

Wren perches on the edge of the bed. "Where you scared?"

"No, well at first, because I did not know what would happen, but once I saw the light, Wren, I cannot explain how wondrous it felt, like I belonged, totally accepted. No judgements, no animosity, just, just love. It is the only way I can describe it."

Chapter 15

Wren

Picking up the empty tankard from the table, I slump onto the stool. "A drained cup, that's how I feel." Kneading my back, little kicks inside my stomach. I smile wearily. "There, there, little one, it will not be long now before I see you." I rub my expanding belly, excited at the thought of holding our baby in my arms. The hour is growing late, the last rays of Sun lighting a small patch of floor, shining through the small bubble glass window of the cottage. The main room houses the fire, a table, bench, and two stools. "It may not be a design as grand as one of Inigo Jones, but it is home." A line Lockhart often repeats, proud of his workmanship. In the evenings, Lockhart returns from a hard day on the fishing boat with Aeron, or grubby from working with the animals. After eating, he stretches his long legs, dozing in front of the fire, and I read to him, the way I did after his injury. The First Folio of William Shakespeare, one of the few possessions I saved from the family home. Being a special reminder of my time with Lockhart, I hid it under my pillow. It is showing its age, the red binding split and fraying, the pages yellowed. I take it from the shelf and open it at the section of, *As you like it*. Which I will read tonight. "I like this place and willingly could waste my time in it." I do love this place. Occasionally missing the lovely dresses, I used to wear, and the beautiful home shared with my parents. I accept this is my life now, and like how druid women are seen as equal to their men. I'm allowed to do the same work, even having the same rights, but with the growing baby within me, it is becoming increasingly hard to move around, and therefore I spend most of my time at home. I waddle like an oversized duck to the crib; my hope is that the baby will be a boy. Lockhart wants a son. Initially I worried whether he would be happy should I bear a girl, but he had laughed. "If it be a girl, she will steal my heart just as her mother has."

Above the crib, the love spoon hangs from a nail. Taking it down, I look at the intricate design of the twisted stem and heart shaped scoop, turning it over to read. "Cariad, sweetheart." Tears fill my eyes. Constantly emotional, and unsure of everything, I wonder if it is just the pregnancy? We still make love, occasionally, but Lockhart is cautious, caring but not passionate, perhaps afraid of hurting me and the baby. I worry he does not find me attractive anymore. He claims tiredness, long hours. Taking advantage of the light summer evenings and the extra coin, the mackerel season brings, I see little of him. Any free time he spends with the sisterhood. I cannot help but wonder what happens in that woodland hut, he doesn't tell me much. Does he have feelings for Sian, or Glenda? They are the prettiest. I sigh deeply. I will feel happier once the baby is born, maybe then he will spend more time with me, with his family.

The room has grown dark. With no sign of Lockhart, his food ruined, Shakespeare left unread, I retire to bed, but my mind will not rest. Images of Glenda offering a cup of wine, Sian fluttering her eyelashes. Then I hear the creek of the door. He pulls off his boots, the noise of him so familiar. I cannot hold back and sob, angry, scared, wishing to express my fears, but afraid. Mother always held her emotions in check, but on reflection I wonder if this the cause of her headaches. Father was always reluctant to involve himself in what he saw as women's weakness. Lockhart said it would be different for us, our marriage was based on the druid's belief in truth, but old unease of father's angered reactions when I have been outspoken live on within me, anxiety laced through my internals. Lockhart enters with a tallow candle in hand. "Why are you crying?"

I face him, eyes red and puffy. "Look at me," I wail. "I am fat and ugly, and you do not want me anymore."

"Wren," he says tenderly, but I am in no mood for his excuses and explanations, words tumbling uncontrollably out of my mouth.

"You would rather be with Glenda and Sian than me, you spend all your time with them, which is your favourite?" Venom spills. "You tell me nothing Lockhart, what do you do there, what do you do?"

Lockhart appears shocked by my accusations, but I do not care. "Wren, how could you even think such a thing, what do you take me for, some philanderer?"

I cross my arms. "Pray tell Lockhart, are you?"

He glares, shaking his head, but says nothing.

"Am I to take it you have a guilty conscience, as you appear unable to give me an answer?" I spit the words.

His eyes narrow, jaw tenses. "You are lucky I am not punishing you for speaking to me like this, I am your husband, and you have no right to question me in this way."

"Oh, I wondered how long it would take." I kneel in the bed to face him. "All these ideals of being a druid, men and women being equal. Now when it comes to it, you want the freedom to take any woman you wish and expect your wife to say nothing of it."

He flails his hands. "I have done nothing wrong. Can you not see I am working myself into the grave to keep a roof over our heads? Believe me Wren, I am aware we do not live with the finery you are used to, and I am sorry I am unable to provide more, but I thought you understood. I thought you realised going to the sisterhood was something I must do. It is not a harem Wren; do you think I am working my way through all nine of them?"

His crestfallen expression dissipates my anger, and I stifle a grin. "Would you know what to do with nine women?" I ask with a snigger.

The mood broken, Lockhart shrugs. "No, it would scare the life out of me."

He sits on the bed and pulls me to him. "Wren, I do not want anyone but you. You are my wife, you carry our child within you, I could never wish for more."

"Oh, Lockhart." I sigh. "I just feel so big and uncomfortable, and fear losing you. My mind plays havoc when you go to the sisters, I imagine all sorts."

"Once the baby is born you must come with me, see what we do," Lockhart says. "They can help you too, I know you are a healer, Wren; you have healed my life. I want to share this with you, I want to share everything with you, but it can be hard to explain what happens."

The baby kicks and I place Lockhart's hand against my stomach. He smiles, feeling the movements. With one hand on my stomach, his other arm around my shoulders, I snuggle against him. "Please try and explain, it is such a big part of your life, and I want to be a part of it too, we both do."

"Well, let's see," Lockhart starts. "At first the sisters would, what they call, channel healing into me with their hands, and I would feel very relaxed, sometimes floating away to another world, a world so beautiful, but I have told you that before." I nod, warm and relaxed, his heartbeat against my ear, comforting me. "Anyway, after a few weeks Ranulf began coming also, he has been showing me how to read the colours around people, to understand what ails them. He says I have a natural ability to do so. He told me not to speak to anyone of what I saw, until I was sure I was seeing the truth. The thing is Wren, I am now realising that what I see, is true." He pauses. "That is not all." I look at him questioningly. "I know we are to have a boy; I have been shown."

I let out a small gasp.

"Really, you really know that?" Lockhart nods. "You wait and see; I will be right."

"What else?" I snuggle closer.

"Well, as you know, sometimes the feelings of other people overwhelm me, especially if their thoughts are of sadness."

"Do you feel it all the time?"

"No, not anymore, Ranulf and the sisters have shown me how to control it. I visualise a white hooded cloak around me and ask for protection, that way I can feel the emotions but to a lesser degree. I do see a golden light in my dreams at night sometimes too, but it brings comfort, it feels familiar. It is nothing to fear Wren, it is good, not evil."

"Does anything else happen?" I ask tentatively, and Lockhart laughs.

"Lessons Wren, that is all. Druids do not write down information, it is taught, and you must keep it in your head, all of it." He sighs, his chest rising and falling. "There is a lot to remember."

"Tell me some more," I ask sleepily.

"The summer solstice will be the next celebration," he explains. "A time to give reverence to the bounty provided by the sun." He details the sacred ceremony. "And did you know, druids believe we are reborn amongst the same people over and over, until we learn our lessons. Isn't that amazing?"

I do not reply, my eyes closing.

Damp warmth stirs me from slumber. My eyes flicker, registering darkness they close again. My back aches with an uncomfortable tightening. My eyes shoot open again. "Lock," I whisper, entwining my fingers within his. "Lock." I push his shoulder. "The baby is coming."

"The baby," he mumbles, then the news hits, and he pulls himself upright from the groggy depths of sleep. "Are you sure?"

It is a stupid question, the fluid holding our child cosy in nourished protection, seeps around the bed. "Quite sure," my reply tinged with fear.

Scrambling out of bed, removing his sodden nightwear, he pads barefoot to the fire hastily lighting the tallow candle. I am laid on my back, navel pushed outwards from my distended stomach. I can barely see over the nut-brown line running towards my mound. No one knows the reason for it. "Fetch Branwen," I urge, a grimacing pain inside.

Lockhart hastily pulls on breeches and boots. "I will be quick as I can."

The door slams, and I am alone with our child. I stroke my stomach. "Whatever happens little one, know I love you." I breathe deeply, another contraction rising. I imagine Lockhart running through the dark night, a waxing moon to light his way. "Branwen will come, and all will be well." I tell the baby, for I fear otherwise. Lockhart's mother died birthing him, as many do, or the child may become stuck, or never take its first breath. My mind will not rest, another contraction tightens. I pray Lockhart will hurry. Branwen said to ask assistance from the faerie midwife. Although sceptical, right now I will accept any comfort, and call out. "Queen Mab, please surround me in your faerie magic, that I might live, and our child be born healthy."

Lockhart returns with Branwen; I am relieved to see them both. "You cannot stay," she frowns at Lockhart. "Make yourself useful and fetch Aneira."

He kisses the top of my head, whispers "I love you" in my ear, and is off again.

"I should have all we need." Branwen peers into the small sack she has packed. "Pulsatilla, and sepia, arnica for the bruising, and horse parsley, to expel the afterbirth." She nods, satisfied with her selection.

The pains grow over the next hours, Aneira holding my hand, rubbing my back, wiping my brow, Branwen reassuring me, but their voices are distant, I belong to another world, where there is just me and my child, nothing beyond the relentless contractions, the excruciating pain and the belief I can take no more, that it will never end, and then Branwen is telling me to push, and it feels my whole insides are threatening to expel from between my legs. Then a slipping, and the rush of warm water.

"He is here." Aneira smiles, Branwen holding a scrap of arms and legs.

I hold my breath, until… He cries. Branwen hands him to me, we have made it.

Lockhart returns and sits beside me on the bed. I am contentedly rocking our precious child. He peeps at the baby and his face radiates love and awe, at the tiny button nose, and small pink lips suckling from my breast. He kisses my cheek. "Are you alright?" he asks.

"I am now." Our eyes return to the child. "I cannot believe he is ours, isn't he gorgeous," I remark. Lockhart nods. "Now he is here safely he needs a name, any ideas Wren?"

"Lockhart after you," I suggest.

"Um, I feel his first name needs to be one of his own." Lockhart strokes the child's hand; the baby grips his finger. "He's a strong boy." There is pride in his voice.

"Gwilym is a good Welsh name," Branwen proposes, "the meaning is protector, same as the island."

"Yes, I like that, what do you think Wren?"

"I agree, it suits him. Croeso, Gwilym Lockhart Edwards."

The child suffers with colic. I grow tired, rocking the child to prevent him waking his father. A few small spoonful's of mint seeped in water, and a warm compress massaged on his tummy help enormously and burping him after food. It is odd how relieving gas is seen as positive in an infant, how it is encouraged and cheered. Branwen brought an infusion of fresh chamomile, growing excessively in these parts during the summer months, to calm my nerves, and in turn calm the baby through my breast milk. I find it fascinating she knows all this, and I am eager to learn. My initial fears of druids being witches, and tales of human sacrifice, have proved unfounded. Where these ideas come from, I do not know, but it is clear these people are misunderstood. Their ways may be seen as old fashioned, but they work. I place Gwilym in a sling, and we set off to see Branwen. She tells me today is special but would not reiterate. A warm breeze blows, clouds white and fluffy in a bright blue sky, a pleasant stroll.

Branwen welcomes us with a smile. "Come in." She gestures. "I was just preparing for the Coll moon celebration."

"What does Coll mean?" I sit on the stool, rubbing my aching back. Gwilym is asleep, his cheeks pink from teething.

"It is an Irish word and translates to the life force inside you." She props the door open with a broom; streaks of sun lights the dust floating in the air. "They are there all the time." Branwen remarks, "we just don't notice."

"Sorry, what are you referring to?"

"The dust particles. Without the sun we are blind to them, as with most of life. There is much more than the eye can see."

I don't understand what she means. She sits opposite me and takes my hands. "I have an admission; I have invited you under false pretences." I tense. "I feared you would worry, should you know, about the ceremony?"

"Ceremony!" My heart beats faster. Branwen squeezes my hands.

"There is no need for concern, I assure you. Let me explain."

She fiddles in the pocket sewn to the front of her skirt, handing me a leaf. "Hazel," she explains. "Hazel moon is an alternative name for Coll moon. Do you understand the relevance to druid tradition?" I shake my head. "There are said to be nine hazel trees at the centre of the Otherworld, branches overhang the well of wisdom. When nuts are shed, they drop into the water, making it magical, and should you drink from it, whatever you need to see, or divine, will be revealed, for hazel is the tree of knowledge."

"You wish me to take part in this ceremony?" I am forging excuses in my head of how to avoid doing so. "Will I travel to Annwn, as Lockhart does? I'm not sure I would like to."

Branwen ponders. "I feel your journey, although interlaced with Lockhart's, has a different purpose and therefore I expect your experiences will be different."

"Do we have to wait until it is dark? I cannot keep Gwilym out so late." Panic is rising.

"No, we are going now."

"Now, no, really, I cannot. I need to go home; I will leave you to it."

Branwen touches my knee. "This is for you, Wren."

"I really don't think…" I begin, but she cuts in.

"Did you know your name means ruler, and in Welsh, Dryw, means both druid, and Wren, symbolising wisdom, divinity, healing and the Otherworld of Annwn."

"My name is connected to druids!" I cannot comprehend how this can be.

"It is magical, synchronistic, a sign." Branwen takes my hands. "Please, be open to possibility."

I chew my lip. Branwen says this is for me. Nothing is ever for me, always another. Lockhart, Gwilym. I feel confusion, unsure of who I am. Conflicting ideas. A druid, or a Christian. A wife, but at the expense of being a daughter. I stare at Gwilym sleeping peacefully, overcome with love. I am a mother, and he belongs here, on the island, and Lockhart believes I do too. This place is part of Lockhart's life, and if we are to integrate into the druid community, I must be willing to play my part. With reluctance, I relent.

We walk towards the sister's hut, but do not enter, veering to the left through a coppice of budding elm, birch and sycamore. Spotting a clearing on the right, I wonder if this is where Lockhart was brought for his ceremony. He explained what happened and fear pricks inside me. It looks calm now, but I could imagine at night, in the dark, it would be terrifying. We walk on, coming to a small clear lake, and beside it, two hazel trees, new leaves of bright spring green fluttering in the breeze.

"Sit with your back resting against the tree," Branwen instructs, "until the sisters arrive."

Gwilym has woken, and I feed him whilst we wait.

"The trees will impart their wisdom to you." Branwen sits beside us.

"How can they do that?" The bark is rough but warm against my back.

"We are connected to all, Wren, the tree transfers to you, and equally you transfer to it, so be careful of your thoughts."

Minutes later three of the sisters, Abefa, Caitrin, Everlee, along with Aneira, emerge from the trees. Gwilym finishes his feed and Aneira reaches for him. "I will take him." She turns.

"Where are you going?" I ask in panic.

"I will be in the sisters hut, this is women's business, no boys allowed." She smiles.

The three sisters sit with their back to the corresponding hazel tree. Branwen explains the power of having three sisters in attendance. "The trinity, a symbol of body, mind, and spirit. Past, present, future. The virgin, mother, crone. All is three. Light and dark, with you at the centre. The capacity to see beyond the appearance of the solid world, for you are equally, human, faerie and druid. The trinity."

"Me! Really Branwen, I don't think I can do anything out of the ordinary."

"Only because you do not believe you can. Your upbringing has taught you to be small and meek. That you are nothing more than a feeble woman. Which could not be further from the truth." She smiles kindly.

"How do you know?"

"I know for it is the same for us all. We all have the capacity to see beyond the illusion."

"Illusion? I don't understand, Branwen."

"Annwn, the otherworld, is not below us, or above us, but here. It surrounds us, and I, in fact, Ranulf and I both agree, that you and Lockhart, especially together, hold the capacity to break through the deception."

All the sisters have been given a separate task. Abefa collects water from the lake into a small cauldron, Everlee lights a small fire, proceeding to heat the water. Caitrin adds herbs, pours some into a cup and brings it to me.

Branwen answers my questioning look. "Belladonna. Only three sips though, that is enough."

I do as she instructs and then lie on the earth, looking through the branches of the tree. Sunlight flutters through the canopy of bright spring green. A spider weaves a web of intricate design. "A gossamer veil invokes a tale, of hidden truths which shall prevail."

"How do you know that ode?" Branwen smiles.

I shrug. "I don't know, it just came to me." Branwen nods in her knowing way and the three sisters sing a sweet tune. "We call upon the faeries of Annwn, the knowledge of the Hazel, and the gift of sight. Welcome Ceridwen. Goddess of grain, nature and moon. I have drunk from your cup of magical brew, bestow me with your wisdom, as the Hazel moon unfolds." They scatter wildflowers around the tree base as they sing, daisy, violet, may flowers. Unable to keep my eyes open, allowing them to close, relaxing, deeper and deeper. In my mind's eye I see a woman, a daisy chain of flowers threaded in wheat coloured hair. Ceridwen, I decide. Thoughtful hazel eyes, symbolic of the earth, fertility, regeneration, and poetry. A lyrical voice, within my head recites, "Through the echoes of time, I come to you. Through the breeze, I whisper, I call. Invisible threads connecting. Our hearts, our essence, our soul."

Chapter 16

Lockhart

The cottage door rattles in the wind, rain sweeping with a vengeance across the island. The familiar smell of leeks, potatoes, and onions fills the room, bubbling in the large black pot over the fire, my stomach grumbling at the wait. Wren stirs the vegetables, hitches Gwilym a little higher on her hip. A cosy domestic scene, except, time has moved with remarkable speed, another year flown by, Samhain once more upon us. Wren is content being a mother, and happier with her growing involvement in the spiritual aspects of life. Branwen, a frequent visitor, offers advice and teaching on the healing properties of the herbs and plants growing in the area. Wren is developing a small garden behind the cottage. Aneira has become a close friend, bringing her young son Griff to play with Gwilym. The only blight on our peaceful life, the recent declaration of civil war. Most of Wales backs parliament but Tenby and Pembroke have pledged allegiance to the king, dividing opinion, tearing apart families and communities. Gwilym's big blue eyes are drooping, and Wren lies him in the crib, rubbing her hip, aching from the weight of the growing infant. I am agitated and take my cloak from the peg beside the door.

"You can't really be thinking of going out in this?" The rain smacks against the window. "You will be soaked."

"Wren, there are fences which must be fixed."

In truth, I am averting my mind from the evening's plans, for whilst the veil between this world and Annwn, lays thin, I will undergo a spiritual journey, with intent to enter the mystical world for the first time. Ranulf has explained it's the next stage in my development. What will happen is unknown.

My hopes of foregoing the planned ceremony due to the weather has been thwarted, vanishing clouds leaving a clear starry night. With the usual festivities over, the island's inhabitants are retiring to their beds. Geraint pats me on the back. "I look forward to hearing your tale on the morrow." He offers a lopsided smile.

"I feel like a lamb led to slaughter," I confess.

Ranulf stands on the pathway leading into the woods. "Are you ready?" He looks strangely ethereal with the glow of moonlight behind him.

"As ready as I am going to be."

Wren places a warm comforting hand on my face. "Safe journey Lockhart, Gwilym and I will be waiting for you." Her smile is unable to hide the smear of anxiety and fear, within her rainbow.

I want to reassure her, but words fail. I gulp the lump in my throat, turn to Ranulf. "Let us get on."

The swinging lantern casts an eerie shadow upon silent trees as we travel deeper into the wood. The moon, almost full, helping to light our way. I trudge behind Ranulf recalling my first visit to the woodland, so long ago, so much has changed. I ponder how much has been of my making, how much destined. "A good sign," Ranulf points to the moon. He appears excited by what may take place, in the glade tonight. Says my progress in such a short space of time is unheard of. Ranulf believes I hold within me the power to move through time and space. Tonight, offering the best possibility of success. I am not sure his faith in me is well founded, and I have no wish to disappoint.

Reaching the glade, I pull the white gown over my clothes and sit crossed legged on cold damp earth. It seeps through the thin fabric, and I wriggle. The sisters, along with Branwen, circle Ranulf and myself. "You are wearing the onyx?" Ranulf has explained the stone removes the veil of illusion, that all is separate, aiding my ability to converse with the Otherworld. It hangs around my neck, warm against my chest. Ranulf draws a circle in the soil with his dagger, drawing a further two circles around it. In the centre, three rays, with a dot atop each. "The Awen," Ranulf explains. "The Welsh druid symbol representing the polarities. Male on the right, female on the left, the ray between, balancing the opposing powers, a state we all strive to attain. Equality, symmetry. Only then will we be worthy of a place in Annwn."

Ranulf raises his hands to the moon. "I call upon Rhiannon and Pwyll, Lord and Lady of the kingdom of Dyfed. On Math Ap Mathonwy the great wizard, and Arawn, Lord of Annwn, Lord of the Otherworld. I pray for your protection and guidance for my druid son. With the deepest respect and honour, we ask you to escort him to your world, to experience the beauty, splendour, and wisdom, of which it holds. Bless him and grant his safe return to us, so he may share what he has seen and therefore, guide us all."

Ranulf stands behind me, hands resting on my shoulders. "It is time; you know what you must do. Project yourself through your mind into the circle, see nothing but the circle and the symbol. I will hold your physical body safe, whilst you are away."

I proceed to repeat the practised words of Taliesin, my heart racing. "Not of mother nor of father was my creation. I was made from the ninefold elements.

"From fruit trees, from paradisiacal fruit. From primroses and hill-flowers. From the blossom of trees and bushes. From the roots of the earth was I made. From the broom and the nettle. From the water of the ninth wave.

"Math enchanted me before I was made immortal. Gwydion created me with his magic wand.

"From Emrys and Eurion, from Mabon and Modron. From five fifties of magicians like Math was I made. Made by the master in his highest ecstasy. By the wisest of druids was I made before the world began.

"And I know the star—knowledge from the beginning of time."

Concentrating on the symbol of Awen, the lines shift, smooth slithering snakes of colour. I watch, my lids growing heavy, until I can resist no more. In my mind's eye, the serpents remain, merging into the familiar swirling spirals, followed by the bright white light, which effortlessly I travel towards. A tunnel holds me safe as a baby in its mother's arms. Peace and calmness envelope, no distinction between myself and the light. A merging of energy, an overwhelming expression of love, the breath of a warm breeze. Total acceptance for all I am or will be. A vision moves into my awareness, of trees and grass of vivid green, birdsong, and blue cloudless sky. This is the boundary, as far as I have come, never entering this beautiful place, which I believe to be Annwn. Beyond doubt, this world is not the imagination of poets, folklore or legend, but real, as the earth. Breathing slowly and deeply, calmly, but with conviction, I ask for entry. I sense a pull, an invisible thread drawing me, and I am drifting into the beautiful world, a leaf in autumn, carried on a gentle breeze. Natural, without fear, with wonderment, reverence, and a little confusion. Rolling hills of wildflowers, sheep grazing in distant fields. I know this place. "Welcome home Lockhart." A brilliant golden light has appeared, radiant, in the form of a woman, though her features obscure.

"Who, what are you?" Dazzled by her essence, she is somehow familiar.

"Lockhart," her words wash over me. "You must trust all is for a reason, everything holds the gift of a lesson, which develops your soul. One day you will see, one day you will remember me."

"I do not understand?" I ask in frustration.

"You came here for wisdom, so hear this Lockhart. Always follow your intuition, no matter how much it goes against your sense of logic, listen to your heart, and follow where it leads, it will not let you down, will not trick you. Align yourself with the power that permeates all things, take responsibility for your life and who you are. Life will present challenges; how you deal with those challenges, serves your soul."

"But I still do not understand what you want of me?" She does not answer my question, replying in rhyme.

"Remember you are immortal, this, just a lesson for your soul.

"Through the troubles and strife of earthly life, remember you, are not your form.

"During pain and heartache, do only what feels right. Do not be swayed by others, live simply, from your heart.

"I am with you always, Lockhart, you are never alone. Be still, listen, and I will guide you home."

"Forget to remember," she whispers. "It's the way it has to be."

I open my eyes, find myself home, Wren rocking a crying Gwilym. Needing a moment to ground myself before questions begin, I am struck with an overwhelming realisation, that my love for these two people expands further than the here and now, developing throughout time. We are as one, no beginning or end, a cycle of life, death, and rebirth, druids do hold the secret. Late autumn sun bursts from behind cloud, a shaft of light streaming through the window, showering Wren and Gwilym in its glow, sunlight enhancing the gleaming colours. Wren's shimmer, greener, her healing abilities, shining through. Gwilym's array is like his mother, he too will be a healer one day. Slipping out of bed, I cross the room wearing nothing but my shirt. Wren opens her mouth but placing a finger to her lips, I say, "Hush, not yet." Her eyes question as I take Gwilym, the child instantly quietens, closing his eyes to sleep. Laying our son gently in his crib, I turn back to Wren. "I love you." I whisper, sealing her mouth with a kiss before she can reply. Taking her hand, guiding her across the room, indicating for her to sit on the edge of the bed. Grinning cheekily, I push her backwards, disappearing beneath the folds of her skirts, working my way up the inside of her leg with small kisses, primeval need, and longing, as old as time.

After the initial burst of energy, I sleep. The room has grown dark by the time I rise from slumber. The smell of cabbage and potato drifts under the door. Entering the main room, Branwen stares aghast, and Ranulf circles me, shaking his head.

"My, my, amazing, can you see, Branwen?"

Branwen nods, her mouth agape.

Ranulf bows. "We are honoured with your presence."

"What, me, what are you on about Ranulf?" I ask.

"Not you," Ranulf tuts. "Your guide, I am talking to your guide."

Branwen grabs my hands. "Your guide is clearer than before, she is beautiful."

Wren is sitting by the fire. "Can you see her?" I ask, and she shrugs.

"No, I wish I could."

I look back at Branwen. "Why can I not see her, if she is my guide?"

"Because she stands within your energy," Branwen explains. "Not separate, a part of you."

An insipid sun hides behind cloud, the metallic sea serenely trickling against the shore, creeping across dry sand, only to be pulled back, consenting to the rhythm. I breathe in the calm. Despite the time of year, it is mild. Across the water, my eye is drawn to a bobbing grey object, and I focus on the area. Where has it gone? There, I spot it again, closer. A seal, playfully diving in and out of the water, accepting life; why am I incapable of doing the same? My body is present, breathing, heart beating, so why is my head always elsewhere? Imagining the future, remembering the past, or wishing to be back in the Otherworld. Since my journey, I have struggled to settle back into earthly life, barely registering one day sliding into the next. Nothing feels real, or solid, leaving me with the odd sensation of disconnection, from the earth beneath my feet. It irritates like an itch. Whenever I gain relief, it moves again. Having worked hard to reach the goal of entering Annwn, expecting it to bring answers, it has brought only more questions. Wren, it appears, is the opposite. Since her experience in the woods, she is more grounded, more in tune with the earth. I hear her humming tunes when in the garden. Laughing with Aneira. I worry we are growing apart. "Why am I different, why am I here?" I shout into the wind.

"To lead us." I spin round; Ranulf is settling against a rock. Sometimes I'm sure he can shapeshift. "To help others understand there is more than what they see. Prove the existence of the cycle of life, death, and rebirth." Ranulf points to sea. "The seal is a symbol bringing a clear message, to allow your creative nature to come to the fore and follow through on your dreams. What is your dream Lockhart?"

I shrug. "I spend a lot of time dreaming of Annwn, wishing I was there."

Ranulf nods emphatically. "The Otherworld Lockhart is a place where souls rest between earthly incarnations. Only when the soul has sufficiently evolved can it rest eternally, but we do not remember this place, for it seems better than this." He sweeps his hand. "This is the danger when you travel there. Having glimpsed its beauty, the earth plane appears wanting, but remember Lockhart, if you are here, there is a reason. We all have more to learn, our souls are not ready to rest yet."

Slumping onto the sand beside Ranulf, I am hit with realisation. "You have been also, to the Otherworld, haven't you?"

"Yes, Lockhart, I have been there." He stares out to sea.

"Why did you not tell me?"

Ranulf sighs. "It was a long time ago; I did not live on Wills Mark then, nor in Tenby, not even Wales."

I am surprised. "I thought you had always been here."

Ranulf laughs. "Yes, it appears that way to me also at times, but no, I come from another land."

"Where?"

Ranulf pats my arm. "I am a voyager Lockhart; I came across the ocean in a boat from the west, and when I have come full circle, I will leave the same way, but then I will be facing the setting sun. It is the way for all of us. We are all a link between this world and the Otherworld, and although we have the privilege of journeying there, we must remember our responsibilities here. The key is balance Lockhart, the balance between spiritual and material, between body and spirit. This is the reason druids take only what we need from the earth, no more. By achieving balance, we are best placed to teach others."

"Annwn is so beautiful Ranulf, how can I continue in this drama of duality, knowing there is a better place?"

"You must understand Lockhart, the Otherworld is not a place of death, nor a heaven, it is life of a different sort, part of the cycle and each cycle has its turn. The wheel is always turning, but right now, we are here, even the enlightened must live this life in a physical body. As travellers, we seek the wisdom of spirit to use in the here and now, not for us to escape it. Do not make the mistakes I made, what you have here is precious, cherish it."

Ranulf walks away across the beach, his usual colourful shimmer fainter, greyer. I push it to the back of my mind and consider Ranulf's words. I belong here, with Wren, have responsibilities to her, and our son and consider myself lucky, to have so much joy in my life. Blessed with the knowledge that a guide stands close behind me, all I need is here. What I must do is take heed of my guide's words, listen to my intuition and heart as she advises. My time in the Otherworld will come again at the end of this earthly life. Wren, once again with child, needs my presence. I must live the best life I can, in the present, with my family.

Chapter 17

Wren

Fingers of ice cling to bare branches, hedgerows sprinkled with white, sparkling in morning sun, sky of the brightest blue, though over the distant hills, heavy cloud warns of failing weather, before the day is through. Lockhart kisses me on the cheek and ruffles Gwilym's wispy hair before mounting his horse, the long woollen cloak wrapped tightly around him.

"Remain on grass verges, avoid the icy pathways," I call to him, and he winks at me, causing my heart to flutter. Market day in Tenby, and he doesn't want me to venture far in this weather, not in my condition. I stroke my stomach affectionately.

"I think it may snow." I yawn, settling Gwilym into his crib for a nap. Though it seldom falls in this part of Wales, incoming clouds are building. "Once I have finished preparing the meal, I think I will join you. I could do with some rest before your father returns, let's hope he makes it back before the weather changes." I set about preparing vegetables, adding them to an iron cooking pot. With jug in hand, an icy gust blows through the cottage as I open the door, and I pull my shawl tighter. Finding the water in the outside barrel is trapped under a thick layer of ice, I curse, berating not asking Lockhart to fetch water before he left. Carefully making my way to the store at the back of the cottage where Lockhart keeps his tools, searching for something to break the ice, I find a wooden hammer, and head gingerly back to the cottage, when I feel my foot slip. The ground moves up to meet me, and I spread my hands, protection from the fall, landing face down, my ankle twisted beneath me. I lie in shock, cold seeping through my clothes. Shakily I attempt to right myself, but I can put no weight on my throbbing ankle. A rising panic beats within my chest, frozen ridges of mud sucking warmth from my bones. I raise my head, wriggle onto my elbows. In the far distance, Halwyn, tall for a boy of ten and two, with a shock of red hair, earning him the nickname rooster, tugs a rope wrapped around the neck of a mule. Feeling foolish I cry, "Help!" Expressing disgust at being ousted from the barn with expletive hee-haws, the mule drowns my voice. Sickly, breathing slowly and deeply. I see Halwyn remove the rope, the mule walking off sullenly to the far end of the field to stand in a semi-circle of grass beneath a large evergreen, untouched by frost. Halwyn blows into his cupped hands, turning to retrace his steps. I must make him hear. "Help. Halwyn, please help me." Fear enveloping me. He cocks his head on one side. I shout as loud as I am able. "Help." He turns in my direction but cannot see me on the floor, so I continue to shout over and over, when he appears.

"Are you alright?" He runs over to me, attempts to help me stand, but I squeal in pain. "Perhaps you have broken something, I will get help." He turns to the cottage.

"Lockhart is not home," I tell him.

"I will get father."

Once Geraint and Aneira arrive Gwilym is crying, and I am shivering. Geraint lifts me easily as a corn doll, and carries me into the house, sending Halwyn for Branwen. Aneira helps me into dry clothes, and it is then we see, exchanging worried glances.

When a crisis looms, all options lost, prayer is all we have. We pray to Queen Mab but when Branwen arrives it is as we feared, the baby is coming, too early. I pray to all the goddesses I can think of, and to God. I don't care who hears my plea. However, prayers are not always answered in the way we hope for, and by the time Lockhart returns it is all over.

"You cannot come in here, it isn't right," Branwen tells him.

He stands defiantly in the doorway. "This is my house and Wren is my wife; I shall do as I wish."

"It is hardly fitting Lockhart," Branwen pauses. "But under the circumstances, I see no reason to deny you." She stands aside.

He moves to the bed and takes my hand. I know this, feel the cold of his fingers, and yet, I am a shell, my sense of self shattered like glass, impossible to restore.

"Too early," is all I can say, my lip quivering.

He turns to Branwen for explanation, though deep in his heart, I am sure he knows.

"I am sorry." Branwen's voice cracks with emotion. "We did all we could."

Aneira is wrapping the bundle in a scrap of clean cloth, wiping tears with her sleeve, she turns to the door.

"Wait!" Lockhart crosses the room. Aneira holds the bundle protectively against her chest. "Boy or girl?" he asks quietly.

"A girl," Aneira replies.

"I want to see her," Lockhart holds out his hands.

Aneira glances at Branwen, who nods, and Aneira carefully places the bundle in Lockhart's arms. I see the events from a place of detachment, not fully present, numb. He carries her to me, but I do not wish to see, cannot look, it is too painful. I turn.

"Wren, are you going to hold her?" he says gently to me. I shake my head, afraid. "This will be your only chance to meet her, you need to do this." He places the baby in my arms and unwraps the linen cloth. Together we investigate the face of our stillborn daughter, small, and light as a feather. Lockhart removes more of the swaddling; her skin is tinged with blue, but she is perfect. Ten little fingers and toes, a shock of dark hair. Willing my mind to imprint her features in my memory, Lockhart kisses her forehead. Tears well in his eyes, but he is a man, and I know he will not cry, turning to look out of the window. I follow his gaze. Silent snowflakes fall, a blanket of pure white descending across the island, the room cloaked in calming pale pink light. Sheltered by the fence a clump of green leaves with delicate white petals, their heads drooped. "I wish to name her." My voice choked with emotion. "Eirlys, Welsh for snowdrops." Lockhart cups my head, rests it on his chest, and with the motionless child in my arms, I weep, from the depths of my soul.

In the weeks that follow I cannot be reached, sinking further and deeper into my inner darkness. My heart is broken. Lockhart takes Gwilym with him to tend the animals, allowing me time to rest, brings me presents to cheer me. I catch him searching what he refers to as the arc of light around me, and when I question, he says the colours are pale with tendrils of black mist. If he is looking for recovery, he will have a long wait. The sisters have given healing, the gloom receding momentarily, only to return. Lockhart says he misses his wife, but I remain lost to him, and myself. Going through the motions of daily life in a blur. After my experience under the Hazel tree, I felt blessed with protection. I was deluded. I appeal to Branwen, "I feel so helpless, all faith in life has left me. I have tried everything to lift this dark shadow, but it remains..." I falter.

"Grief affects people differently you cannot rush these things. Time, what else is there. Growth can be very painful, Wren, living in a world of duality, with light and darkness, health and illness, love and hate, birth, and death. We cannot fight or deny it, only live through it the best way we can." She hands me a clay pot. "Try this, it will ease your symptoms."

"What is in it?" I ask dubiously. "Lavender, saffron and Hypericum perforatum."

"Obviously I have heard of Lavender but not the other ingredients. I do not wish to take anything which will make me drowsy when I have Gwilym to attend to." I hand the pot back to her.

"Hypericum perforatum is also known as St. John's wort so a common plant, and saffron is something I have only recently purchased from a seaman. Just take it, trust me." She smiles warmly, putting the pot on the shelf by the window. "I need to be off," she says, heading for the door.

I cross to look out of the window determining her reasons for the brisk exit. She is talking to Lockhart. I open the door a little to listen covertly to their conversation. "Have you considered returning to your learning. You had made such progress. Or maybe the sisters, they have offered you healing, why not try it?"

"No Branwen, I cannot." Lockhart folds his arms. "I have lost my faith in all of this."

"Your guardian, still stands with you Lockhart."

"Do not speak to me of my guardian," he growls. "I asked for her help, and this is what I got. Why did she not warn me? I believed Branwen; I really did. In the teachings, everything you and Ranulf told me about thinking right, guides and healing, and now I see how foolish I was to do so." I hear his rage. "I felt powerful Branwen, in charge of my destiny, everything was good, but it has been ripped from me. I do not understand why this happened; I do not understand any of it. What is the point of showing me another way to live, only to realise, that no matter which path you take, life is full of pain and anguish?"

"It is difficult to understand some of our life lessons Lockhart; we cannot always see the bigger picture."

Late summer, the sun dipping in and out of cloud reflects my cyclic mood. Wiping the newly dug potatoes with bare hands, the earthy smell of damp soil collecting beneath my fingernails. I gather the crop into a sack. My eye notes a small, shrivelled specimen. I examine it in my palm. Tears dampen my eyes, and I am overcome by despair. Clutching the wrinkled potato to my chest, the nourishment needed for growth denied. As Eirlys had been forced from my womb, warm and nurtured, too early. I rebury the potato, cover it with loose soil, attempting to undo the damage I unwittingly caused digging it up before it was ready. "I'm sorry, I'm so very sorry." Briefly I look around, ensuring no one is near, and I will not be heard, collapsing forward, head in my hands, grief building inside, and I gulp for air. Finally relenting, accepting the inevitable sadness which always follows, the tears, the incessant spinning thoughts. As a child, I witnessed a tornado. Only a small one, father had said. Nothing compared to ones in distant lands, but it frightened me. The power of an unseen force gathering everything in its path. Grit, soil, twigs, leaves, swept high into the vortex, unable to escape the pull. Intense feelings whirl within my head, pulling up every pain and hurt from the past. Perhaps I deserve the pain, after all, my stupidity killed the child. Or maybe Emlyn has cursed me for loving his brother.

Lockhart is unable to grasp how I feel. "Many women lose babies." His intention, no doubt, to reiterate I am not alone, but his words sting, and it takes all my will not to lash out with fists and words. "I know you are angry," he will say next. "A red mist has just descended over your rainbow." That doesn't help either. I am irked he can read my emotions clearer than I. I am not even sure I love him anymore. My mind twists, tumbling into reliving the events. The fall on ice, the swift labour, a child, born without breath. Branwen rubbing the scrap of arms and legs like a new-born pup. The desperate prayers for help, forgiveness. Thoughts spin out of control, and I pummel my stomach, bereft, begging for the emotions to cease. Eventually tears run dry, and I wipe my eyes with grubby hands leaving streaks of grey soil across my face, but I don't care, accustomed to what comes next. Numbness encasing me in a shell without feeling. Although liable to break open again at any given moment, for now, all I feel is empty.

Civil war in England threatens the stability of Wales. Lockhart ordered to return to Tenby, didn't take much persuading, despite Ranulf explaining that as a druid he could not be called to fight. Lockhart feels protecting Tenby is imperative, something he must do. To be honest, I believe he is secretly pleased to be away from me. Or at least I thought so, until the messenger arrived at my door this morning.

"How dare he summon me?" I angrily fold my gown into the chest. "This is just to save face."

"He just does not know how to deal with his emotions," Branwen acknowledges. "He thinks he can run from them and return to what he was, in time he will see, he cannot."

"I do not want to leave," my voice cracks. Branwen places a comforting arm around my shoulders. "I cannot bear to leave Eirlys; I visit every day."

Dabbing tears with my apron, Branwen smiles. "I will tend her grave, I promise, and maybe distance will help, for a while at least. I am sure you will return, you and Lockhart."

I hang my head. "I am not sure I want to return with Lockhart, after all this." I tuck stray hair into my coif. "I have been thinking, Branwen. As a druid, I can divorce my husband, can't I?"

Branwen lifts my chin. "You could divorce, yes, but think long and hard before you make your decision, this has been a difficult period, for both of you, it does not mean you cannot grow from it."

I turn my head. "I am not sure Branwen, if we can ever return to how we were."

"That is not what I said," Branwen replies. "You are right, you will not be the same, either of you, or can you expect to be. However, love can still grow, even flourish, through trauma. You will find a way to reconnect; I am sure of it."

"How can he not see what this is doing to me, expecting me to leave Eirlys and my home, go back to living in Tenby castle?" Anger tightens my chest. "Does he not remember what happened there, does he forget Emlyn? It holds no happy memories for me."

"He will remember," Branwen empathises. "But he has been called to fight, and as a man, that is what he must do. This has been hard for him also Wren. He is doing what he thinks he should, whether that be right or wrong, it is his way of dealing with it. Do not give up on him."

Gwilym has come to sit between us, lying his head on my lap. He is a sensitive child, and I stroke his soft hair.

Branwen continues, "You once told me; your heart opened the moment you laid eyes on Lockhart. That you felt you already knew him."

I sigh, recalling the scene in the hallway, blood dripping from his wound. How for a moment the world stopped. "Yes, I did."

"I believe you have been together through many lifetimes, and you sensed that recognition from the depths of your soul. But, as Emlyn discovered, love cannot be forced, it must be given freely, and right now; your heart is closed; you are afraid to release the pain you hold there. A lock cannot be forced without causing damage, but the potential to love is always within you. I genuinely believe, your husband holds the key, after all, his name is Lockhart." I squint, puzzled. "I open locked hearts. That is the meaning behind his name." Branwen smiles. "So, let him."

A trickle of warmth seeps into my heart, melting the ice, just a little, breaking through the heavy weight of storm clouds, pressing on my troubled mind.

"You still love him?" Branwen asks.

I look down at our child, the product of our creation, forged from love. "Yes, I do."

"Then love will find a way to reunite you."

I must admit, Lockhart looks dashing in the black felt hat with an ostrich feather. It's blue green eye, bright as a summer sea, bobbing up and down as we walk. Dark grey breeches, and red doublet, black boots, turned over at the tops, complimented by a short black cape.

"I have been promoted to Captain," he says excitedly. "Tom said any man can become an officer through ability and allegiance, which is much fairer than being a right of birth, don't you think?" He hurries on. "Tom said it is hard to find men trained as well as I, with sword, and horse." He reminds me of a young boy with a gift at Christmas time.

Our room is impressive. A large oak bed with embroidered coverlet, complimenting the wall hanging of golden fleur de Lys, on a dark blue background. Not as elaborate as the room shared with Emlyn, but comfortable. A shiver runs down my back at the thought of Emlyn. The past must remain there, I remind myself.

"Are you cold?" Lockhart notes my shiver. "I will put another log on the fire."

This is worlds apart to how we have been living on the island. I am unsure that is good.

"I am happy you and Gwilym are here." Lockhart takes my hands, turning my palms up, he kisses each wrist tenderly, searching my face. "I feared you would not come."

I force a smile.

Lockhart's footsteps echo the corridor. I always know it is him, long confident strides. The aroma of roast lamb enters through the door with him, and my stomach rumbles. "Not that I will be able to eat much," I complain to my reflection in the mirror. "These stays are so tight I can barely breathe, let alone enjoy a feast."

Lockhart does a double take, smiling lustily. "Gwilym, please fetch your mother, she has been replaced with an enchantress, and I am not sure I will be able to resist her beauty."

Ellen, who looks after Gwilym, grins, and distracts him. Lockhart crosses the room.

"My lady," he says, bowing, "you are most beautiful."

I curtsey. "My Lord," I tease, "your admiration is most welcome, however, if you do not hurry, you will be late for your appointment with Lord Carbery. For right now you resemble," I sniff the air, "and smell, like a stable boy."

Lockhart pulls a face and hurries to prepare.

Major David Hammond, puffs with self-importance. Gushing to Lord Carbery, the extent of repairs to the fortifications of Tenby. Governor Tom Griffiths, the Mayor Evan Williams, and Lockhart, sit at the same table. "The task is yet incomplete, but we are almost there." His voice reverberates around the cavernous room. I hear every word, despite being sat a fair distance away with the other wives, who have made it quite clear I am not in their league. Nor do I wish to be, and with tendrils of dark hair in loose waves resting on my shoulders, the length braided and pinned at the back, I am feeling attractive, increasing my confidence. I don't care what they think, at least I am genuine. My gown is the colour of red wine, white lace kerchief, and cuffs. An apple red stomacher pinching my small waist. I feel Lockhart's eyes on me, raising his glass he winks. He has trimmed his beard into a point; the latest design suits him. I smile shyly; tummy fluttering as it hasn't for some time.

Carbery, in gold doublet and wide red sash, looks drained and tired, slunk in the cushioned chair. Dark shadows, under deep brown eyes. Carbery addresses Lockhart, "Are you a relation of James Lockhart?"

Lockhart pulls back his shoulders. He does this to appear more confident, a nuance only observable to one who knows him well. "My mother was a Scottish descendent of the Lockhart family, but I know little of her ancestry."

"Indeed," Carbery remarks. "What of the Lockhart amulet? Are you aware of such a thing?"

"I am afraid not my Lord."

"That's unfortunate, I hoped to be enlightened on the reasoning behind its power. Presently on loan to Newcastle, as protection from the plague, by order of King Charles. I believe it is having a significant effect."

"My Lord," Tom Griffiths cuts in, "What are we to do with regards to Poyer, and Laugharne?"

Bored by talk of war, and the witter of women discussing the latest designs in fabric and gowns, interspersed with gossip of others' troubles, their feigned concern, thinly disguised. It is not the fine clothes which make you, but the company you keep. Branwen's words repeat in my head, and with that, I make my excuses. Lockhart later finds me talking to a serving girl I find more interesting. He guides me to our room, for I am giddy from too much wine. Easing sore feet out of red satin slippers, Lockhart takes both feet onto his lap, kneading them with warm strong hands.

"I used to do this when you were pregnant, do you remember?"

"Yes, I remember," I reply sleepily.

"Wren, I want you back." His pale blue eyes reflect my own pain.

"That Wren is no more Lockhart," I reply earnestly. "However, the Wren I have become, would like to be loved, as much as the old one."

"But I do love you, how could you think otherwise? I just want things to be, how they used to be."

"I am afraid that is impossible Lockhart. What happened, Eirlys…" I choke back the tears. "How can I be the same? I know it is difficult for you to understand, as a man, you don't feel the loss as I do, you couldn't possibly."

"Hold it there." Lockhart stands, folding his arms across his chest. "I know I did not carry the child, nor gave birth, and I agree, I could never feel the emotions the way you do, it isn't the same, it cannot be the same, but to suggest, I do not feel deeply the loss of Eirlys, is frankly, unfair."

"You never showed any grief," I shoot back. "You didn't cry yourself to sleep every night, for months on end."

"This isn't a competition of who hurts the most Wren. I didn't show my pain because, well because, men don't, they are expected to be strong, carry on, support their wives. That doesn't mean I haven't, haven't…" He crumples onto the bed, head in his hands. "I am not for one minute suggesting, my pain has been more than yours, Wren, but I tried hard to be there for you, and you pushed me away. I thought you did not want me, that you blamed me for Eirlys, I could not reach you."

My face, flushed from the wine, eyes no doubt a little glazed, but the alcohol helps me speak openly. "It was the only way I could cope with the pain, to withdraw, can you understand that?"

"I tried hard to understand Wren, really I did, for as long as I could."

I stiffen, irked. "I have found it exceedingly difficult to understand why you chose to leave the island, to come back to this." I sweep my hand around the room. "Now I see, you signed up to be a captain, so you could get away from me."

"No, yes," he stumbles. "I thought maybe distance would help, and we are at war, Wren, in the end we both knew I would be called to fight. Believe me, being under the command of Tom Griffiths, leaves a bad taste in my mouth, but I have no choice, I must defend Tenby, and Tom is governor of the castle, there is nothing I can do about that. I couldn't fight for the opposition."

My voice catches. "So how do you feel now? Do you still wish for distance between us? Is that what you want?"

"No, of course not." He rakes a hand through his hair. "I could have left you on the island if I did, but I wanted you here, I missed you. You and Gwilym, my family, my life, I do not ever want to be apart from you." He looks up at me, his anguish clear, yet I did not see it, until now. A tear spills onto my cheek, his heartfelt words touching my soul.

"Can we start again?" I hear his sincerity. "Eirlys, has changed us, life, changes all of us, but it is how we move forward from the grief; the next chapter, is it not?" Love, wells in my heart. "I want you Wren, no other, for all eternity."

I reach to touch his face, teasingly tug his beard. "A Van Dyke, just like the king." I sniff. "You are my king Lockhart, my prince, my husband, and I love you." I kiss him. He smells of stale tobacco and alcohol, but I don't care. Returning my kisses eagerly, he pulls back a little. I know he is scanning my arc of colour.

"I know what you are doing, Lockhart Edwards."

"Sorry, I just, wondered if… I mean, I will be gentle."

I bite my lip and whisper in his ear, "The answer is yes."

Chapter 18

Lockhart

The army manoeuvre through the narrow streets of Tenby, townsfolk cheering, shopkeepers clapping as we pass. Down a narrow alleyway the blacksmith, two dark eyes against his sooty face glances, frowns, returns to the hammer, clanging the metal on his anvil. Not all agree with loyalty to the King. Children run alongside horses, excited expectant smiles. They see uniform, banners and drum. A show. War, the dire circumstances awaiting us, incomprehensible to their youthful souls. Tom Griffiths leads the cavalry, foot soldiers and baggage train. I focus into the distance, back straight in the saddle. My confident air belies the fear snaking through my internals, turning my stomach, threatening to release my bowels. No trace remains of the vomit purged but an hour ago, except the reflux burn in my throat. I was not alone, blaming a bad batch of ale we almost convinced ourselves it was true. A rapier hangs at my hip; two pistols housed in the saddle bag, my heart hammering beneath the armoured back and chest plate. A chilly wind blows across the Atlantic, pressing against my face, a warning to turn back, unacknowledged. Yesterday I stood at Eirlys's grave. A small clearing overlooked by oak, sycamore, and yew trees, planted to ward off evil spirits. A peaceful place, the first time I had visited with Wren. Since our daughter had been laid to rest, we grieved separately, each believing the other unable to understand the pain. No more, we stand like pillars, our two children, one in life, one in spirit, the bridge connecting us. Pebbles from the beach mark the outline of the grave. The name Eirlys, scratched into a larger rock with my dagger. Wren scattered wildflowers over the small mound. I sigh unconsciously, cannot but wonder if I will soon join our baby beneath the ground. I fear leaving Wren and Gwilym, more than my own death. As life appears to be coming right again, will happiness, be once more snatched away. The tall west gate is dragged open, ministers offering prayers as we pass. Women resiliently waving, fear etched into their brows, knowing as well as I, not all will return; silently hoping, it will not be their husband or son who falls. Drumbeat carried on the wind, reminds me of the druid drum, and I ache for the peaceful life I had not so long ago.

At Colby Moor a thousand Roundheads stretch ominously across the grassland with horse and cannon. "We are still mightier in number." The Colonel speaks with reassurance. The air is still, sun shielding behind cloud. Over my shoulder the army of Royalists await instruction. Mounted cavaliers in green sashes, or blue. Most of the foot soldiers, the pikemen, wear nothing to distinguish them, few even possessing a pot helmet. The Parliamentarian troops wear the favoured russet colours, but their foot soldiers are dressed as ours, in farm clothing. Recruited not for the cause, but for food and a wage. How are we to tell which side they are fighting for amid battle? I wish my hands would stop shaking.

Looking across the peaceful green pasture, I return in my mind to Wills Mark. Ranulf and the sisterhood holding hands around the young oak known to instil strength, king of the forest. Nuts and fruit placed around the base, sacrificial food to nourish the soil. I often sit beneath the tree in quiet reflection; therefore, Ranulf believes, imprints of my energy are held within the roots, representing the past and strength to grow. The trunk, the soul of self, steadfast, branches, reaching in expectation of new growth. In the hollow of the tree, Branwen placed the Glain Neidr, a small piece of flint, a hole through its centre. Passed down through the generations of druids, a part of the island. Ranulf's words repeat in my head, "Protect and guide our druid son, Lockhart. Bring him strength and courage, in the deed ahead, and bring him safely, back to the island." Offerings were made to Bran, God of war. To Gwydion, the greatest warrior, and Dewi, God of the red dragon. Saying goodbye was hard, acting the part of a confident captain, when inside the dread eating away my resolve was almost unbearable. Ranulf squeezed my shoulder.

"You are a valiant man Lockhart; you strive to do that which needs to be done, with honour. Devotion to your cause, may bring triumph or your downfall, we are all but human, unable to stop a bullet; your courage to do what you feel you must, to protect Tenby, your friends, neighbours and family, I admire." Ranulf had embraced me, whispering, "Do not fear death, Lockhart, remember you are a druid, remember the dragon, it will bring you the strength, you undoubtedly will need. Fight to return to us, there are people here who need you, do it for them." I had been unable to answer with the lump in my throat.

Beneath my buff coat, I wear the short red tunic marking me as a druid warrior. I admit I was surprised, having thought druids were people of peace, not warriors. Ranulf reiterated that druids would fight to protect. How in times past, they have been known to come between armies and prevent war, but I doubt King Charles or Cromwell would hear our words. I do not feel brave or audacious, inner demons feasting on my conflict. The men across the moor, the enemy, must be defeated, clashing with the druid teachings, of all being connected, all one. Am I fighting an aspect of myself? Shifting position in the saddle, I find no comfort, knowing what I am about to do. Snap out of it. I scold. Remain focused on the task. I can ill afford to see these men being a part of myself, with women and children at home praying for their return.

Taliesin's words float into my mind. "The haft of a knife, or a spear in battle clearly shall I prophesy. Of battle where smoke comes drifting. Five battalions of lads will dance on my knife.

"Six yellow horses, the best of the breed. Better than any is my cream-coloured steed, swift as a sea-mew along the shore.

"I myself am a power in battle. A cause of blood from a hundred chieftains. Crimson is my shield, gold my shield-rim.

"Only Geronwy, from the dales of Edrywy, is better than I."

Absently touching my breastplate, the onyx warm against my chest. "Awaken dragon, I need you." The familiar warmth emanates in my stomach. "And guardian," I continue. "Do all you can, to keep me and my men safe." In my pocket, the well-worn pages of my almanac, read over and over for reassurance. It clearly implies the king will be victorious, but I have heard rumours of another almanac in circulation, claiming the opposite.

The day draws on, sun silently moving across the sky. Soldiers deployed to the east and west, pikemen and musketeers in the centre. We wait, pregnant with expectation. At 6pm Commander Laugharne launches a cavalry charge for the opposing parliamentarians, horses galloping with haste across the grassland. Raising my loaded pistol, a signal to my men. Emotion buried, the fight for survival instinctively taking precedence, we charge forward, hooves thudding on the dry soil. Pikemen, foot soldiers, lock in combat, the air crackles, musketeers firing matchlocks, the moor descending into chaos. Jaws set hard, faces stern, shouts, grunts, war cries. Terror, confusion on both sides. My pistol jams, refuses to fire. I circle back, reload the second, damp gunpowder renders it useless. A man lunges at my horse with a pike, the animal brought down, I with it. My heart is hammering, and pulling the sword from its sheath, I lash out indiscriminately, scramble to my feet, clashing against another man's blade. Adrenalin coursing through my muscles, burning with fatigue. The sword is heavy, holding it with both hands, sweat pouring from my brow, anger at Emlyn, at losing Eirlys, finding its outlet. The air is thick with smoke, fighting in a fog descending over the terrain, a cacophony roaring in my ears. Gunfire, men's screams, injured and dying.

The tooting bugle calls retreat, defeat. Fearing capture, I run, sword dripping with blood, stepping over corpses, of gallant men, who fought until the end. A young farmer boy, sinew spilling from his shattered cheek, mouth open in its final cry, someone's son, unrecognisable. The sight repulses me, embeds in my brain. I keep on running, away from visions clouding my head, dazed, afraid, until my chest screams for air. Short painful breaths, the metallic taste of blood, and my legs buckle, cause me to stumble. Scrambling to safety behind a bush blooming with early blackcurrants, looking back at the moor, I am shivering. Hell spewed across the landscape; grass turned red with blood. Bodies of men, massacred like plagued rats, some cry for their mothers or wives, others howl in pain, it chills me to the bone. This, the vision in the flames, the first night in the woodland. How can it be? Rubbing my face with grubby hands I notice among the plumes of smoke, bright circles of light. I think of Emlyn, question if they are Angels, come to take the dead. Peace emanates from the iridescent balls, incongruent with the torturous sight. A heavy hand presses into my shoulder, and I spin, eyes wide. "Come on man, we need to get out of here." Merek grabs my arm, pulls me to my feet. He drags me along a dirt path, round the circumference of a field, sheep grazing, scatter as we hurry by, to an abandoned barn. Grateful for Merek's presence, to know he is alive, for his concern. We hunker down in silence, catching our breath, but it is too dangerous to remain, we will be found, held as prisoners. We hear voices close by, and huddle in the darkest corner to listen. Merek whispers, "It sounds like Tom Griffiths." He spies through a hole in the wood. I never expected to be happy to see Tom, but I am.

Night falls in swathes of metallic sulphur, remnants of pungent gunpowder clogging the air. Through the shadows, exhausted, bone-weary, grubby, and stinking of sweat. Boots and coat muddied, caked in other men's blood, we trek through the dark night in silence. The fight no longer with sword and musket, but haunting images of battle, loss of friends, brothers, sons, a hole impossible to fill for the remainder of our lives. The walking wounded will be imprisoned. The rest, I do not care to think.

Without horse I trudge, head hung low. Under no illusion, it will not be the last we see of the Roundheads. Reaching Tenby, gold stretches across a sky of purple cloud, the castle welcome, but the war far from over.

Cleaned and fed, I sleep for ten hours. Gwilym wakes me, tugging on the coverlet. Opening an eye, my son is pointing a wooden sword at my face.

"Gwilym, come away, leave your father to rest," Wren reproaches.

"No, leave him." I pull him onto the bed. "Son, you only point a sword if you, or one you hold dear are in danger."

"Ranulf said you only fight if you have no other choices." He tilts his head, observing me with big blue eyes.

"Ranulf is right, he is very wise."

"When can we go back to the island?" The child scowls at me.

"Why, do you ask?"

"It is nicer there." He sticks out his bottom lip and continues, "I miss Griff, and Branwen too. I want to live like we used to."

I exchange a smile with Wren. "Out of the mouths of babes."

Pale light dawns. I stoke the fire, adding a further log, sitting crossed legged and pulling my cloak over my shoulders, staring unseeing into the dancing flames. Muscles on sustained high alert ache with tension, but I cannot rest. The anxiety of waiting for the inevitable has brought another sleepless night. We have learnt that over seven hundred royalists were captured at Colby Moor, and Cromwell's army grows daily in number, marching the length of Wales, destroying every castle in their wake. Clearly, it can only be a matter of time before they reach Tenby. Slowing my breathing, the warmth of the fire upon my face, the druid training to bring a sense of peace, simply isn't working. Thoughts looping, a continual figure of eight, circles in my head. Justification for my allegiance to the King, brought into question. Hearsay suggests the King will be tried for treason. Marrying a catholic and dissolving parliament, has undoubtedly created much division and unrest. The parliamentarians promise a better life for the poor, but can they be trusted? There appears little evidence to support their claims. I chew it over like a piece of tough steak, no amount of masticating or gnawing makes it any easier to swallow. One fact remains; the castle, and much of the town, are Royalist. Then there is Wren, pregnant with child. My attempts to persuade her to return to the island, met with refusal. I look at her sprawled across the bed, dark hair unkempt, feathered around the pillow, the halo rainbow of my sleeping wife shines brightly. I rake a hand through my hair, decide with conviction to return to Wills Mark once the war is over, continue my druid training.

"We shall all return," I whisper, crossing to the bed, stroking her swollen stomach. Wren stirs.

"Are you awake already?"

"Are you asking me or her?" I smile.

Wren's lids shoot open. "Her, you said her, do you know that, are you sure?"

"Yes, we are expecting a daughter."

Wren smiles a little sadly. "That is wonderful, but what about Eirlys?"

"Eirlys is also our daughter. She will not be replaced; merely gaining a sister."

Wren brightens. "Can we call her Cerys? It means love in Welsh."

I laugh. "I am aware of its meaning, and it is indeed a beautiful name. Hello Cerys." I kiss Wren's tummy and the baby responds, rolling inside her. We laugh, a moment of joy before another day under the shadow of war.

Cerys arrived in the world swiftly a little over six weeks ago. A contented baby, bringing calm and hope to a fraught situation. Her first smile, just for me, and the memory of it appears behind my closed eyes, momentarily lifting the heavy tension. The dawn chorus of birdsong, floats through the window, our daughter suckling on her mother's breast. Wren insists her own milk is the best. I am fully clothed, sat in the chair by the fire. Wren says I am like a Welsh hillman dog, always on guard. She is right, I rarely sleep deeply.

There is scuffling in the corridor outside our door. "We are under attack," someone shouts, followed by the bugle call to arms. Men are running, boots echo on the stone steps. A loud thud shakes the walls, a reverberating rumble. Gwilym and Cerys cry. Hastily I fasten the scabbard around my waist.

"You know what to do." I glance at Wren, who nods fearfully, but there is no time to reassure. A further cannon ball strikes the outer wall.

Sprinting up the steps, Jarin Evans, still unforgiven for breaking my tooth, hands me a loaded musket, swiftly filed by the younger boys. "Ships!" Jarin points southwest. Shadows of masts and billowing sail, push through the sea, monsters of wood heading up the Bristol channel. With Tenby in view, they separate. One remains close to Caldey island, away from the rocks, another coursing around St Catherine's Island, a third around the headland to the harbour. The deafening boom from the castle cannons release into the awakening day. Soldiers on the parapet, every available man in the town, clamber onto the town walls, firing guns and canon, but a further blast by the enemy, penetrates the north wall, crumbling like a castle made of sand, a shoddy repair by Carbery, but it is Emlyn I curse, allowing the defences to fall into disrepair. Men alight from ships, onto the beaches, soft sand slowing them down, some we strike down, they never reach the town walls. The musket is empty; I drop it on the floor.

"Take this." Jarin passes me a flintlock, and falls forwards onto me, a strangled cry, face bloodied, eyes staring, shot dead. I push Jarin off in horror. Red kites circle overhead, in lieu of rich pickings, a bright blue sky, white cloud. Why? I ask my guardian, but it is the dragon who responds, filling my belly with fire, determination, strength.

Roundheads break through the north gate, followed by the west gate, racing through the town, up the hillside like a swarm of angry wasps, battering down doors, stepping through the rubble of walls, storming the castle with swords and musket and pike. With my beloved family so close, I must not lose this fight. Sprinting down the steps, I come face to face with a man pumped with muscles, tight as a drum. He lunges with murder in his eyes. The stairs run clockwise, disadvantaging the right-handed rebel. I take a swing, the man dodging my every advance. He steps back; I step forward. I am gaining until we are in the corridor, where he takes his sword in both hands and swings over and over. I can barely keep up with the relentless momentum, avoiding the steel of his thrusting blade, now it is I who steps back, realising too late, I am against the wall. The man sneers, victory for the taking, raising his sword to strike the deadly blow. My throat, tight with fear.

"Go, now."

The woman's voice in my ear clear and forceful, propels me to action. I sidestep, duck under the man's outstretched arms, and run. Cutting away from the ensuing battle in the hall, I race up the back stairs, hammer on the door. "Wren, it's me." She drags the heavy chest away. "There are too many," I say breathlessly edging round the small gap. "You must leave, now." Tying her shawl into a sling she places baby Cerys inside, I grab Gwilym, sit him on my hip. Scanning the corridor, beckoning Wren to follow, we move gingerly down the winding back staircase. Hearing voices below, we press against the wall. A finger to my lips, indicating silence, I hand

Gwilym to Wren, and slowly edge down the steps, peeping around the stairwell, into the corridor below. Aelwen, the sword of a puny Roundhead, pressed into her back, her three boys huddled round her skirts. I sneak up, grab the man from behind, pulling him to the ground. The sword flies from his hand. I place a foot on his breastplate, the tip of my sword to his throat. "Your choice." I scowl. "I can kill you, or you can run." Removing my sword and foot, the man lies in momentary disbelief, before scurrying to his feet and fleeing. I grab Aelwen, call up the stairs to Wren, lead them to Emlyn's study and push them inside. Running my hand down the side of a wooden panel to locate the hidden catch, it creaks open. A dark corridor of stone lies beyond.

"Make sure you keep to the right, eventually you will see daylight. There will be a boat, go to Branwen." I light a torch from the fire, handing it to Wren.

"Lock." She touches my arm.

"I will follow, when I can," I reassure.

"Find Merek," Aelwen pleads, clinging to her boys.

"You have my word." I promise, urging them to hurry.

They disappear, a flicker of light sways in the darkness. Reluctantly I replace the panel and lean against the timber. "I know you are still with me guardian; you still stand behind me, please see them safe." Taking a deep breath, I head back into battle in search of Merek.

I scan the hall, Gethin lies dead, eyes and mouth agape. A memory sparks, of a moment previously seen, but more pressing matters prevail, and I step over him. Eyeing Merek slumped against a bench; my heart tightens. "Merek." I shake him. No response, blood pumping from a deep gash in his leg. "Gwydion, druid god of magic and healing, please assist me." I grab Merek's hair, pulling back his head. "Merek get up." He groans, and I am relieved. "Come on," I demand forcefully. "You must get up, we must go."

Merek groans. "Aelwen."

"She is safe, now move you great lummox." Merek forces himself to his feet, wincing he leans heavily on me. "Through here," I indicate, half pushing, half dragging Merek into the study.

Through the confined space of the damp dark passageway, I scan for signs of Wren and Aelwen, Merek hopping, cursing, groaning. A small scrap of red material clings to the rough stone wall. "They must have made it through." I show Merek. "This is from Wren's shawl." We come out inside a cave, behind the parliamentarian ships, anchored offshore. Tell-tale signs of a boat recently dragged. "That's my girl." I cautiously scan around the edge of the cave, but I see no sign of them on the water.

Heading back, Merek shakes, moving into shock, losing too much blood from the wound; the flow needs to be stemmed. Untying my collar I secure the narrow laces tightly around Merek's leg, using a twig to twist it. "It's the best I can do," I apologise, wiping bloody hands on my breaches. "You will not be able to walk far with that injury," I surmise. "But there will be no horses this far from town."

"Donkey's," Merek mumbles.

"Donkey's!" I frown.

"In Gavin Johns field behind us."

Stepping outside the cave, edging cautiously around the rock, I look up. On top of the cliff, two donkeys chew happily on grass. "Not very regal, but they will do."

We duck and dive behind rocks, remaining out of sight, guiding the animals along a narrow path, away from the town. It is a miracle we have not been spotted, and I heave Merek onto the back of the slightly larger of the two grey animals. "I apologise, for giving you such a heavy load to carry."

"Hey, do you mind; it is all muscle you know." Merek huffs.

Looking back, the castle is aflame, orange flickers and black smoke disperse into the morning sky, leaping from windows and arrow slits. My conscience pricks.

"Do you think I should I go back and fight, leave you to go on alone?" I run a hand through my hair.

"Too many Roundheads, the castle is lost, no point wasting your life." Merek rubs his leg. "And though it pains me to admit, without you, I doubt I will make it either."

Around the coastline we trot towards Penally. "Dai Price lives around these parts and keeps his coracle nearby. He takes it up the river to St. Florence. I have seen him, and if memory serves me well, we are almost there," I reassure Merek.

It is oval shaped, the weave old and weatherworn. "Do you think it will let in water?" Merek sits slumped, skin clammy and pale. Getting him to Branwen soon, imperative.

"We are just going to have to chance it." Not designed for the sea, and only to seat one, I drag it to the water's edge returning for Merek. Squeezing in beside him, grateful the water is calm, the tide in our favour. "I hope Dai will be reasonable when I explain why we stole his vessel, and Gavin for that matter, when he finds his donkeys, miles from home." I instigate conversation. Keeping Merek awake is paramount.

"Not stolen, Lockhart, merely borrowed," Merek reminds me. We have spoken casually, since my return to the castle, though not in the easy manner we had previously. When I first arrived the meeting with Tom Griffiths had not gone well when I laid out my terms. "As a druid I am under no obligation to you."

Tom swept his hand across the table, sending tankards of ale tumbling to the floor. "You had better retract your words right now and remember your duty as a soldier."

The mist around Tom darkened, but I refused to be intimidated. "I am no longer a soldier at this castle, that role died with my brother, remember? Therefore, you currently have no jurisdiction, but as a native of Tenby I feel it my duty to protect where I can."

Leaving the hall Merek followed. "You were always a good man," he jibed. "What the hell has happened to you? Living out on Wills Mark, wearing your druid robes, has made you soft. I never thought you would be a coward, but that is what you have become." Merek pushed me and I almost lost my footing, taking a backwards step to steady myself. "You are no brother of mine." He spat on the floor before turning.

Our present predicament, perhaps, a good opportunity to set matters straight. "Am I forgiven?"

Merek shrugs. "I don't know."

"I am not even sure why our friendship has become strained," I grumble.

"You have changed." Merek's teeth chatter.

I ask. "How so?"

"Well, you used to be fun, you liked nothing more than a good brawl in the tavern and a drop of ale."

"Aye." I smirk. "But things happen Merek, life changes you, none of us stay the same."

"I'm the same," Merek snaps.

"No, you are not." I laugh. "You are wed and father to three strong boys, how can you possibly be the same?"

Merek shrugs again, changing the subject. "I didn't even know about the other tunnel through Emlyn's office."

It was one of the few secrets Emlyn shared only with me.

The sun peeps fleetingly from behind cloud, briefly warming us. Unused to the steer of a coracle it is a slow journey to the island. Merek rubs his aching leg and takes up the conversation. "I thought you had no backbone, all this druid rubbish, instead of fighting like a man."

I look at him in surprise.

"I was wrong. On the battlefield you fought with the strength of two men, knew when to strike, when to turn. You have always been a good swordsman, but I was impressed. Not that I had much chance to watch of course, I was a bit busy myself."

I consider if the strength I found in battle, had anything to do with my dragon.

"You a turncoat." I am seething. "I cannot believe what you are saying, how can you even consider fighting for the parliamentarians?"

Merek bares his teeth. "Because they pay well Lockhart. There is no king's army anymore and I have a family to feed, I do not really care about Cromwell's politics and ideals, I work for whoever pays the best price."

I shake my head. "You do not care? Parliament's men make their own rules, no one sees fit to stop them, taking from rich and poor alike." My voice rises with every word. "I hear, even the great English houses are eating naught but potage and gruel. They are scum, have plundered and pillaged the church, in fact the whole town, and then, have the audacity to use the remnants of the castle as a garrison."

Merek leans on his stick. Branwen has worked diligently on his leg; however, he still struggles to walk unaided. "Times have changed Lockhart; the royalists are defeated, Wales stands with the parliamentarians and rightly so, in my opinion."

I fail to understand. "Men are turning traitor to the king daily, but I never expected you to be one of them, I thought you would remain loyal."

"Come on Lockhart, wake up man. Tom Griffiths has defected, disappearing like a shadow in the night. Rice Powell, drafted in from Cardigan, now governs Tenby for parliament. The King arrested for treason, yet you expect me to be loyal, why?"

I remain defiant. "What about Emlyn, he would have remained loyal to the cause."

Merek laughs humourlessly. "Emlyn, you think Emlyn would have been loyal, only if it suited him. He cared about only himself; he even arranged your slaying; he wasn't even loyal to his own kin."

I stare open mouthed. "What did you say?" I ask slowly.

Merek averts his eye. "Tell me," I demand. "What do you know?"

Merek shakes his head. "I promised myself I would not reveal this to you, but you are so darned sure of yourself, so self–righteous, maybe it is time you heard the truth." He sneers. "The day we were attacked on our way to Llandovery, to find the cattle rustlers." I wait for him to continue, a heavy stone in my gut. "The men had been sent by Emlyn; he wanted you dead."

A stab penetrates my heart. "I don't believe you, why would he do that?"

Merek shrugs. "He probably just wanted you out of the way, he never did care much for you."

My chest tightens, bilious stomach threatening to purge the words before they take root. Brothers, spawned from the same parents, expelled by the same loins, loathing running deep as a festering sore, red, burning, angry, but to arrange my murder? A memory floats into my awareness. Emlyn's study, before leaving for Llandovery. "You may have to keep an eye open as you sleep." That was Emlyn though, always sharp with his tongue, they were just words, I argue with myself.

"If it were true," I conclude, "he would not have left the job unfinished but tried again."

"He did you fool; do you think he meant to get himself killed when they stormed the castle? You were the target; he arranged it with Tom Griffiths."

"Arranged what exactly?" I cut in.

"I am not party to the full details. I just know that if Emlyn had not double crossed them, it would have been your blood spilt not his. Lucky for you he was such a miser, if he had paid the agreed price, you would be the one cold in your grave."

Merek's malicious tone smacks of indifference. What have I done to my friend, to Emlyn, for them to behave so? My mind flits like the wings of a startled bird. Did Emlyn genuinely believe I had been having an affair with Angharad? Was that reason enough to cut me down? He knew my distaste for Niamh, she would never have been a concern, but if he were under the illusion that I had slept with his first wife, had he wanted me out of the way before he wed Wren? My stomach lurches. Was Emlyn afraid I would steal her away? Jealousy, was that it? I wouldn't have been the first man to succumb to his fate, through envy. Anxiety and guilt shred my internals. The very thing Emlyn feared, came to pass. I did fall in love with her. Still, to arrange my death, surely, he wouldn't go to those lengths.

"Caprice, why would Emlyn gift me a horse, if he didn't care?"

Merek sighs wearily. "Lockhart, he won the old mare in a game of dice, he had no use for her. The gift, if that is what you wish to call it, was to appease you, keep you on side, she was worthless. He told the men who attacked us on the road to Llandovery to sell her on, make it appear the horses where the target. With the poverty of war, the cob has no doubt become some-one's dinner by now."

"You seem to be well informed on what was taking place," I challenge.

"You hear things." Merek shrugs.

"Yet you didn't think to come to me?"

Merek fails to meet my eye. "As I say, I wasn't aware of the full details, but rumour suggests, Emlyn was to disappear when the castle was stormed, allowing Tom to take up residence, but unbeknown to Emlyn, Tom, underhand as he was, had arranged for him to be arrested."

"From my recollection, the night Emlyn was killed you only appeared after the event. Where had you been?" I fist my hands. "Were you expecting to find me dead?"

"Of course not."

"You were also insistent we leave the castle and come here to the island. Was that to enable Tom Griffiths time to take up residence?"

"What if it was, the town has fared better without Emlyn; you can't deny that. Well, it had until the war came." Merek's nostrils flare, spitting out his own defence. "If you must know, until the castle was taken that morn, I knew nothing, but I was dragged from my bed, and when someone is pointing a blade at your chest, you tend to agree to the terms being offered. The man who murdered Emlyn said there had been a change of plan. Told me to get you and Wren out of the way and say nothing, or he would come after my family. I couldn't take that chance."

"Then it appears you are right; I have been a fool." Anger replaced with a heavy heart. "I believed that regardless of our differences, Emlyn still thought of me as his brother. I also believed you were my friend; it appears I was wrong on both counts."

"I saved you when we were attacked, didn't I?"

"I am no longer sure whether to believe a word you say," I reply sadly. "But tell me Merek, what have I done that is so wrong, why has our friendship turned bitter?"

Merek furrows his brow. "I cannot believe you are unable to see for yourself what you are," he snarls. "You think you are so high and mighty, that because you are a druid, you can pick and choose when to fight. I have tried to accept the changes in you Lockhart, believe me I have, but you must see what others see?" I remain silent. "No, then allow me to enlighten you, friend." Merek grimaces. "You allowed your own brother to be murdered before your eyes; you did nothing to help him. So, I ask, which side where you on? Did you double cross your brother?" My head shakes in opposition, as Merek continues. "And we all know why, do we not? We all know why you wanted him out of the way. So, you could claim his wife for yourself, you make me sick, you and Emlyn are cut from the same cloth; you are no better than him."

I see red and lunge at Merek. Unsteady on his feet, he falls, grabbing my shirt, taking me down with him. I swing the first punch, square on Merek's chin. Merek hits back with a side swipe to my face, my mouth fills with blood. We wrestle on the gritty soil like dogs.

"That's enough men, leave it." Geraint grabs Merek's arm.

"Pathetic, you are not even worth it," Merek growls, staggering to his feet. He grabs his stick, and hobbles away.

Geraint holds out a hand to help me up. "What was all that about?" Wiping bloodied lips with the back of my hand, I fail to reply.

"I cannot believe it, Wren; I risked my own life to save him, and this is how he repays me." Wren bathes my cheek, dabbing gently beneath my eye. It is burning, raised, angry as my temper. "Sit still," she scolds. "How am I to tend your wounds when you wriggle like an eel?" She wipes my swollen lip, and I wince, batting her hand away.

"Leave it woman." I pace the small room relaying my argument with Merek. "Can you believe he had the audacity to suggest we are even?"

Wren looks puzzled.

"He saved me, I saved him. Can you believe he even thinks that way?" Slamming my fist down on the table, Cerys begins to cry.

Wren picks her up, sitting her on her hip. "You need to calm down, you are upsetting the children."

"Calm down, how am I to calm down?" I throw up my hands.

"Then I suggest you go for a walk, to clear your head," she demands.

Slamming the door on my way out, striding towards the beach, I sprint across shifting sand, fast as I can. Heart thumping in my chest, lungs burning and shaky from the exertion, until I can go no further. By the water's edge, I bend, hands resting on my knees, the warmth of the sun on my head. The sea washes over my boots, soaking my feet. Irate, I move away and sit on the soft warm sand, sifting grains through my fingers.

In the distance, Wren walks towards me, holding up her skirts to keep them dry, sunlight accentuating the brightness of her array of colour. Reaching me, she sits, tucking wisps of dark hair into her coif, and taking my hand in hers. We watch the surf in silence. Grey sea rising, folding into small white waves, spilling across the shore, the sun blinking in a billowing cloud. I gaze at the distant horizon.

"Do you think I had Emlyn killed?" This worry prays on my mind.

"Of course not," Wren replies. "I know you loved him, despite his faults. I have seen the guilt which eats away at you, for his death."

Licking my swollen lip with my tongue, I look at her. "Merek is right though; I did nothing."

"You told me you were unable; your head smashed against the wall repeatedly, rendering you dazed and confused."

"What if I didn't try hard enough?"

"Remember your druid teaching Lockhart, the goddesses spin a web through life, attracting to you what lies hidden within, enabling you to become aware of that which needs healing. You try so hard to be a good man, to do what is best for your family and the community on Wills Mark and Tenby. Yet you never feel you are doing enough; guilt sits with you always. Merek showed you what you have hidden inside of yourself, the guilt you feel. He merely revealed your reflection."

Considering her words, I reply sadly, "I know you are right, I seem to have always felt guilty, for even being alive, when my life, ended our mother's. I know Emlyn never forgave me." I sigh deeply. "Then father dying, I thought Emlyn had taken me in because he cared. Now, I wonder if it was because he felt obligated to do so, to placate our father on his death bed." I laugh mirthlessly. "Can you believe Emlyn accused me of having an affair with Angharad?" I turn to judge her reaction. "I didn't," I say quickly. "She taught me to read; he had it all wrong but wouldn't listen."

"I believe you husband, but once someone has convinced themselves they are right, it can be very difficult to change that view."

"He knew I loved you. I guess that stirred old feelings, I think Emlyn hated me."

"I did not know Emlyn well. During our short marriage he remained a closed book, distant. Had built a wall of protection so high; I doubt anyone could have entered. I do know he was very unhappy; he didn't like himself very much. Bullies never do. They use aggression to cover their true feelings; they are afraid to appear vulnerable. I do not believe Emlyn hated you, but I do believe he was jealous of you."

I pull a face. "Jealous, why would he be jealous of me?"

"Because you are the man he wanted to be. You are well liked by the people of Tenby, a good soldier, skilled with sword and horse, strong of body and character and rather dashing." She bites her lip. "You are everything he was not. Remember all reflects what is within. You showed him the things he could have been, the characteristics hidden, waiting to be recognised, but for whatever reason, refused to acknowledge; that is not your fault."

Teasingly I ask, "when did you get to be so clever?"

She laughs. "I listen to the teachings Lockhart, that is all, I listen to Branwen and Ranulf and the sisters."

"Are you saying I do not?" Hands on my hips, in mock defiance. She smiles and I draw her close. "I have felt guilty for loving you," I confess. "It hurts that Emlyn had to die, for us to be together."

Wren places a finger on my bruised lips. "Hush Lockhart, some things are meant to be."

I kiss her finger. "So, my clever faerie, what do you suggest I do about Merek? We have never fought since we were young boys."

"Nothing, we know the truth but if he does not want to see it, that is his problem. We each have our own truth, our own views, you cannot force another to think differently, they must come to that decision by themselves." Adding, "I am sorry, I know you have been friends a long time but when your paths lead in different directions, it is no use clinging to what was. Standing up for what you believe is not easy, especially when others deride you, but you must remain true to what your soul shows you, trust what feels right in your heart. Let Merek go with your love, do not vilify him for his viewpoint, it will not serve you." She reaches to touch my face. "You will have a black eye tomorrow, if I don't see to that soon."

Chapter 19

Lockhart

Carefully placing his few precious belongings into a square of sackcloth, Ranulf ties the ends, slumping onto the floor, breathless from the small exertion. Owning little by way of possessions, he is happier for it. "Possessions do not make the man," Ranulf always says, "What you hold in your heart and your everyday actions, are what define you."

"You are not fit to go anywhere." I lean against the cave entrance with my arms folded.

"But I must make peace with my homeland before it is too late." Ranulf rubs his chest.

"You belong here Ranulf, the people of Tenby and Wills Mark are your family," I protest.

"You do not know who I am, or how I came to be here, you know nothing of me," Ranulf says wearily.

"Then stay, tell me."

Ranulf sits hunched, a tight smile across his lips. He picks up a feather lying at his feet, studying the size and colour. "Blackbird, a spirit messenger, symbolising change, magic, death." He twirls it between his fingers. "I have not been entirely honest with you Lockhart." He looks up. "I haven't lied, but, neither have I revealed the full story. This," Ranulf indicates to the feather, "is my prompt to do so." Intrigued, I cock my head. "You had better sit, it's a long tale but one you deserve to hear, before I leave." I sit on a smooth rock facing Ranulf. "Where to begin?" He strokes the feather. "My name, like yours, is Scottish, did you know that?" I shake my head. "It means advice of the wolf, the wolf being my animal, as yours is the dragon." Ranulf winces, rubbing the pain in his chest.

"So, where are you from?"

Ranulf smiles serenely. "I come from the Isle of Arran, which lies on the western coast of Scotland." Ranulf's eyes cloud dreamily. "A spiritual place inhabited by druids, equally as powerful as the Welsh, no doubt related in times past. It is the place I was born and tutored from a young age by the head druid." His forehead tenses. "He was elderly and taken back to the Otherworld suddenly, unexpectedly, and I was to step into his shoes. I didn't feel ready, for such responsibility, barely a man myself. I covered my insecurity with arrogance and self-importance. Others in the village made their feelings known, challenged my authority and the old ways. Christianity, had become the way forward and most were choosing that path." Ranulf pauses. "I had a sweetheart at the time, Muira. Auburn hair and deep grey eyes." He sighs dreamily. "I became embroiled in the task of head druid, so pretentious." He shakes his head. "Does a man no good, to become too big for his boots… I thought I was powerful, that I could control the village as the old master had, but I was brought back down to earth when Muira left me for another. Adding insult to injury, her new man was a Christian. Not that I have anything against them, it's just choice. There should always be a choice." Ranulf shakes his head. "I tried everything to win her back. Gifts, poems, even spells, nothing worked. When their marriage was announced I knew I could not stay. The thought of them bearing children was too much; I lost my faith in druidism."

"Lost your faith?"

"Yes, I didn't get my own way you see, and more and more of the village were turning towards Christian teachings, I began to doubt. Saw what was happening as proof druidism was not the right way to live after all. Of course, the real problem was my self-righteous behaviour. I was being shown a lesson I did not wish to face." He smiles sorrowfully. "We all have tests Lockhart, things to overcome. Living is the challenge." He falls silent.

"How did you come to be in Tenby?"

Ranulf looks off into the distance. "The same time this was all happening in the village, your father's boat became lost in a storm, the crew drifting many days in open water." My mouth falls open in surprise. "By the time they arrived on the shores of Arran they were weak and famished. They stayed several days to rest and recuperate and fix the boat."

"Did you come to Tenby with my father then?" I ask eagerly.

Ranulf gives me a small smile. "More than that Lockhart, I came with both your parents."

My brow furrows. "I don't understand."

"Your mother, Brigid, we lived in the same village. She fell in love with your father, Ifan, during his time on the island."

My past slips like sand through an hourglass. The truth regarding my origins shattered, invoked by nothing more than expectation and false belief, no longer contained in protective glass from where I can observe the contents. Upturned, spilling across the floor, spreading further than expected. Not the true Welshman I thought.

Ranulf continues, "Your mother and I were both selected by the great druid teacher. She held promise."

"You are telling me my mother was a Scottish druid!" I exclaim.

Ranulf nods. "The druid teachings spoke to her deeply."

"I always assumed mother was Welsh. That I was Welsh, with a distant Scotch ancestry. Why has no one thought to enlighten me, until now?"

"Because if you had known it would have influenced how you saw me, how you saw her, and more importantly, how you saw yourself."

"Why does that matter?" I frown.

"We are shaped by the connections to the people we share this journey with, and sense of belonging to a place, to make a difference to that place. Tenby is your home. Your father, Welsh, therefore, so are you. It is vital your decisions are based on messages from your soul, your dragon. Not from a place of grandiosity, where wisdom is fed by a jumped-up importance because you are descended from a line of druid healers. Do you see?"

"Yes, I understand what you're saying. I must learn for myself without preconceived ideas."

"Exactly, now shall I continue my tale?"

"Yes, please do."

"One night, Brigid confided in me, she was leaving Arran and returning with Ifan, to his home in Wales. She too, was tired of the village politics and wanted more, adventure I suppose. I told her I would come too, but she wouldn't hear of it. That is, until I threatened to tell and scupper her plans. I am not proud of it." Ranulf dips his head.

"I cannot believe I have never known these facts." I rake a hand through my hair.

Ranulf fiddles with the sackcloth. "She wasn't happy that I forced her hand, wanted a new beginning I guess, away from her old life, I was a constant reminder." Ranulf sighs. "We went our separate ways once we arrived here. Brigid made a life with your father, but I found myself drawn back to the old ways when I discovered the druid community on Wills Mark. Your mother rarely used her skills, a shame really, but she wanted to fit in, didn't want to appear different. Dafydd's daughter Rhia was one of the exceptions. She wouldn't be grown with a child of her own, if it hadn't been for your mother's intervention."

"Did you speak to my mother at all?"

"Not until your birth was imminent, did she seek me out. I don't know if she could foresee her own demise, but something was amiss. She told me she was to have a son who would inherit her healing abilities. Asked me to offer you protection, should you need it. She wouldn't elaborate, but I have kept my eye on you, from afar, as promised."

"Have you?"

Ranulf rubs his chest. "It hasn't been easy I can tell you; I never saw any indication of your healing abilities. In fact, I had pretty much given up, decided your mother must have been mistaken. That is until the day we met under St. Catherine's Island. I was shocked to see your golden essence, I swear it hasn't always been there. I knew instinctively I must give you the onyx for protection. If I hadn't, maybe you would have been killed when the castle was sieged. Then…" he pauses.

"Then what?" I ask with growing excitement.

"I am not sure, how I can explain it." Ranulf shrugs.

"Try."

"Two lives intertwined," Ranulf reflects. "The night of Samhain, I saw an image of a different life, where your choices were not honourable."

"But what does that mean?"

Ranulf shrugs again. "As you know Lockhart, the images and messages we receive, are not always clear, not like sitting with a friend in conversation. We must try and interpret the meanings ourselves."

"Then how do you interpret it?" My heart races; will I finally have an answer?

Ranulf merely replies, "All I know, is that the answers lie within you."

Fatigued after the short journey from the island, Ranulf slumps against the harbour wall.

"It is a long voyage Ranulf, fraught with danger, what if you become even more unwell. Have you been to the sisterhood?" I lean on the wall beside him.

"The sisterhood have done all they can, and I am well aware I may not last the trip." Ranulf offers a lopsided smile. "If I do not, they will throw me overboard and the tide will take me instead, either way, I will make it home. I told you once, that I came on a boat from the west and would leave the same way."

"I remember," I recount. "You said, when you have come full circle, you would leave, but this time you would be facing the setting sun." I sigh.

"Now I understand what you meant."

"It is my time Lockhart, nothing to fear, we both know what lies ahead for my soul."

"You truly believe that your soul lives on?" I ask hesitantly.

Ranulf shakes his head. "You of all people, ask me this question, have you learnt nothing? What you believe to be true becomes your life, and, what you find upon your death. If you believe people are generally good, do all you can to be good yourself, you receive goodness in return. If you believe you are worthy of love, you will receive love. If you believe you have a soul, then it will save you at your point of death, for even the next life, is what you expect it to be, the soul immortal. Death is not the end but the beginning, as all things are, whether that be in this world or the Otherworld, as sure as sunrise follows darkness." Ranulf sighs. "Remember the words of Shakespeare. *As you like it.* Your favourite play." Ranulf clears his throat. "All the world's a stage, and all the men and women merely players. They have their exits and their entrances; And one man in his time plays many parts." He pauses. "A very wise man Lockhart, he knew the truth."

"But what will I do, without you to guide me?" I ask. "There is so much I still do not understand."

"You have Branwen, she will help, and the sisters." Ranulf rubs his chest. "But in the end Lockhart, you must take responsibility for your own journey. Guides, either living or in spirit, can only lead you so far. From now on it is up to you, to make use of what you have learnt, use wisely what you already know. The time for you to do so is way overdue." Ranulf smiles. "You are here for a reason, the opportunity to help many souls has been given to you, it is up to you to figure out how. The message I am given over and over, is that you must remember why you are here."

"How do I do that?" I ask.

"You continue to learn, fall, pick yourself back up and remember, that everything which happens, has the gift of a lesson, if you are wise enough to see through the illusion of the event, to the hidden message beneath. If you follow that guidance, you will not go far wrong. If you take my advice, the first thing you must do is release your guilt over Emlyn's death, it is holding up your progress."

The crew are hoisting the sails, time short. Slowly we make our way along the pier to the gangplank. "There is one other thing." Ranulf purses his lips. "Druids understand the power of the wren, revered even by the great Taliesin, he believed they could shapeshift."

I laugh nervously. "You honestly believe Wren can shapeshift? I would have noticed."

"She won't do it all the time," Ranulf considers. "She may even keep the same form for a lifetime, but then I guess that makes us all shapeshifters. At death we all move on from one form to another." He looks smug.

"Do you believe, as Branwen does, that Wren is a faerie?"

"It seems a reasonable assumption, given her sparkling colours."

"You are seriously suggesting, I am wed to a faerie?"

Ranulf shrugs. "You wouldn't be the first Lockhart; there are many myths and legends of faerie folk and humans interacting."

"Yes, myths and legends," I cut in. "Not facts."

Ranulf places a hand on my shoulder. "Go back in your mind to the day we met under the rock of St. Catherine. What did you think of me?"

I fidget. "I am not sure."

"You know perfectly well, that is why you wriggle so." Ranulf laughs. "You thought I was a mad man, wandering around Tenby with my spells and predictions, in exchange for a few coins."

"But I didn't know you then," I say in my defence.

"Exactly, I have not changed Lockhart; it is your perception which has. It is the same with all of life. The stories we tell ourselves are not fact, merely interpretation."

"What has this got to do with Wren?"

"Myths and legends Lockhart, stories weaved by bards, altered over time. Each storyteller adds and takes away; therefore, we must look to the root of the story, and if everything must come from somewhere, it begs the question. Where does anything come from?" I shrug. "The invisible Lockhart. Every idea, every thought, appears as if conjured by magic, therefore, all things are possible. Listen from the core of your being, for this is where the truth lies, feel the answer before you think it. Now, is Wren a faerie?"

The billowing sails catch the wind, the ship drifting away from Tenby, across the ocean. With Ranulf's words fresh in my mind, I watch until the stern becomes simply a spot on the horizon. "We will meet again in the Otherworld," Ranulf told me. "You still have work to do here, but my time is done. Do not make the mistakes I made Lockhart. The Otherworld is enticing, and I became hooked, spent all my time there, instead of in this world. When my sweetheart found another, I left Scotland to mend my broken heart, but running away never works. My heart is still broken, and if we suppress our feelings, they come back to haunt us." He touched his chest.

"Are you saying that is why you are ailing now?"

"We think we can hide, but our body knows and finds ways to remind us. Use the wisdom of spirit to help you in this life, cherish what you have, and for goodness' sake use that dragon."

I had held out my hand to shake Ranulf's, but he pulled me into an embrace, whispered in my ear, "Neither your past nor your future, is set in stone Lockhart. Remember my words and live from the heart."

Knelt with hands resting in my lap, I will them to stop shaking. Branwen stands behind me, hands on my shoulders. Wren kneels with one hand over my heart, the other on my back. I am relieved she is here. The sisters form a circle around the three of us.

"Are you ready?" Branwen asks, and I nod. "Then relax," she scolds. "I can feel the tension in your body, take a deep breath." Breathing deeply in through my nose, holding, for, 1, 2, 3, and releasing. "Again," Branwen urges, "in, 1, 2, 3." I sense my heartbeat slowing. "Again," she repeats more softly, moving her hands to my head. "Look at the candle and still your mind."

On an old stool, a small white candle in the centre of a chipped blue and white plate, patterns of fish running around its edge, a crack through the centre. Concentrating on the flame, flickering light, gold, blue, smoke rising, shadows. Having promised myself I would not return to Annwn, ungrounded for so long after the last visit. Branwen says it may be the only way to release what holds up my progress. Reluctantly I agreed. Deryth, the older woman of the group, her eyes and hair darker than my onyx, insisted I walk barefoot to keep my connection to the earth. I wonder how it is women boss me around, not the other way.

Branwen's soothing words wash over me. "You feel relaxed, drifting effortlessly, calm and serene." Focusing on the flame, my eyes become heavy. "See the flame with your inner eye," Branwen whispers.

The dancing flame flickers behind my closed lids, growing, filling my vision. A sense of leaving my body, floating, moving towards the light, calming, natural, energy merging with the vibrancy emanating from the light. An overwhelming peace, acceptance, and love expands my sense of self. Unsure how long I stay within the light, I become aware of falling, gently, into the same beautiful landscape I visited before. A presence beside me appears from nowhere, but does not surprise me, everything feels… right.

"Hello Lockhart," I know the voice. "Follow me," she whispers, her warm hand taking mine. Without fear, my trust implicit, we walk in silence. Passing through a forest of verdant green, a body of water on the right sparkling with crystalline water. "Do you remember being here before Lockhart?" she asks, coming to a clearing. A throne, the legs carved with engravings of sprite and naiad, sits in the centre of a labyrinth. The circular path interlaid with small white stones. "Do you remember me Lockhart?"

Unable to distinguish her features, or place how, but knowing, somehow. "Yes, I feel I know you, and this place; it seems very familiar."

She laughs. "You have been here many times, some call it the Otherworld, some Annwn; its name is not important." Looking to my left, a translucent stream bubbles over small pebbles, the caressing water forming a trickle of memory, of scooping water into my hand, splashing the girl beside me.

"I was with you!" A statement not a question. I know I am right.

"For now, it is not important." Her voice whispers over and through me, "There are other matters, and you cannot stay long."

"I am confused. Nothing is making sense."

"That is because you are looking at life with your human eyes, through a human brain, not from your spirit."

I sense her within my head. How? "You are doing it now," she gently scolds; I sigh in exasperation.

"I go around in circles, swing between belief and disbelief, never to find an answer."

"It is not easy," her voice a whisper in my mind. "Being human never is, for anyone. I see your confusion, for I am always with you."

"You are my guardian, the one who walks with me?"

"Yes, I try to encourage you to make the decisions that will develop your soul, it does not always work." The sweet sound of her laughter resonates with every part of me.

"Are you, my mother? I have often wondered."

"Your mother watches over you, but no, I am… part of you."

"Part of me, how can that be?"

"I cannot explain, it is something you cannot understand with words, you have to feel it."

I consider. "When bad things happen, is that because I have done something wrong?"

"Some things are meant to be Lockhart," she impresses. "You cannot control everything in your world, only your reaction."

"That is what Wren tells me also, that some things are meant to be."

"Then listen to her Lockhart, she is a very wise soul."

"So, I am not responsible for Emlyn's death? Could I not have prevented it?"

You must stop blaming yourself, neither you, nor Wren are responsible, it is important you tell her that. The guilt you share, sits like a heavy weight between you. It was imperative Emlyn return to us, preventing his death would have gained nothing, only repeated the same cycle. Rest assured, we are working to heal his soul."

"What do you mean, repeated the same cycle?"

"That is for you to work out Lockhart, but remember, you are never able to see the full picture when you are earth bound."

"What about Eirlys?" Emotion amasses in my throat. "Was her death my punishment for Emlyn, or for loving Wren?"

"We never punish Lockhart," she assures. "There is no vengeful God, only steps along the path to enlightenment. Eirlys chose you and Wren as parents because she knew your love, would heal her wounded soul. She was deeply hurt through a previous incarnation and was not ready to live on earth again. You still love her, don't you?"

"Of course."

"She feels that love Lockhart, for love crosses time and space, has no boundaries. The love you feel is helping her, just continue to love, guilt only breeds more guilt. Forgive yourself, let it go, for what you give out you receive back in like measure, that is the law. Choose your thoughts, words, and actions wisely."

I am no longer listening, thoughts of Eirlys filling my mind. "Is she here?" Fervour burns in my chest. "My daughter, can I see her? Please, just one more time," I beg.

"Rest assured she is safe, your mother cares for her. You cannot see her, but you are able to connect to her," she explains tenderly. "Look within your heart and soul, she is there. Close your eyes, think only of her."

I picture Eirlys, her tiny body, closed eyes, peaceful expression. From deep within a flutter of butterfly wings vibrates, and I remember. When Wren had been pregnant with Gwilym and Cerys, I was aware of their presence, with Eirlys it had felt different, delicate, light, like butterfly wings. It is her; I am connecting to my daughter. "I love you, Eirlys." I swallow a lump in my throat, but grief snakes up, building. I let go of the pain and despair. Suppressed sadness and anger. A mother never known, a father barely remembered, Emlyn. Comrades in battle, so many men.

Merek's friendship, all taken. None compares to the pain of losing Eirlys. Sorrow unleashes in a torrent of anguish, the mourning I refused to allow. Men, expected to remain strong, bury their feelings. Sobbing so hard my heart hurts, my head hurts. Opening my eyes, Wren cradles me in her arms crying also.

"I felt her too," Wren sobs. "I felt Eirlys."

We cry and laugh with joy, knowing our daughter lives in another time, another place, but also within our hearts.

Chapter 20

Wren

The last day of April marks the beginning of Beltane. It is a warm day, and I gather hawthorn, breathing the sweet fragrant white flowers. By the lake, beneath the Hazel tree, I come as often as I can. The sisters tell me the more time I spend here, the more connected I will become to it, and in time, it will speak to me, for they believe I am fae. This is something I find difficult to digest. My mind recalls a conversation with Lockhart.

"It seems to me Wren, you must be a faerie, it all adds up."

"Don't be ridiculous," I snapped, for I become fearful whenever it is raised. I do not have wings, and although small, I am far from being an elf. A fierce need to protect my sense of self, my humanness.

"Then how come you have a rainbow of colours?" Lockhart asked.

"You said everybody has them," I'd shot back.

"They do, kind of, yours are different."

"I am not discussing this any further."

"Why are you refusing to admit this to yourself?"

Lockhart fails to understand my fears. It is true my uncle is an apothecary, said to be a direct descendent of the physicians of Myddfai. Using herbal medicine, which, as Lockhart can testify after his own recovery, works exceptionally well. Branwen often comments how easily I learn the properties of plants, how it appears second nature. Is that because I have inherited an innate knowledge for such things? Yet I come from the female line, and the skills are said only to pass through the males. Even so, what if Lockhart is right, and my blood is not human, or only part human, what does that mean for the children? The lake is peaceful, still, tranquil, but my mind jumps around like fleas. Look into the water, Everlee says, become one with the water, for immense energy is stored within. I like Everlee, she is quiet, some might say reserved, but she has granted me her trust, revealing her story, and through this we have become friends. Her husband failed to accept her grief at the loss of their child, spending more time away from home. Overwrought with loss, she found her way across the water, as many do. Begging Branwen and the sisters for help. She never left, made her home here, amongst those who offered care, and the time needed for recovery. Caitrin, I am told, although she has never confided in me herself, tired of being used as a punchbag by her husband, boarded a boat in Pembroke Dock. We all have reasons for being here. The place draws lost souls. An impulse arises to submerge myself within the cool calm waters. No one is around, so I quickly undress, the lake surprisingly warm. I lie on my back, dark hair splayed, looking into the sky. White cloud overlaps like ruches on a gown and circle the island. The centre clear, bright blue. It is beautiful, I cannot help but wonder why God allows such tragedy, illness and sadness whilst creating such splendour. For despite my druid learning, deep down, I still believe God to be the creator of all. Lockhart is more accepting of the druid way, believes he has a dragon and a guide who speak to him. I admit, I am jealous. The only voice I hear is my own, chattering. Branwen explains we are each on a collective and individual journey. Abefa has always lived on the island. Daughter to Deryth, the crone, chosen to aid Lockhart. As powerful as her mother, she agrees spending time barefoot absorbs the earth energies into your being. I am to listen to the rustle of leaves, the whisper of trees, my work, to heal, not just people, but the earth; a faerie, at home in the forest where the naiad and sprite play. I come full circle, back to the constant festering worry. Do I believe it possible; I am of faerie blood? Druids believe we create what we are; if that is the case, why do I continually create bad things? Lockhart has faced many challenges since I came into his life, and what of the daydreams I used as respite during marriage to Emlyn. I got what I wished for, but at what cost? Cromwell was stolen as a baby, by a monkey. Faeries too, are known to steal human babies, swap them for a changeling who wreaks havoc. That is the fear I keep close to my heart, what if that is who I am?

I adorn the outside of the cottage, never the inside, for this is bad luck, with my pickings. Aneira arrives with Ffion, and we head for the sister's hut. Tonight, will be spent separate from the men; they will hold their own secret ceremony. Bringing offerings of shells, pebbles and crystal from the beaches, and wildflowers. Hyacinth, cowslips and bluebells, we gather round the fire, talking, laughing, singing. As the sky darkens, we hold hands. Abefa bangs the drum, slow steady beats. We sit in silence, eyes closed. Deryth, despite her stern appearance sings beautifully, a melodic tune, calling in Creiddylad, the May Queen. I sense the energy, the song heightening in pitch, the drum beating faster. My heart expands, joyful, loving. Connected to all in this room. We chant, Creiddylad, Creiddylad. Then silence. Branwen thanks the May queen for gracing us with her presence. Then we dance, and eat, and the comradeship of these women is like no other. How could I have seen this druid life as primitive, less, when I have never felt happier? The night ends with the story of Creiddylad. Gathering around Branwen like children, we listen intently to the tale. "Daughter of Lludd Llaw Eraint, the most beautiful of maidens in the three isles of Britain. Two rival lovers, Gwyn and Gwythyr, battle on May Day for her hand, for on this day she becomes Queen of Annwn."

Tomorrow, the men will act out the scene of the belligerent lovers, and we will dance around the Maypole, a stick of birch garnished with colourful ribbon. The men will watch, and we shall choose, if we desire. After Eirlys, I learned, and continue to, from the women of the island, opening my view to a way of living and dying I would never have thought possible. Now I cannot imagine living any other way. The fire dwindles, and we each scoop ash from the dying bonfire into jugs, cups, or bowls, and say our goodbyes, the waning moon casting shadows along the path as I hurry home. Around the door, sweet hawthorn greets me. In the hearth, embers glow, enough light to move easily through the familiar room. I add twigs, sprinkling the pot of ash collected from the ceremony. The fire spits and crackles, warmth presses against my face. On this night of Beltane, the veil between this world and the faerie kingdom thins, allowing access to the esoteric wisdom of Annwn. Excitement flutters in my chest, flames jumping like woodland sprite, my eyes growing heavy and closing. I breathe deeply, expelling presupposition. Slowly, bright colours flicker across my inner vision, vibrating, rearranging into a sequence of numbers on a scroll of yellowed parchment. "Druid goddess Creiddylad, guide me," I whisper, and wait, trusting assistance to unravel the meaning. A pattern emerges, then letters, the connotation clear, and I read. Beltane marks the emergence of the new, a man aided by the fertility of spring falls in love amongst the blooms. I, Creiddylad, bring prophecy, healing and reincarnation, for the revenant, you have been chosen to assist.

It has been a magical day of activity and community and once we arrive home the sun is low, colouring the clouds with an artist's brush of orange and gold, a shimmering reflective hue across the water. I sigh, admiring the beauty. Cerys on my knee, is teething, and I constantly wipe dribble from her chin with a cloth. Lockhart sits beside us and rakes a hand through his hair. We have brought the stools outside; reluctant to see the day end.

"Any ideas Wren?" He looks at me.

"About what exactly?" I enquire, sipping honey mead.

"How we can help people." He opens his hands.

"Well, the people of Tenby are suffering that is for sure. All the promises from Cromwell of a better life have led to nothing. There is more poverty for the majority, it pains me to see their suffering, Lockhart. We have precious little here, but at least the land remains fruitful."

"Do you think we should offer healing?" he suggests. "There is much sickness and anguish with the war, surely it is only right and fitting we use our skills."

"I agree, Lockhart. There is little point learning to heal, then not using it to alleviate suffering, but how can we? People come to the island to visit the sisters, or Branwen for healing, what can we offer that is any different?"

"I was thinking we should set up in Tenby somewhere. I am sure more would come if we were on their doorstep."

"Do you think that is wise, what of Cromwell's army?"

"I understand your concern Wren, and how it will be received, remains to be seen, hopefully people will see the benefit." Lockhart strokes his beard. "We must take heed though, although the town accepted seers such as Ranulf, and tolerate the druids, many of the soldiers at the garrison are English, they may not be open to such things."

"You think they may associate it with witchcraft?" I ask uneasily.

He nods. "That is my concern. I hear they hang women for having a hairy lip in England. It beggars' belief."

"I guess we can but try." I shrug a little fearful.

"That's settled then." He leans over to kiss me.

"Yuck, that is so soppy, father." Gwilym, hands on his hips, pulls a face.

"Oh really," Lockhart is trying to look stern. "And what would you know about it, young man?"

Gwilym narrows his eyes and purses his lips.

"You had better start running," Lockhart is failing to sound serious. "I am going to tan your backside when I get hold of you, for your insolence, young man." Lockhart raises an eyebrow, a grin tugging at the side of his mouth. "Are you ready? 1, 2, 3… Go." Gwilym sets off, fast as his legs can take him.

"Time for one more kiss," Lockhart bends to touch my lips.

I slap his arm. "Behave yourself and go and catch our son."

“Oh, I have time, he cannot run so fast.”

I point where Gwilym has run. “Now,” I demand, but Lockhart does not move. “What are you waiting for?” Then I realise. “Oh alright.” I sigh. “1, 2, 3… Go.” Lockhart turns on his heel, chasing the giggling boy. Trying to corner Gwilym near the fence, the child ducks under his arm, and is off again across the field. I laugh, standing to watch the happy scene, lifting Cerys onto my hip. I rub noses with our daughter, who chuckles. Lockhart grabs Gwilym by the waist, bringing him gently to the ground, tickling him. Our son’s laughter fills the air. A moment to capture and keep in your heart. “I do wonder,” I say to Cerys, eagerly chewing the ties of her bonnet, “if your father is from this century, or even this world. He is unlike any other man I have met; we are incredibly lucky.”

The women work diligently by the harbour, huddled around baskets in black hats and shawls, undisturbed by the stench of fish. Their gnarled knuckles and chilblained hands sorting cockle and winkle.

“We can help ease your aching muscles, supply ointment for your hands,” Lockhart attempts to explain.

“We have no time for your nonsense, be on your way.”

In the town, shopkeepers offer excuses, others outwardly rude, none accept our offers of healing.

“Now what?”

“We wait,” Lockhart says. “They will come.”

“How do you know?”

“I feel the heat in my stomach.”

Our patience is rewarded an hour later, when a young woman peeps around the door of the old wooden hut Aeron has kindly provided for premises. “Come in,” I offer, but the woman shakes her head, remaining in the doorway.

“I was wondering, if you could help my mother.”

Weaving through the narrow streets of Tenby we arrive at Bethog’s house, positioned on a steep incline, nestling between a row of equally dilapidated wooden dwellings, leaning at a precarious angle towards the harbour. The young woman shoves open the splintered door with her shoulder. Her mother is on a wooden pallet by the fire, curled like a resting cat. Myfanwy explains, “She has barely moved since father was killed in battle; she seems unable to accept it; I do not know how to help her.”

I squat by the side of the pallet. “Mistress Bethog.”

“I do not need help,” the woman barks. I indicate for Lockhart to try.

“Mistress,” he begins, “holding your feelings within your heart is causing you pain, allow us to help you release them.”

Bethog stirs, raising her head a little, her face etched in deep furrows of anguish.

“Please mother, try,” Myfanwy pleads.

“You have a look of my Cynfor.” Bethog smiles weakly at Lockhart, her eyes distant.

Lockhart takes her hands in his. “Place your trust in us and we can help you.”

“You have nothing to lose mother.”

Bethog’s mouth is twitching. Then a look of hope eclipses her anguished face, and she nods. Lockhart closes his eyes, concentrates. He waves me over, and I stand behind our first patient, working as a team, equals. Bethog sighs deeply. When we leave, she is sat in a chair, and by the end of the week, she ventures outside for the first time in months. The news spreads.

Chapter 21

Lockhart

I wake in a cold sweat, heartbeat drumming against my ribs. A dream, though I am only partly convinced. The images replay. Bethog was wading into the bitterly cold sea. My words to call out to her would not come, and doggedly, she continued. The grey surf drenching her skirt, hands outstretched. I was running, scrambling across the soft sand of castle beach. Bethog struggling against the power of the ocean, dragged off her feet, goes under, disappearing beneath the swirl. I cannot swim, and search for someone to help, looking up at the castle. I see Wren watching from a window, my eyes penetrating the walls, for I see the scene within. Wren sat with a child upon her lap. A son, but not Gwilym. Dark shadows under sad eyes, her complexion pallid, the arc of rainbow drained of colour. Emlyn stands behind her laughing. The laughter filled my head, and I woke with a start. I rub my temples; the images disturb me. "It makes no sense," I mutter. "Bethog is alive, Emlyn dead, and Wren did not give him a child."

It is early, birds singing their dawn chorus beyond the window. Wren sings too, a ditty to the children, dressing a wriggling Cerys by the hearth. "Hey, ding a ding, and ho ding a ding. The parliament soldiers are gone to the king. Some with new beavers, some with new bands. The parliament soldiers are all to be hanged." She tickles Cerys, who squeals with delight.

"Wren," I begin uncertainly, crouching beside her, passing the child's woollen stockings airing by the fire. "Bethog, she is alive isn't she, we did heal her?"

Wren looks at me questioningly. "Yes," she says slowly. "I spoke to her at the market only yesterday; she relayed the news she is to be a grandmother."

I blow out a long breath. "Thank goodness."

"Why?" Wren asks.

"Just a dream." But dreams are messengers. What can it be making me aware of?

"Sacrilege," the minister yells. "That is what this is."

Forcing myself to remain aplomb, I speak calmly through gritted teeth, "People are suffering, in pain, how can it be wrong?"

"God is the only one who can save us, how dare you suggest you have the power of God? This is the devil's work," the minister spits out, looking to the mayor, Evan Williams, and two officials, Derwyn Reece and Einion Bale, for their agreement.

Fear of God and the church keep many away from our door, but slowly the trickle of people has increased, bringing our healings to the attention of the minister. I appeal to the mayor, a serious but fair man. "I am not saying I am God; I was raised a Christian and have no desire to disrespect the church. However, if I can aid people, how can it be the work of Satan?"

Derwyn Reece eyes me cautiously, elbows resting on the dark oak table stained with ink. "It seems to me," his heavy moustache twitches, "that all this healing ability, as you call it, has only arisen since you took up with your brother's wife." I gulp the lump in my throat. "Your brother did not live very long after his marriage, I understand." He raises his bushy dark eyebrows. "So, I find myself asking if your wife is in fact some sort of witch?"

Murmurs pass among the small congregation of men in the town hall. My muscles tighten. "No Sire," I begin. "I can assure you she is not a witch; she is a woman of high moral standard, with a Christian upbringing, as I am sure you are aware."

Silence hangs expectantly, and I am just deciding to say more in Wren's defence when the mayor unexpectedly stands and beckons me. "I wish to speak with you privately." This warrants disapproving stares. Squaring my shoulders, I follow him into a private office. "Close the door and sit." Evan Williams is a short, ruddy man. He wears a curly brown wig of the latest fashion. "You understand," the mayor begins, "that you are not under arrest, and that if your wife were found to be a witch, it would matter little in Wales. If we were in England, things would be different, you will be aware of that, I am sure." I give a small, almost indistinguishable nod. "However," Evan Williams continues, "if the church becomes involved, we must investigate; we cannot upset the minister, do you understand?"

I rake a hand through my hair. "I am not sure I do, Sire."

Evan sits back in the chair. "I am saying, you must be aware of the impact your, err, healings," he emphasises the word, "has on the town, and particularly the minister."

I eye the man cautiously. "But we are helping people, Sire."

"I believe you are, but you must tread carefully, discretion is called for, Sire, many fear what they do not understand, believing demons walk amongst us, superstition is rife."

"Are you suggesting we continue, but do so, quietly?" I am perplexed.

"Yes, you understand my meaning." His nose twitches. "There is a farm building I could make available, which would suit your requirements. It is beyond the town walls and therefore not as visible. That I feel would be preferable, out of sight as it were."

My eyebrows rise. "Are you offering it to us, Sire?" I hadn't expected this. "What of the garrison? Parliamentarians are everywhere."

"Indeed," Evan replies. "I am afraid the Roundheads appear to be here for the long haul; we will just have to get used to that." I await the terms of this arrangement; there must be a catch. "Of course," Evan continues. "There is still the matter of the minister. Perhaps a fine would be in order, that may silence him, money usually does."

I scowl. "I have no way to pay a fine Sire."

"Then I suggest you find one, I am prepared to offer the building free from charge, I can do no more than that. If you are as good as people say, they will pay for your services."

I shake my head. "The people we help, have less money than I, they cannot pay."

"This is not open for discussion." Evan lowers his voice, "One other thing." He leans over the table, gesturing me to follow suit. He smells of stale tobacco. "My son, he ails; I request you visit him. In return I will ensure the building remains at one's disposal."

"Are you asking me to?"

Evan holds up a hand to silence me. "Discretion Lockhart, I trust I have your discretion on this matter?"

I nod. "Yes Sire, of course."

"Oh, thank goodness you are home." Wren greets me with a peck on the cheek. "I was worried when Geraint returned from Tenby without you." She ushers me to the stool by the fire. "Tell me what happened."

I hold my hands to the heat, arms resting on my knees. "I was not arrested Wren, just asked to attend a meeting in the town hall. The mayor, with his two cronies, Derwyn Reece and Einion Bale, in attendance. The minister began spouting accusations, accusing me of doing the work of the devil, can you believe that?" Taking my hands, she rubs them between her own to instil warmth as she does with the children. "Where are we to find money to pay a fine Wren?" I search her face for answers.

"We will find a way," she offers a small smile. "I do not understand the reasoning of the church." She sighs. "We offer healing and hope, I cannot see why this is any different to what the church offers, it is two sides of the same coin."

I lift my head slowly. "What did you say?"

"I cannot see why," she begins.

"No, not that bit, the last bit."

"Um, oh, that was it, I said…"

"Two sides of the same coin," I cut in. Wren nods. "Wren, you are amazing, do you know that?" I kiss her cheek and head out of the door, collecting a spade propped against the wall.

"Where are you going?" She runs after me, holding up her skirts. At the back of the young oak tree, close to Eirlys's grave, I pace steps, eight nine ten. Slamming the spade into the ground, I dig. The wind whips around the small clearing, and Wren watches, tucking stray whisps of hair into her cap. My spade hits something, I raise my head and smile.

"I suppose that will be treasure?" Wren grins.

On my knees, I move the dirt with my hands. Wren comes closer and looks down into the muddy hole. Eventually, I have scraped away enough earth to loosen the box, lifting it triumphantly, brushing soil off the lid. "Come," I beckon, and she kneels beside me. Taking the dagger from my belt, I prize it open. Wren gasps, hand flying to her mouth. I grab a handful of coins; they trickle through my fingers.

"How could I have forgotten?" I laugh. "It was only when you mentioned coins, that I remembered. Now we have enough to pay the fine, with plenty to spare."

"Where on earth did it come from?" she asks, once back inside the cottage. We sit staring at the open box on the table. I put my arm around her shoulder.

"Do you remember when we were at the castle, how I was unable to sleep, waiting for the parliamentarians to attack?" Wren nods slowly. "Well one night, I was led there thinking about Emlyn, when I recalled a conversation. He told me the tapestry of the phoenix rising from the ashes, which hung in the hall, held a secret, but I couldn't understand what he meant, and he wouldn't reiterate. He was very drunk, and never mentioned it again, but it was a bit odd, so it stuck in my mind. Anyway, that night as

I lay in bed, an idea came to me, and I crept down to look. Behind the tapestry was a loose stone, it was hard to see at first because it was quite high up, I had to pull the table across to stand on so I could reach. I took my dagger and began chipping away until it finally freed, and I felt around inside and found this." I point to the box. "No wonder Tom Griffiths could not find the coins."

"So how did it end up here?" Wren asks.

"Well, I had to get it out of the castle, so praying the Roundheads would not attack while I was absent, I escaped through the secret tunnel and brought it here. I knew Eirlys would keep it safe." I kiss her cheek. "We must be careful though, we need to keep some for our children, but can also help feed the children in Tenby, what do you think?"

"I think that is a very good idea," she agrees, snuggling closer.

Turning off the main track I head to Penally. Slowing the horse to a trot, following the instructions I turn right along a tree lined path. Ruts in the wet ground from carriage wheels, a good indication I am heading in the right direction. In the distance I glimpse the house through a spread of leaves. A grand mock Tudor design of immense proportion, characterised by the pitch gable roof, and half-timbered framework. Passing neat lawned gardens I pull up at the entrance. The decorative door opened by a butler. He ushers me into the hall and leads the way up the stairs adorned with wall hangings and family portraits. "This way, Sire." Along a long dark corridor of doors, he stops abruptly at the last one and knocks, opening it inwards without awaiting a reply. Light from the large leaded windows floods the room.

Evan Williams moves from his desk to greet me, shaking my hand fiercely. "Thank you for coming, please, sit down." The high-backed chair with barley-twist legs, is cushioned in red velvet. Dark wood cabinets fill most of the back wall, lined with red hardback books. This room alone, as big as our cottage on the island. Beyond the window, a ship in the distance, sailing towards Tenby harbour. Evan sits behind the walnut desk; his shoulders slumped. "I am not sure what you can do." Tension creases his forehead. "Master Aled is my only heir, a sickly child since birth," Evan explains. "Always suffering a cough and weakness. However, these last few weeks he has deteriorated. I know not what has taken hold of him." He hangs his head. "We have paid for the best apothecaries. Bloodletting and all manner of concoctions have been tried, but alas." His despair fills the room.

"I will do all I can," I reassure him.

Aled spits into a bowl, his skin grey and clammy, his frame childlike, not that of a boy on the cusp of manhood. Sinking back against the pillow, exhausted with the small effort. Bloodied phlegm is not a good sign. A maid covers the bowl with a cloth and leaves the room. I introduce myself, "Good morning, master Aled, my name is Sire Lockhart Edwards."

"Are you another apothecary?" The boy's red rimmed eyes survey me.

"I am not."

"If you are not a physician, how can you help me?"

I consider. "I am a druid and have been blessed with a gift, a gift which heals people."

The boy visibly recoils. "Do you invoke magic, like a wizard?"

"Please, do not be afraid master Aled, your father believes I may be able to assist you, if you will allow me to try."

The boy softens. "Then what will you do?"

"Well, we could start gently, if you like. Perhaps I could hold your wrist or touch your shoulder."

"It is my chest which hurts, not my shoulder."

I smile. "That may be so but believe me the healing reaches where it needs to go."

Aled's brow furrows. "How does it know?"

I shrug. "I have no idea. Why don't you allow me to show you?"

Aled cautiously removes a slender arm from beneath the coverlet and holds it out, closing his eyes. "You may try."

My hand circles his small wrist.

The following day, at Wren's suggestion, I bring a syrup of Agrimony to ease Aled's cough. I am pleased to see progress, the boy sat a little straighter, no longer huddled in pain. By the fourth day, a small portion of clear soup remains in Aled's concave stomach.

"I am in less pain Sire Lockhart; your funny healing helps me."

I return Aled's smile with a lopsided grin. "Don't do too much too soon, master Aled, perhaps a little reading."

"Very well," Aled yawns.

"I can see you are tired; I will return tomorrow."

At the door I glance back into the room, my eye drawn to the far corner of the ceiling. My heart plummets.

A candle is lit, although it is almost midday when I return. Condensation clouds the windowpane, as though preventing the bad weather outside from being seen. "Greetings Master Aled, how are you feeling today?" I point to the open book on the bed. "Shakespeare, proof you are an educated man."

Aled beams delightedly. "I am reading Hamlet."

"A tragedy," I note. "Would a comedy not be more uplifting?" I prepare a tincture for his chest.

"I enjoy the drama," Aled says seriously. "Hamlet is full of grief, and longs for death to appease his misery." I glance to the far corner of the room; the sphere of white light remains. Aled continues, "Hamlet is afraid to die. Do you fear death, Sire?"

I stop, consider my answer. "I believe death is simply moving into another room. The body may cease, but the spirit remains."

"Will I go to heaven?" Aled asks forthrightly, and I face him. Angelic in his white bedgown, fair hair resting on his bony shoulders, I sit on the edge of the bed.

"I believe we all go to a better place, when it is our turn."

"I am at the end." His innocent blue eyes forlorn, old before their years.

"Of the play?" I hold his gaze.

"No, like Hamlet." He picks up the book and reads. "To die: -to sleep: No more; and, by a sleep to say we end The heartache and the thousand natural shocks That flesh is heir to, tis a consummation Devoutly to be wished." He stares into the distance. Words to lighten Aled with hope, speak of becoming well, to lie, will not come forth. Aled closes the book, and shuffles under the coverlet, closing his eyes. "Grandmother came to see me yesterday."

"It is enjoyable to have visitors." I search the child's fading misty colours, hankering for a positive sign.

"She died many years ago." The boys' eyes remain closed. "I could never tell father, but you understand, don't you?"

Reeling from the passing of Aled, having failed him and his father, I arrive in Tenby for the healings, when I would have preferred to sit at home, turn my back on a world which makes no sense. Wren refused to allow me to be maudlin, reminding me of those I have helped. She is right, as usual. I must not lose faith. Kittiwakes rest on St. Catherine's Island. I watch them, and wonder if they mourn their dead, as we do. If birds are messengers from God, and all animals sentient beings, as Ranulf believes. I dreamt of him last night, or at least, I suppose it was a dream. He was smiling, a full set of teeth, younger, hair a coppery red. "I'm home." I woke wondering if he meant he had made it back to Arran, or if he meant Annwn.

"Lockhart." Wren breaks my reverie. "This gentleman," she indicates a young Roundhead, "wishes to speak with you."

Despite our proximity to the castle the soldiers keep their distance, and therefore, his attendance is somewhat a surprise. Wren offers him a stool, but he lifts his hands in protest. "No mistress, this isn't for me; I just want to talk to him." He points in my direction. Wren has heard it often, men, women too, often trust their secrets to me more than her. As a man I am deemed more knowledgeable. I am aware it irks her, but she accepts it, discreetly leaving us to speak privately.

"How can I help?" I ask.

"Can you come and see someone at the castle, you on your own Sire, if you will."

Scorched wood is strewn across the courtyard, doors swing on their hinges, corridors dirty with mud. Only the north and west of the castle remain intact. The wooden soles of our boots echo the castle corridors. Lit wall sconces cast dark images across the floor, a reminder the shadow self always walks with you. Parliamentary soldiers huddle around the fire in the great hall, wall hangings in tatters on the floor, except for the phoenix remaining stubbornly on the wall. The once splendid room looks and smells like a stable. The soldier pushes through the men, who eye me cautiously. At the back of the hall the door opens into a makeshift sick room, men foetal on pallets. At the back, a man lies alone. Abscesses and ulcers disfigure his face and cover his body, naked bar a thin linen sheet. He groans.

"How long has he been this way?" I ask, shocked by the sight of him.

The soldier shrugs. "Weeks Sire, and he isn't getting no better, if anything, he is worse."

I sit on my haunches to take a closer look, reeling in horror.

"Are you alright Sire?" The soldier squats beside me. "I know it is a bad sight to see. His name's Macsen, always a jester, often had us laughing. I feel right sorry for him. Can you do anything?"

I can barely believe, but it is him, the toothless attacker, here all along; how could I not have known? Struggling to piece together conflicting opinions of this man, the caring young soldier having no knowledge of the man's violent acts. I imagine my revenge, stabbing the abscesses, causing him further affliction, but, writhing in pain, he is surely suffering enough. Rising above these baser instincts, and without touching him, I move my hands above the man's body, forcing myself to remain impassive.

"I will leave you to it." The soldier backs away.

When he rests easier, I pull up a stool. "Macsen." It feels odd to know his name. "Do you know who I am?"

"Aye, I know."

I steel myself. "Was it Emlyn? Did he pay you to kill me?"

Macsen opens his eyes briefly, closing them again. "Nothing personal, Sire, just business."

My heart tightens, so it is true. "What of Tom Griffiths, was he behind Emlyn's death?"

"He was behind all of it, wanted your brother out of the way." The man falls silent.

"Go on." I encourage. Macsen shudders. "Tom warned Emlyn of the unrest in Tenby, offered him the chance to disappear under the guise of the castle being stormed. Tom would then take his place, but your brother wanted you out of the way first, and Tom arranged for it. When you returned after, well after our meeting." His face tightens.

"Continue."

"Well, it was decided your throat would be cut during the siege."

"But Emlyn didn't pay the agreed price, am I right? Is that why you murdered him?"

"We did you and the rest of Tenby a favour, you can't deny it."

My jaw is clenched, nails digging into the palms of my fisted hands. "Why didn't you kill both of us, you had the opportunity?"

Macsen shifts, wincing. "I intended to, but let's say I had a change of heart. Emlyn was the bigger fish, and if you had both died it would have looked suspicious. The locals speak highly of you, they might have objected, caused trouble, it wasn't worth the risk."

My mind is awash, and we fall into uncomfortable silence.

"Sire, why are you helping me after everything I have done?" Macsen asks sombrely.

"Why indeed. You like your bible quotes, it seems, so hear this. Let he that is without sin cast the first stone. John 8:7 I am a healer, but also a mortal, I have made mistakes, none of us are perfect. There is a power greater than I who determines our fate, it is not for me to decide."

"Do you feel it's too late to repent my sins?" He mumbles, and I scowl. "Ye shall know the truth, and the truth shall make you free. John 8:32."

Needing time to organise my thoughts before heading back to the healing room, I make my way to the north beach, rarely having the opportunity to visit now that I live on the island. Collecting a handful of shifting sand, the warm dry grains slip between my fingers. I think again of Ranulf, wonder if the onyx ensured my survival during the castle siege. "I hope you made it home to Scotland." Observing a honeybee bobbing around a clump of striped pink and white sea bindweed, it reminds me of something Ranulf said during my training. "Bee wings beat so fast you can barely see the movement." I hear his voice in my head, "To the observer the insect moves serenely from flower to flower, but her work is of the upmost importance, for it ensures the survival of her companions in the hive." I acknowledge a kinship to the bee. Serving others, appearing calm, serene but with a buzz of activity few see, not all of it kindly. Repressed anger at Macsen has whipped up frustration and fury towards Emlyn and Tom, who tricked me into believing my promotion to captain was down to my skills. I feel used by them, and it rankles. If a bee feels threatened, she will strike, and you will feel the sting in her tail. I too wish to lash out, hurt another, reveal my poisonous venom, but like the honeybee, to do so would cause my death. I will no longer be the person I have worked hard to become. Ranulf told me anger is fear in disguise, of not being worthy, not enough. Right now, I don't care. I am irate and feel justified.

Wren sits me on a stool and offers wine, which I gulp in one go.

"Pray tell what troubles you, husband." She sees my tetchiness, always knows my mood.

I rake a hand through my hair. "I went to the castle." I pause. "A man in much pain," I turn to her. "Emlyn's murderer; I cannot believe he has been no more than a breath away and I did not know."

Wren frowns. "If you had known, what could you have done?"

I shrug. "I was asked to help him, but how can I help a man when he killed my brother?" I refrain from revealing what else I learnt.

"How can you not?" she replies. "We do not know his reasons, Lockhart, do not know why he chose his path, you tell others we are all equal, all a part of the whole. So how can you go against that now, just because it is personal?"

I furrow my brow. "He has the French disease, Wren, punishment for his behaviour, you know as well as I, you get the pox from whores."

Wren blushes, and I regret speaking to her of such things. "Yes, I am aware of that, but you are judging him and who are we to judge?"

“So, you do not believe he is being punished for his acts? For murdering my brother?” I say angrily.

She glares at me. “You appear to forget that Emlyn was not only your brother, but my husband.”

I open my mouth to speak but think better of it. Wren sighs. “I may not have loved Emlyn, but it pains me he died in such a horrific way.” She pauses, tucks hair into her coif. “I can understand your dilemma Lockhart, but you must overcome this, by not letting go of hatred you continue to punish yourself, you need to forgive.”

I return to the castle early the next day. The young soldier meets me in the courtyard. “Macsen died last night,” he informs me sadly. “Perhaps it is just as well, his suffering is now over.”

Walking away I curse myself. If I had not been so self-righteous, done more for him when I could, maybe the outcome would have been different. The voice of my guardian floats into my head. “You did enough and learnt your lesson, he is at peace.” I often wonder if my guardian is real, or if I am making it up. For if I am powerful, why do I often fail. “You do have power, Lockhart, but do not get above your station. You are merely the facilitator, something greater uses you to bring forth healing. If it does not come, we must accept it was not meant to be. We are not able to decide the fate of others, that is not our task.” She speaks wisely, is right, always right, that does not make it any easier to live with.

Evan Williams edges his way along the queue, the line of people stretching beyond the door. Doffing his hat to the ladies as he passes, he rarely visits the healing room, and I am surprised to see him. “Sire Lockhart, Mistress Wren.” Evan bows politely, appears flustered.

“To what do we owe this pleasure?” A cloak of dread falls across my shoulders, fearing Evan’s removal of accommodation and trust, after Aled. So far, other than the run in with the minister, there has been no comeback to our unorthodox methods. Yet a constant vigilance remains. Since the introduction of chemical medicine only licensed physicians are allowed to medicate. Using herbs and plants to aid healing virtually eradicated. Anyone using such methods seen as charlatans and soothsayers, risking prosecution, even death. Having the mayor, a man of influence on our side, has certainly kept the wolves and apothecaries at bay.

Evan rummages in the pocket of his buff coat. “I have brought you a gift, I thought it may help increase your knowledge, enabling you to heal even more.” He surreptitiously hands me a book with a quiet word in my ear, "It is written in English, not Latin, therefore it should be easier for you to follow."

It is unexpected. "I am most grateful to you," I read the title. "*A Physicall Directory* by Nicholas Culpeper. But why? I let you down."

Evan's eyes darken. "Aled passed quietly, with little pain. His lips quiver and he touches them with his fingertips, as if pushing the despair back inside. "I believe you helped him all you could; he was no longer afraid. I trust he resides in heaven now, that God would not turn him away for using what grows upon his sacred land, what nature gives freely to aid." Red spider veins of misery thread across Evan's dark eyes, his cheeks hollow with anguish. "May I sit Lockhart; I feel a little discomposed?"

"Certainly, Sire," I bring a stool. "Is there anything I can get you?"

Evan steeples his fingers, tapping the tips. "A moment of your time, if you please."

"Is something wrong, Sire? Your wife, mistress Williams, is she well?" I sit beside him.

"She is as well as can be expected at this time." He brushes away my concern. "There is another matter, one I need to confess, unburden myself as it were." He picks at a speck of fluff on his doublet, and I wait patiently. "You may not be aware," Evan begins, "but your mother used to work for my family, as a personal maid for my dear mother." My eyes widen, and Evan shifts uncomfortably. "My mother suffered greatly towards the end, her liver was failing, her skin and eyes yellowed. Brigid, your mother, aided her with a tonic. What it included I cannot be sure, fennel certainly one ingredient, you could smell it, and unfortunately that is what gave her away. Father was livid. Using what he called, concoctions of the devil, but there was no doubt in my mind, that mother had made a remarkable improvement whilst taking it." He smooths his moustache with a finger and continues. "Father would hear none of it and dismissed your mother from service. Henceforth, my mother declined, rapidly. Father blamed Brigid for her death, which followed shortly afterwards, spewed accusations of a curse." He looks up. "I didn't believe it, not at all."

"Why are you telling me this?" I frown. Evan shakes his head, eager to continue.

"Father sought revenge, he was grieving, lashing out at the unfairness of losing his beloved wife. I tried to make him see reason; I really did."

"Revenge?" My eyes narrow, heart drumming wildly in my chest. "What did he do?"

Evan takes a handkerchief from his pocket and wipes his face. "Father summoned Brigid to the house. I was in the room, heard every word. He told your mother he would have her arrested and tried for witchcraft, which as you know is rare in Wales, but father said because she was Scottish not Welsh the same laws did not apply. Your mother, at the time, was carrying yourself, and she begged for the life of her unborn child. Father eventually agreed proceedings would be delayed until after the birth." Evan appeals for understanding. "See, he wasn't all bad, he showed some leniency."

My jaw is tight. "But she didn't survive the birth," I remind him. "Is this why you help me now, to appease your guilt?"

"No, no," Evan protests. "I have read Culpeper; he too advises fennel for treatment of liver complaints and the yellowing associated with it. I believed in your mother, I believe in Culpeper, and I believe in you." Evan's shoulders slump. "I knew in my heart Aled could not be saved, but he certainly improved under your care, as mother did under Brigid's, all those years ago. When the angel of death comes calling, there is no way to avert it. The way mother died, in much pain…" he trails. "With your mothers help, that could have been averted, as it was with Aled." He wipes his nose with the handkerchief. "I am sorry Lockhart, about your mother, but I feel you are now blessed with the ability to alleviate unnecessary suffering, and I wish to help you with that."

My thoughts swim. I wonder if my mother had ensured her own death rather than face a hanging. Conjectured, if she had disclosed her plight to my father? Was this her reason for asking Ranulf to keep an eye on me, knowing she would not be alive to do so? What of Evan, is it right to hold him responsible for his father's wrongdoing? That would be equivalent to me being held to account for Emlyn's misdemeanours.

There is no mistaking the information deemed from Culpeper aids our work, even overtaking Shakespeare as the choice of read. Wren helps me study the suggestions, and plants a varied array of herbs and flowers in her garden to accommodate what is needed. I flick through the pages for recommendations. "Ah, this should do it." Returning to my patient with a linseed poultice to heal an arm injury. "Put this on the sore, it will disperse the puss leaking from within and cool the heat." The day's queue slowly decreases. "Yes, Mistress Priddy." I follow the last patient to the door. "Continue to wear the woody nightshade around your neck and the dizziness should clear up."

Outside, Merek hovers, his youngest son Bowen perched on his hip, the child's pallor red and blotchy. "Please Merek, allow us to aid him." I take the child, leaving him no choice but to follow me inside, and I ask the child's symptoms. Moving my hands over the boy, after a few minutes the child calms and sucks on his thumb. I hand him back to Merek and cross to my wooden case. Through observation of symptoms and coloured mist surrounding patients, I am guided to the treatment needed. Culpeper isn't always required. "Are you still at the castle?" I ask conversationally.

Merek shrugs. "I am, though I am not happy with recent events being what they are."

"So, it's true then. That Powell has pledged his support to John Poyer at Pembroke?"

"He is a fool. Declaring in favour of the King and expecting us all to just go along with it. Humph." Merek scowls. "I suppose you are still Royalist?"

"I prefer to remain neutral." I produce a balm of calamine, handing it to Merek.

"Use this on his skin, it will remove the itch and ease the redness." I touch the forehead of the infant in his arms. "He is a strong boy; I am confident his health will be restored."

"What do I owe you?" Merek roots in his pouch.

"Nothing." Our eyes make contact. "You owe me nothing."

An understanding of mutual respect passes between us. Our paths have grown apart but for there to be no ill will, is enough.

Summer sun blazes. The turquoise sea is calm and ripples along the shoreline. Wren has added the remainder of the spiced bread to the picnic, and I poke it. A bit dry, but with the mead it will go down a treat. Removing my boots and stockings, warm sand eases the tension from my feet. Taking in the view of Caldey Island and Tenby, breathing salty air deep into my lungs, my shoulders relax, the ambiance working its magic. Wren insisted we share family time, and I am glad I was persuaded. Gwilym is paddling, watching the surf cover his feet. I grab Cerys by the hand and chase Gwilym into the water. Hitching her on my hip, Gwilym scoops at the water, splashing me and Cerys, she screeches. After we have eaten, I find a stick, write, I Love Wren, in large letters in the sand. She helps the children write their own names while I rest, shielding my face from the rays of bright sun with my hat.

"Lockhart!" Wren pushes my shoulder. "Wake up, we have company."

Her tone is sharp, and I pull myself up onto my elbows, summer haze shimmering across the golden sand, a figure making their way towards us. "What does she want?" Wren hisses.

I rake a hand through my hair uneasily. "Afternoon, Nerys," I say politely.

"Hello Lockhart, and Wren."

Wren sits like stone beside me. Having inadvertently mentioned the episode at Merek's wedding, my tongue loose one night after too much ale, and regardless, we had not been together at that time, Wren was not amused and does not trust her.

Nerys curls a strand of hair around her finger. "Lockhart, may we speak privately?"

Wren sends me a warning glance, but I can hardly refuse. "Of course," I find myself saying, scrambling to my feet. I feel Wren's eyes burning into my back as we walk away. "How can I help you?" I ask once out of earshot.

"I was hoping you could give me a healing; I have heard you are very good Lockhart, that your hands hold magic within them." She looks at me from under her lashes, and I cough awkwardly.

"We will be healing again tomorrow, if you would like to come by."

"I am returning to Swansea tomorrow. I was hoping you would help me today."

Her light brown eyes, hard to resist. "Why not ask Branwen?" I suggest. "After all you are on the island to visit her, are you not?"

Pushing out her bottom lip she places a hand on my arm. "I want you to do it, we could go to the hay store."

Nerys sits precariously on a bail of straw. Examining her array of colours for clues, I rub my hands and place them upon her shoulders. A vivid image flashes across my inner eye, of Nerys, the laces of her stays loosened to accommodate the expanding swell. Removing my hands in shock, I rub them on my breeches, take a deep breath, return them to her shoulders, and close my eyes. She is crying, pleading with me, I push her away, she falls. "I want nothing to do with you or your bastard child," I picture myself shouting. "The child is yours Lockhart, there has only been you," she sobs, tears upon her cheeks. Removing my hands again, gulping my anxiety. I may have been drunk but nothing happened between us.

"Is something wrong?" Nerys asks. "Why do you keep stopping?"

"Are you with child?" The words out of my mouth before I can stop them. She twists around to face me.

"You can see that?" She gasps. "No one knows Lockhart, do not tell," she pleads. "I believe this is why I am sickly, especially in the mornings." She bites her bottom lip. "I am afraid Lockhart, what should I do?"

"Who is the father, Nerys?"

She lowers her eyes. "Hywel Talbot. He is a stable hand where I work."

"You are sure of this?"

Her head snaps up, glaring at me. "Of course I am sure, he is my sweetheart."

"There has been no other?" I ask tentatively. Nerys' mouth falls agape, momentarily speechless before she shoots back.

"Lockhart, how dare you suggest such a thing?" Whispering, "I know we, you know, had that incident at Merek's wedding." She blushes. "But you know as well as I do, nothing happened between us, I was just a foolish young girl. So, despite what you think of me." She glowers. "There has been no other, what do you take me for?"

My panic abates. "No, I mean I believe you, of course, I meant nothing by it, I apologise."

"Can you help me or not?" Nerys asks huffily.

"I am sure I can help ease your sickness, but you must promise me to speak with your mother about the baby, you cannot keep the secret for very long."

Nerys sighs. "I guess you are right about that, but mother will kill me, and father disown me."

"That won't happen," I reassure. "You are not the first to find yourself in this predicament, nor will you be the last."

"Will you come with me, to tell them?" she asks.

"I think Hywel is best placed to take that responsibility, don't you? Will he do the honourable thing?"

"I think so, yes." She brightens.

"Then you have nothing to fear." Returning my hands to her shoulders, I'm relieved to find the images have subsided, but they remain on the edge of my awareness.

Tenby is in a dire situation. Having retaken the castle for the King, Powell led the soldiers to St. Fagan's, where, drawn into battle by Colonel Horton, Powell and the remaining men fled back to Tenby defeated, hotly pursued by Roundhead forces who soon surrounded the castle. They held out for ten weeks until ailing and starving they surrendered unconditionally. Powell frogmarched to his fate at the hands of the justice system. All seems lost. Royalist supporters defeated at every turn. Scandal, hearsay, and half-truths surrounding King Charles. Unable to bring about a change in fortune he was arrested and tried for tyranny and high treason. Beheaded outside the Banqueting House in Whitehall, on the 16 January 1649. It had been bandied around that it was a possibility, but he was the King, you cannot murder a King.

"Cromwell is behind this," I seethe. "It is deplorable what that man has got away with, the lands are no better for his meddling."

"Aye," Geraint agrees. "His promises have come to naught."

Aneira pipes up, "He wants to ban Christmas. Now I may not be Christian, but it cannot be right to take such things away from people that are."

Geraint raises his eyebrows. "He does not plan to ban it completely, only the frivolities. Says there is too much drinking and not enough praying."

"We should pray for his soul; it may just go to hell after this," Aneira remarks.

"We must pray for the soul of King Charles." I say quietly. We mark his passing with a simple druid ceremony, forming a circle, holding hands, our eyes closed. "We pray for our king; we pray for his soul. We pray he rests in peace, in the Otherworld."

Lichen creeps along gaping castle walls. Cromwell, having arrived in Tenby the previous day, is rallying support, before continuing to Pembroke. I am escorted by two Roundhead soldiers in russet coats, to the same room where I met Lord Carbery. The room furnished with dark wood panelling smells of beeswax, the stone floor scrubbed and laid with a Turkish rug from the times of Henry VII. Gold, red, and purple thread, bringing a touch of elegance and opulence, the only part of the castle remaining in its finery. It is imperative I hold my tongue, to apportion blame will not serve my cause, but hatred for Cromwell, gnaws at my brain. For the impiety and increase in taxes which make Emlyn's appear meagre by comparison. It is a miracle I have been granted an audience with Cromwell and consider, as Branwen suggested, if my mind rehearsals have ensured it happening. One thing is certain, Tenby residents suffer under parliamentarian rules. Men, unable to work with the injuries sustained in war, families of men who died in battle are left impoverished. The coins only go so far, and healings do not put a roof over people's heads.

"Lockhart Edwards?" A short man in curly wig and buckled shoes clicks along the stone floor towards me.

"Yes, Sire," I instinctively straighten, gaining full height. The man rattles off profuse instructions on the expectations of my conduct, before offering me a seat. Tenby dignitaries sit straight backed with pinched solemn faces. I sit at the end of the bench. Cromwell enters the room blank-faced; his features give nothing away. His once brown wavy hair now sparse and greying, eyes hooded and tired. Evan Williams sits to the right of Cromwell in his mayoral cloak of deep purple. Each man on the bench beside me, councillors and officials, leading figures in Tenby, air their views, express their devotion to parliament, suckling like a lamb on its mother's teat. I swallow the bad taste in my mouth and await my turn.

"Sire Lockhart Edwards." My name announced by the curly wigged man, I stand, bow.

"My Lord, thank you for allowing me this opportunity to speak. Please understand I come not for myself, but for the people of Tenby." Cromwell sits in a high backed heavily embroidered chair. Wearing a black velvet doublet with silver buttons, the sleeves trimmed with lace, arms resting loosely by his side. He nods imperceptibly. I continue, "There is much poverty and great sickness, if you could find it in your heart to in anyway help."

"Who did you say you are?" Cromwell asks.

"Lockhart Edwards Sire." Beside Cromwell, Evan Williams speaks into his ear. Cromwell listens vacantly, remaining focused on me, waves Evan away. "From what I understand your brother was once custodian of this castle," he remarks.

"That is correct Sire." My head is held high, but my stomach churns with anxiety."

Cromwell continues, "Therefore, you are a royalist, if I am not mistaken, with no authority to request anything."

After recently hearing Powell had been tried under court- martial for his ill-thought-out defection from parliament to royalist, I feel no desire to follow him. Although he had eventually been pardoned, I might not be so lucky. "I care not, my Lord, for politics, I speak only for the people of Tenby."

Evan Williams mutters further words into Cromwell's ear, and his eyes narrow. Silently I ask my dragon and guardian for help. "So, you are a druid now?" Cromwell remarks with surprise.

"Yes Sire," I reply. "We are peaceable people."

Cromwell continues to eye me passively. I shift, a bead of sweat trickling my forehead, but I dare not wipe it away. "I have no time for men such as yourself, who have turned away from the Christian teachings. Your strange ways and beliefs hold no merit in today's world. In fact, I have recently passed legislation which will see an end to the village maypole. A heathenish vanity, generally abused to superstition and wickedness." He is belittling me, and I do not like his tone. He knows nothing of our beliefs. "However," Cromwell concludes, "I have seen for myself the dire situation of the people in this town, I will see you have your money. Ten pounds, I feel will suffice." Cromwell waves his hand. "You may leave, but a word of advice. I suggest you forgo your strange druid customs and return to God."

"Thank you, Sire, my Lord, thank you. I will give your request consideration" I can barely believe it has been so simple. I had expected argument, having to plead my case. Evan Williams gives a small smile. Realising then, Evan ensured I was granted the opportunity to speak to Cromwell. Knowing Evan, my unexpected ally, believes in me, fills my heart with a wave of gratitude.

Closing the door behind me, I let out a deep sigh of relief.

"Good afternoon son." I barely recognise the gaunt figure, leaning against the door frame.

Chapter 22

Wren

"Oh, Lockhart, how was the meeting? What is Cromwell like?" I smile excitedly.

"Good, good, he has promised to release some money to aid the people."

I can tell by his tone, something is amiss. "What is it Lockhart?"

He grips my upper arms. "Your father is outside." My eyes widen, and I try to release myself from his grasp, but he holds me firmly.

"Father, I must go to him." Confused by Lockhart's action.

"He is not well Wren, a changed man; you must prepare yourself."

My eyes question as Lockhart releases me and walks to the door. Returning a few moments later with an old man, the sight for which I am ill-prepared. "Croeso father." It is difficult to conceal my consternation. "What a pleasure to see you. Please come in, take a seat." He has aged considerably, skin lined and sagging. He does not look well.

"I hope she has not been here alone?" Father addresses Lockhart.

"No of course not, Halwyn is with us." Lockhart bristles, pointing to the red-haired young man sorting bottles in the corner. "Son of a friend and quite capable. He and his sister Ffion act as chaperone, whenever I am away. Your daughter is a powerful healer in her own right Sire, perfectly able without me by her side."

My heart swells at the pride in his voice.

"Yes, I heard something of these said healings, I pray for your souls." Father scowls, and coughs, a deep chesty rattle.

I bring him wine, and he takes a sip, spitting phlegm into his handkerchief. Once he is composed, I learn he had not stayed long in Cardiff, deciding to seek his fortune in London, where he began working for Cromwell.

"The long journey's I am finding difficult." Father coughs again. "I am not a young man."

"Husband, may I speak with you?" I take Lockhart's arm, ushering him out of earshot. "He cannot carry on; he must come and stay with us."

I sense his unease. "I am not sure Wren, what if the children catch whatever ails him?"

"Do you sense there is a danger of that?" Admitting he did not, I appeal. "Lock, he is my father." I only call him Lock when we are intimate and know he will not refuse me.

I prepare an infusion of hyssop for his lungs, adding ivy leaf for his cough, but he worsens, taking to his bed. Branwen recommends peppermint and feverfew. I slice an onion in half and force father to breathe in the pungent smell, but he becomes irate, tells me he needs a real doctor. Lockhart relents, returning from Tenby with an apothecary at great cost. He takes one look at father, pronounces him incurable, but still, we must pay for this advice. The negative words have a strong effect, father deteriorates rapidly. Complaining of a headache, I give sage. He becomes feverish, I make lemongrass tea. Holding on to life for two more weeks.

The minister professes loudly his distaste at having heathens in his church, but father was Christian, and it is only right and fair he be laid to rest in the graveyard of St. Mary's.

"He will be free now, will join your mother and meet Eirlys," Lockhart offers me comfort.

I lean into him for support. "I know you are right, and I am grateful we were given this time. He knows I am happy here with you, I am sure that knowledge helped him to pass over in peace. We pass Emlyn's grave in the churchyard, realising I have never once visited, and yet it is clean and tidy, obviously tended regularly. Lockhart has not spoken of this, but I know it is him who has left a posy of flowers. Guilt hammers a wedge in my heart.

The mayor paces the healing room, hands locked behind his back. "You must leave. All this trouble, they are blaming me."

"Please sit, let us talk this through," Lockhart urges.

"No, there's little point, my mind is made." Evan looks at me apologetically. "I am sorry Mistress, but I have done all I can and am no longer able to lend support. The town is asking for my resignation, say it is my doing, the town falling into dire times, even claiming my involvement in the weather. Can you believe such a thing?" He throws up his hands.

If it had been only the weather, frustrating as it is, raining almost solidly for two months, Evan may not have felt so agitated, but all is conspiring against Tenby. Crops fail under the deluge of rain, people starving.

Cromwell's money is of no use, when there is little food to buy. Decline in trade from foreign lands due to the civil war, the garrison of Roundheads at the castle, all play their part to increase poverty. Many ail, poverty and disease rife. Smallpox, and spotted fever. Without nourishment, there is only so much the healings can do. Evan sighs deeply.

"The people of Tenby swear it's a curse."

Lockhart folds his arms. "Surely, they don't think I?"

"Not you," Evan explains. "That beggar, who claimed to be deaf and dumb."

Lockhart frowns. "The one who took a beating from Leekie Porridge, before being run out of town?"

"The very same, Lockhart. Everyone was pleased at the time, when I dealt out his punishment. Now," he sighs again, "rumours are spreading that he has cursed the town. The locals proclaiming I had no evidence supporting my belief he was stealing. Therefore, I am to blame. The town is very angry Lockhart, and I wouldn't be surprised if they come for you next."

Life is like a needle, threading in and out, smooth stitches, rough stitches, large and small. Holding the fabric of life together. Or sometimes ripping it apart. Christmas passing with little celebration. Cromwell got his wish. People are praying more, but in desperation.

In the early months of the year 1650, bubonic plague arrives on the shores of Tenby, wreaking havoc in the small community. Men, women, children, rich and poor alike, it cares not. Leekie, and most of his family are amongst the first, adding spice to beliefs of a curse. Dilys, closely followed by Dafydd, soldiers from the castle. It does not distinguish, holds no favour, mercilessly it takes them all. Two hundred and twenty thus far, half the population of Tenby, and rising each day. The symptoms easy to detect. Headaches and fever, weakness, tingling throughout the body. Then swellings, large tender lumps on the neck, under the armpits, and on the inner thighs. Grown men howl like dogs, overcome by the pure torture plague instils on their bodies. Lockhart says it reminds him of the men wounded after battle, their cries still haunt his dream world, he wakes drenched in sweat, and I comfort him as much as I can, holding him, stroking his hair until his night terrors abate. Fear in the town not so easy to contain, many shun the ill. Afraid to be near others who are sick.

With the healing room closed, we take to the town, offering comforting words, alcohol, and wintergreen, to ease the pain. Calling on Edwin, we're pleased to see his plague in remission. His pregnant wife was not so lucky, and we find him weeping over her body. I feel helpless, cannot understand why people must suffer so. Rounding the corner, we see a fractious group congregating in the town square.

"What are they doing here?" I grab Lockhart's arm tightly. A prickle of warning runs up my spine, and he pats my hand.

"Just stay close to me."

"Here they are." A woman from the crowd points. We move towards them with caution.

"What is the reason for this?" Lockhart addresses the mob.

Town councillor, Derwyn Reece, steps forward. His heeled shoes and tall black hat doing little to increase his height. "Evan Williams is responsible for what is happening in this town." He points his nose in the air. "He has failed as mayor, lending his allegiance to you, and your witch of a wife." He spits angrily. Lockhart moves forward slightly, shielding me.

"Responsible for what?" he asks guardedly.

"For the suffering." Derwyn's red cheeks are puffed with superiority, his heavy cloak flapping in the breeze like the wings of an irate magpie. "It's only since you have been doing these healings, this has occurred."

"All the children that have died." I hear a shout from amongst the rabble. Recognising the voice, I search the crowd, my heart sinks, Arlet, I had heard she was working in one of the Inn's, and her smirk tells me she is the one feeding the people of Tenby's fears, spewing her lies about us, and they have ingested her poison. I asked Branwen once of the devil card, learning the meaning is symbolic not literal, representing the scapegoat goddess, Baphomet, who seeks to overcome powerlessness. Yet powerless is how I feel.

"The whole of Wales, in fact the whole of England and beyond are fighting the plague. How can that possibly be our fault?" Lockhart appeals to them.

"The wrath of God," Derwyn growls, spittle congregating at the corners of his mouth. Mumblings of agreement worry me. "The minister warned us not to turn to you. This is punishment from God, that is why we suffer."

"Do you all feel this way?" Lockhart appeals.

"Go, leave us in peace." The blacksmith Crwys Gower pipes up, "You heathens are not welcome in Tenby."

"We have done nothing wrong, only tried to help you." Lockhart protests.

"So, where is the healing now?" Crwys shakes his fist. "When we need it most, you heal no one. You are demons the pair of you."

The agreeing crowd becoming louder in voice.

"Come Lockhart, please, I want to go." I feel much distress, my stomach churning, I pull on his sleeve. He sees the panic in my eyes, and leads us away from the mob, heckles of witch and ogre hurled at our turned backs. A cast stone scuffs Lockhart's shoulder. I am afraid, but he insists we walk at normal pace back to the harbour. Squeezing my hand as we reach the boat.

"Perhaps it is better you remain on the island." Untying the rope securing the boat, he helps me step in.

"What about you, you cannot continue, knowing how they feel?"

"I will take you home, but then I must return Wren, one more time. I made a promise; I must abide by."

I huddle into my shawl. "Why do they think this way Lockhart, why can they not see the truth of it?"

"They are small-minded Wren. When they can find no reason for their suffering, they blame others, it is easier to place it at someone else's door."

"They are fools." I regret my words instantly; they are simply scared. I turn and bite my lip. Those who cast aspersions, I argue with myself. Calling others into question when I am a changeling. "Are we being punished; do you think we are wrong in what we do?"

He tries to comfort me. "We have done all we can, but I am afraid it is out of our hands."

"Perhaps we missed something, perhaps if we had recognised the symptoms earlier, or isolated the sick," I implore.

Lockhart steers the boat away from the harbour. "We tried our best Wren, that is all anyone can do. We washed our hands in vinegar and rubbed it on their wounds, lit brimstone in the chimneys. What more could we have done?"

Lockhart has returned from his final trip to Tenby. Grubby, hollow eyed, the weight of the world on his shoulders. Muscles taut from the days digging. A plague pit, just within view of St. Mary's church. It needed to be big, and deep. He recounts thrusting the spade over and over into the damp soil. Bending to retrieve the larger boulders, hurling them into buckets of excavated earth, the ting of metal against stone, unyielding amongst the backdrop of despair. Foreboding, unrelenting grief. Burying his face in calloused blistered hands.

"It hangs like cobwebs around the town, Wren, penetrating every building, every pathway, every soul."

I can barely take in his words, impossible that a creature smaller than a poppy seed, tiny enough to fit the eye of a needle, has the power to cause such devastation to so many. I wish to close my mind to such devastating tragedy, but I must listen, hear him retell his story, ease his troubled mind from the burden of seeing men he had known all his life, their light snuffed out easily as a candle. He goes on, "Light was fading, the sky awash with swirls of grey and gold from the setting sun, the hole barely complete, but it had to do, such was the hurry to bury the dead. Bodies in burial shrouds, carried on elm planks, laid out in rows. Quicklime spread across the corpses to speed up decomposition and act as a steriliser." He looks up. "I had seen the moment before. In a blinding flash the ceremony in the woods burst into my awareness, the images in the fire. I was able to see this event before it happened." He rakes a hand through unkempt hair. "I shovelled earth over the bodies, deep sadness sucking my strength, wondering why." He appeals to me, "Why Wren. What is the point of showing me future catastrophe when I have no means to prevent it?"

I hand Branwen the box of coins. "You are sure there is no other way?"

Forlornly, I shake my head. She pulls me to her in a tearful embrace.

"There is a druid community on Ynys Mon," Lockhart explains. "Once the children are settled with Alys and Rhys, you will find a good home there, I am sure."

I crouch, sitting Gwilym and Cerys on my knee. "You be good children for Branwen now." I hug them fiercely. "You be a big boy and look after your sister Gwilym." I kiss them both on top of each little head, breathing in their fragrance.

Lockhart slips the onyx over Gwilym's head. "Keep it with you son, it will protect you, I no longer have need of it." Gwilym takes his sister's hand and helps her onto the boat. My heart swells. Rubbing tears with the heel of my hand, I don't want to miss these last moments.

"One final time Wren, are you sure you will not go with them?" Lockhart asks, but I shake my head, lips quivering.

"Come on time to go." Merek calls from the boat, an oar in each hand. He is taking a great risk escorting Branwen and the children to Tenby for the last boat out, when all have been ordered to remain locked within the town. Preventing the spread of disease to neighbouring towns, paramount. Men have been employed to collect goods left by traders on the outskirts of the town walls. For the people of Tenby there is no escape, the walls of protection becoming a prison, like animals trapped in a cage.

"We are most grateful to you." Lockhart shouts to him. We keep our distance, in case.

Merek nods, turning to the children. "It will be a big ship." He grins.

"Will it have sails?" Gwilym asks.

"Massive sails." Merek pushes the boat from the shore. "Farewell, brother."

He waves back at Lockhart, who salutes him, a tear trickling his cheek. Wiping it away with his sleeve, he pulls me to him. "I must not cry; I am a man."

I touch his face. "What is the point of that now, why does it matter when our hearts are breaking?"

He sniffs and nods; attempts to reassure me we are doing what is right. "Alys will care for them as hers, you have given her a precious gift Wren. A family she never had."

Anguish choking like a hangman's noose, I cling to Lockhart's sleeve to prevent my collapse, having known this day would come. The black cat from the Pritchard's farm darting across my path, proved a bad omen, just as I expected. Even King Charles believed the death of his own black cat, forbearer of bad luck, arrested the next day. Lockhart begged me to go with the children, but I have remained defiant.

"I know you have seen the outcome Lockhart; the fear is evident in your eyes."

"I could be wrong Wren, what if I am wrong?"

"You are never wrong Lock and whatever happens, we are together." Now I am submerged in a cascading waterfall of distress, the breath of my life sailing away across the water, taking our precious children to their aunt and uncle in Hawarden castle. I am beaten, bruised, from the reawakening of unbearable grief and loss. After Eirlys's death, it had taken months to reestablish normality and escape the dense fog. Somehow, I had found a way to grow, from the utter despair. A circle of inner strength slowly emerged, encompassing the pain, forever in my heart. Now it bursts forth in a way I cannot describe in words, but Lockhart's eyes have told me the truth of our plight, and I cannot ignore it, risk the children contracting plague. This way, I feel reassured they will be saved. My duty as a mother, to put them first, do whatever necessary to preserve their young lives. I am under no illusion, my desolation will not last for months this time. I don't have months left. Branwen explained that the children will remain a part of me and Lockhart forever. That we are never separated from those we love. Souls remain joined. The death of the body is a form of healing, and only the end if you choose to see it that way. For those aware, it is nothing more than a journey, a sailor far out at sea, gone from view, but not forgotten.

It is but two days later, collecting water from the outside barrel, I collapse. Tired and weak for hours, I had tried to carry on as before, but my head is swimming. Lockhart rushes to my aid. He lifts me into his arms as though I am a feather. The last time I passed the threshold in his arms, had been our wedding night. A blinding headache creases my brow, my temperature climbing, yet I shiver. Finding no comfort, I toss and turn fitfully in our bed, then vomit. Lockhart assists in cleaning me and the mess. He offers tonics but I cannot face the thought. He wanders the small cottage at a loss. It is quiet without the children. Even with my eyes closed I know where he is and what he is doing, taking the book of Shakespeare from the shelf, leafing the pages. "Full circle Wren," he says, drawing the stool to the side of the bed. "What you did for me; I now do for you." His reading is far from accomplished, and I picture him following each word with a finger, as he begins the tale of lovers Rosalind and Orlando. Forced into exile in the Forest of Arden, they become entangled in a beguiling game of love, lust, and mistaken identity. "We that are true lovers run into strange capers." I allow the words to wash over me. I am blessed to have Lockhart.

I must have slept, for when I awaken shadows darken the room. Lockhart lies beside me. "Beltane marks the emergence of the new, a man aided by the fertility of spring falls in love amongst the blooms. I, Creiddylad, bring prophecy, healing, and reincarnation, for the revenant, you have been chosen to assist," I whisper with sadness; only now I understand.

Lockhart props himself on an elbow. "Did you say something?" he asks.

"I have made a mistake, Lock," I admit, unable to look at him. "I was shown these words yet failed to understand, searching for the revenant to assist, selfishly looking to be recognised, to be important. Just as the rich with their fancy clothes, furnishings, and jewels. The poor through their hard labour. Why has it taken me until the end to see clearly, the futility of pettiness, of jealousy and war? For me to finally see Creiddylad was referring to, you." I turn to him, his expression pensive.

"I'm not sure I understand."

"Oh, Lock." My voice is a whisper, but I must speak my troubles while able. "If I failed in what I came to do, we may go to different places, and I cannot bear for us to be apart."

"Annwn is an inclusive realm Wren, we will meet there, I promise."

"Even if I am fae?" I sniff tearfully.

"Annwn is the faerie kingdom, Wren, have no fear."

"You don't understand Lockhart. I am a changeling." I sob.

"A changeling, no, they are known for being mean, cold and aloof, not like you at all."

He takes my hand. "Has that been your concern? Why you did not want to accept your faerie connection, because you thought you may be a changeling?"

"Yes," I admit weakly. "I was afraid."

"Oh, Wren, trust me, you are not, it is impossible, it would have been clear to Branwen and Ranulf if it were so. They would have known." He pauses. "As for Annwn, it really does not matter whether you are faerie, or not. The Otherworld is a kingdom for both faerie folk and druids, for all, welcoming every soul back into the fold. It is incredibly beautiful, Wren. The sky is clear, the water sparkles, and you will be reunited with Eirlys."

His words ease my worries, visions of Annwn dancing in my mind.

I find myself in a magical kingdom, stood on a pathway lined with trees swaying in a gentle breeze, ring-necked doves perching on the branch of a Sycamore. Looking through the leaves to blue sky and pure white cloud. I hear a whisper, the forest beckoning me to move deeper within. Following the trail of a winding path, becoming lighter with each step. The fight to be myself, when the world expects me to be something else, loosens, throwing off the cloak of oppression tied around my neck. Trees of verdant green welcome me. Nine hazel trees shimmer beside a lake, sparkling with crystalline water. Aliveness grows within my chest, my heart expanding, "yes, this is where I belong." Beneath the trees, a throne sits within the centre of a labyrinth. The circular path interlaid with white Selenite. I approach and sit. The legs carved with engravings of sprite and naiad. The hazel warm against my back. I note my attire. A plain white dress, a braid of gold and blue around my waist. The same thread plaited through my dark hair, resting over my shoulders.

A man emerges from the trees, and kneels before me, head bent over a silver sword, a serpent of coloured stones twist around the hilt. "Tyngaf fy ffyddlondeb i ti am byth," he says in Welsh. "I swear my faithfulness to thee, forever."

He looks up, trust and sincerity radiating in his blue eyes. Lockhart's eyes… I peel my lids open, reaching through the darkness to the man who lies beside me in our small cottage. Lacing my fingers through his, I whisper. "A gossamer veil invokes a tale, of hidden truths, which shall prevail. Open your heart, seek, and find. We are never apart, our hearts entwined."

No longer afraid, remembering the reason for everything. "Lockhart, my prince."

Chapter 23

Lockhart

Having fallen asleep leaning across the bed, head resting on my arms, I yawn, rub my stiff back. Noting the swellings on Wren's neck, I gulp the fear in my throat. A golden light is flooding the room. "How long?" I ask aloud.

A gentle voice floats through my head, "She will wait; she will not leave without you."

I pour ale, taking a large swig, there will be no escaping the inevitable. Death is not the concern; I have seen the Otherworld I will return to. It is what comes before. The pain and torture of your body becoming your enemy. Wren's suffering troubles me most, despite offering healing, tinctures, and ointment, I am unable to relieve her pain.

"Are you staying?" I ask my guardian.

"Yes, I will stay."

"Good, I could do with the company."

Wren groans and I bend to kiss her forehead, burning like a red-hot poker. She opens her eyes. "The children," she asks with concern, "where are the children?"

"They are safe with Branwen; she will care for them." The answer soothes her, and she closes her eyes.

I awaken to the hoot of an owl. I am hot, sweating, shivering, and pray to Arawn, God of the dead. To Gwynn Ap Nudd, king of the faeries and the Otherworld. "Allow us entry to your kingdom as we cease this earthly life," I whisper. I pray to Arianrhod, weaver of time and fate, the cycles of life and rebirth. "May we come to you with understanding and wisdom from this lifetime, to use wisely in the next." Hoping I have done enough to appease the gods, and neither of us will linger.

Birdsong and morning sunlight, floats into the room. Weak and shaky, I make my way to the window, nauseous and light-headed, but determined to gaze at the fluffy white clouds in the azure, blue sky, one last time. In the distance, an ebbing tide ripples along the shoreline, golden sand reemerging from beneath the depths of grey blue water. Sparkling grains glistening in the sun, hidden beauty, restored. I watch the birds returning from their winter home, busying themselves in and out of the hedgerows, preparing nests for their new offspring.

"When we are gone Wren, all this will still be here, it is very strange to think so." Unsure if she can hear, I continue, "I wonder where the birds go over wintertime. It is said they travel to distant lands, but how can a scrap of a bird know the way, and when to return?" I sigh. "Will I return? Will I remember who I have been before?"

I spot a small bird darting between the lavender in the garden. A wren, my beloved's namesake waits for her. The colours around my sleeping wife are jagged, distorted in an unusual fashion, and I wish to wipe them away, hold on to the Wren I know, never let go. I am finding the unfairness difficult to justify. The healings we gave, where they in vain?

"I love you Lock." Unsure if it is Wren or my guardian speaking, I turn. Wren, peering through swollen eyes. Making my way back to bed, feet frozen, despite the heat of my skin, I slip under the blanket, try to ignore the buboes spreading over my body.

"I love you too... Forever and a day."

A slight smile, her last, tugs at the corners of her mouth. "Shakespeare." She sighs.

Hours pass in a blur. Wren, writhing in excruciating pain, moaning, her breathing laboured, the swellings under her skin, large and tender. I consider the Lockhart amulet; Lord Carbery spoke of. Wished it was in my possession, and I could use it to save Wren. I keep recalling my conversation with Wren's father. After persuading Wren to take a walk and get some air, I confronted him, asked for his blessing to our marriage, it would have meant so much to Wren.

"Your family have brought me nothing but trouble and strife, why would I give my blessing?" he seethed. "Your brother had his eye on Wren, even before the death of his second wife. Made his vulgar intentions, very clear. Visiting me when his wife passed before she was even cold in her grave, taking great interest in our home. Initially I refused his offer of marriage to Wren; I did not see him as suitable."

"What changed your mind?" I equally wished to know and yet dreaded what he would say.

He continued, eager to confess, "One night I was on a losing streak, every card I turned, getting in deeper and deeper, until I had nothing left to offer, except the house, and Wren. Emlyn offered to help me, said if I would allow the marriage, he would pay off my debts. Emlyn bought the house I had scrimped and saved to build. It was a happy home for a number of years. Your thoughtful brother allowed me to remain in the house and pay him rent, our little secret. When Emlyn died, the deal died with him, and the creditors came knocking. Then you showed up and took the one thing I had left, Wren. I hate you and I hate your brother."

It is obvious now why Emlyn married Wren in haste. He must have felt glee, finding Cedrych in a dire situation. I always suspected something amiss, but thought land was his motive. Now I realise that was a cover, so no one would suspect. He wanted the house, and Wren. No doubt Emlyn had intended to live there, or sell it, take his pilfered coinage with him when his underhand dealings in Tenby, caught up with him. I remember observing Emlyn leaching Wren's rainbow at their wedding. Maybe her inner power was the attraction. I am unsure which I feel the most contempt for, Cedrych or Emlyn. How could they do that to Wren? A renewed hatred for them both, twists in my stomach.

I have become too weak to rise, drifting in and out of sleep.

"Lockhart, awaken." Forcing my eyes open, the golden light in the room is as bright as the sun, but surely, I am not in Annwn yet.

"I am delirious," I tell myself. "A symptom of the plague." Closing my lids.

"Do not sleep Lockhart, time is short, you need to remember." An anxiousness in my guardian's voice, I haven't heard before. Wren lies very still; her suffering will not last much longer. My heart squeezes with pain, whispering the words of Taliesin, "Before I long for my life's ending, before I foam at the mouth, before I am planked, let there be celebration in my soul. Books of learning hardly tell us, of the sufferings after the deathbed. Whoever shall hear my bardic books, shall find sanctuary in the Otherworld."

My mind drifts to Nerys, and the vision when aiding her, of her heavy with child, and I, pushing her away. Though it makes no sense. Nerys and I never had relations, though we came close, and it was before my marriage to Wren… Clarity whips away the fog, memories, clear and intense dart like salmon up the Cenarth falls. A covert conversation with Merek.

"Nerys has been found dead with a newborn baby in her arms, never taking its first breath." The horror and shock at hearing the news reawakens in my heart. "She must have been too afraid to speak of her plight." Merek's face tight. "If I ever find out who was responsible, I will kill him with my bare hands."

"I knew the child was mine, and this was the consequence of my refusal to accept responsibility. I never confessed, felt too ashamed, but how could this be possible guardian?"

I feel my guardian waiting for my limited human brain to catch up. "It belies explanation, unless… I have lived this life before, two lives interlinked. That's how Ranulf described it, but the only way that could be so is… reincarnation!" A snake of energy slithers up my spine. "Is this what I am to remember?"

"There is more Lockhart, but you are looking for the answers in your mind. You will never find them there, look in your heart." Breathing hurts, stress intensifying the pain in my body. "Your druid training." Her words in my head.

The sisterhood taught the art, of allowing my mind to rest, my heart to open, slowing my breathing, moving to a place within, where the pain is bearable, I whisper, "Let me see with my heart, to save my soul."

A burning ignites in the centre of my forehead and abdomen, threading my veins.

"Go back in your mind to a day in the castle when you woke from what you considered a dream, do you remember?"

"I'm not sure," I admit.

"You questioned Emlyn, though you wouldn't normally, commented on the tapestry in the hall, noting the craftsmanship, were kindly to Edwin."

"Yes, I recall now, I ruffled his hair, but surely reincarnation happens at the beginning of a lifetime, not in the middle!"

"Most begin again at birth, you chose otherwise. You invoked Rubicon, which once called cannot be reversed, strongly influencing future events. Such was your determination to come back. Some parts the same, some different," she says.

"Those are Ranulf's words. Are you suggesting I repeated only a section of this lifetime, but why?" Images of the castle siege impress on my mind.

"In your previous life, you fought the attackers and Emlyn survived, which changed the life of so many people. He took Wren away; she became a shadow of her true self. A son born to them, was not part of the plan, we had to call him back, he did not survive."

"The child I saw in my dream."

"Not a dream, your soul remembering." Visions dance behind my eyelids.

"Emlyn was arrested, his dealings caught up with him, and I visited him in gaol. He begged for my help, but there was nothing I could do. I watched him hang on gallows tree hill." Words catch. "I wanted to save his soul this time around, guardian, but yet again, I did not."

She speaks softly, "You were not meant to."

"But I thought all souls could be saved?"

"They can, but it was not your role for this lifetime. Emlyn acted as your shadow, aspects you do not like to admit, even to yourself. Those we struggle with the most in life, hold an image of that darker self. Emlyn was your warning, a reminder, how power can be used for good or ill. Previously, by extending his life, you never became a druid or a healer, as your mother wished. Therefore, you were unable to help Bethog, and you remember now, what happened to her."

"She drowned," I whisper sadly, remembering the second part of the dream which has stayed with me.

"Previously you mocked her, unable to empathise with her grief."

"I never said it to her face." I protest.

"No, but on a deeper level she heard. Our sub-conscious hears everything, even if we are not sure of the sender, we know deep within if we are condoned. The path is slippery Lockhart, many fall foul, decide it easier to conform, wear the mask, and this is who you were before, treating some with contempt, to fit in. Your actions this time, however, have extended Bethog's life many more years. Nerys also will survive, along with Hywel, who loves her dearly. Together they will bring four healthy children into the world."

"She will be alright; you are sure guardian?"

"As long as she continues on the path she is on, yes."

"Is this why I returned? To put right, what I got wrong, previously?"

"Once a deed is done, it cannot usually be undone. However, your death bed plea was heard, and you were granted a chance to fulfil what you asked for. Do you remember what you wished?"

I consider. "I remember lying with Wren, as we are now." I sigh sadly at the memory. "The only time we had was this… We never married or had children; I was afraid of her rejection, did not consider myself worthy, never expressed my true feelings until, it was too late."

"What did you say to her? The answers lie within Lockhart, look with your heart."

"I told Wren, that if I had my time again, I would do things differently."

Forcing my head to turn, the movement agonising. Wren's fingers, face, and neck, black with blood poisoning, spreading through her body. "I promised to make her my wife, we would have children, be happy. I asked that if only I could have another chance, I would be a better man." I sigh. "My beautiful Wren, I am sorry I failed you, not once, but twice. I still allowed your marriage to Emlyn, I should have been stronger, trusted my heart."

"Guilt will not serve your soul Lockhart, you were never expected to get everything right, as a human, mistakes are invariably made along the way, you must forgive yourself."

"Forgive!" I reply incredulously. "How am I to forgive myself when my actions have caused Wren such suffering?" The swellings in my groin and under my armpits are agonising, and believing myself deserving of the pain, I fall into restless sleep.

I wake to moonlight through the window, the golden glow of my guardian, a nurturing beacon in the dark room. "Why can I see you? I thought you always stood behind me."

"I can be in more than one place," she replies, but I fail to understand.

"It is unfair to take me back to Annwn now," I reason. "My druid training, there is much left to learn, has it all been in vain?"

I sense her move closer, bathing my skin in a breath of cool air. "All you have learnt remains within you Lockhart. If you are wise enough to follow your intuition in your next lifetimes, you will find all the wisdom you need."

"Have I done enough?" I whisper fearfully. "So many have died."

"Moved on Lockhart, that is all. Despite the constraints of the century in which you find yourself, you have pushed the boundaries, shown others that there is a different way to live, other ways to see the world, reawakened people to the druid's view of their connection to the earth. Keeping that alive, is especially important for Wales and its people. Few have the power to save the souls of so many, whilst also contributing to save the soul of their homeland." She pauses before continuing. "You can help others only so much Lockhart, you cannot take away their life lessons, each must discover for themselves the truth of who and what they are, your role is only to guide, to inspire and encourage, you can do no more. Remember it is only through overcoming challenges on your journey, that your soul can develop. Mistakes a part of the learning, showing you what to do differently, next time."

"I had plans for the future, so much I expected to do," I grumble. "I was told of a powerful Lockhart talisman, I hoped one day the opportunity would arise for me to visit Scotland, seek it out. If it hadn't been for the pestilence, I may have realised my aspiration." I sigh.

"Humans always expect there will be another day, a chance to fulfil their dreams. It is not always the case, if you resist your inner urges, the opportunity may not arrive. Or maybe, it just wasn't the right time."

"Are you suggesting the chance will come in another life?"

"Everything is possible."

"I still do not understand why so many have to suffer?" My focus wanes through the intense pain.

"There will always be positive and negative experiences, it is how you face them that matters, and you have shown much courage. Every action a human takes affects others, every thought and deed matters, they tend to forget. When the plague struck, you did all you could to help people during their last days, sought to ease their pain and suffering, offered compassion, comforted those who feared death, helping them pass safely into the light. Although your human eyes see only death, you touched their souls, instilled messages which will remain within them, into their next lifetime. They can then help others, a ripple effect. One day, maybe after many incarnations' people will awaken, remember who and what they are. Only then will their souls' full learning come forth. Until that time, all you, and the many others who follow, can do, is express the truth. It may appear they do not hear, but something within, recognises and knows. You did all you could, did not turn away but helped right to the end, except..."

"Except what?" I ask weakly.

"Wren... So much, unrecognised." Her regret tugs my heart. "I understand you did what you felt was right, and within the time period in which you live, you did well, but, you forgot," her voice whispers in my head. "You forgot to remember, the serpent."

Confused, I ask, "What serpent?"

"The symbolism right in front of you, yet you did not see it. The golden phoenix, arises from the ashes, is reborn."

"The wall hanging in Tenby castle, is that what you are referring too, the serpent twisting round the sword."

"Your sword, representing the male, strong and stable, cutting through illusion. A spiritual warrior. The will, when not aligned with our higher purpose, becomes a weapon. The rainbow colours, represent the feminine, the shining one, faerie, Wren," she continues. "The druids revere the adder. The nadredd, sheds its skin, becomes new, reborn, a shapeshifter." She pauses. "Put it all together Lockhart."

I attempt to unscramble the meaning. "The sword is male, the hue of colours female, the snake, the adder is druid, the shapeshifter, transforms, leaving behind the form it once was, yet it looks the same."

"You are almost there," she prompts.

"I don't know." I sigh; the pain making it hard to think.

She guides me. "Consider the Awen. A Welsh word meaning inspiration. The druid symbol of balance. Where does inspiration come from, vision, you must have a vision. Everything emerges from the invisible, your ideas bring it to life. What you see in your mind's eye, everything you think and believe, your words, your deeds, all equally relevant, all shape your life."

My eyes close in exhaustion. "I can't think any more, it hurts too much." I drift towards slumber, letting go of thought, of trying to remember, when, abruptly, the answer reveals itself to me. My eyes fly open.

"I am not unique; reincarnation happens to all. The signs of our life's mission are hidden in plain sight, in symbolism and synchronicity. Names, people, places, each has its reason for appearing in your life. Emlyn represented my feelings of inadequacy and served as a reminder of how not to be. The war, my inner conflict, and anger. The sword depicts the soldier, the serpent is the druid, being reborn, the phoenix, an opportunity to transform. The Awen, the need for balance, between light and dark, physical, and spiritual, yet I was blind. Wren means both druid and ruler, Branwen told me that. Yet I considered my own progress more important. She was, is, much wiser than I, understands people, feels deeply. Why did I not encourage her more?" I berate myself. "Branwen said, right from the beginning, Wren belonged on the island, was insistent I brought her here. Did she know, did Branwen realise, yet I did not?"

"Branwen could not see the whole picture but had learnt to trust her intuition."

"Is this the price I must pay, must I lose Wren as a consequence, for not understanding the relevance, the importance, of bringing forth her wisdom?"

"No," she replies insistently. "You are not losing Wren, this is not a punishment, it is merely time that is all, time for you to return. Maybe, next time, you will see, you will recognise she is more than a woman, more than a faerie."

"More than a faerie! I am confused, is this not what I was meant to bring out in her?"

"Her name tells the truth of it. Wren is a ruler of druids, of the faerie folk of Annwn, a goddess."

"No, no." Tensing against the pain, the realisation of my failure is too much to bear. "If I had remembered earlier, I could have helped her advance further. This was never about me, but her."

"Your heart remembered Lockhart; your heart never forgets. Now you must forgive your mistakes."

I mull it over. "I understand the importance of forgiveness, that forgiveness honours my soul." I whisper into the night. "I forgive you Emlyn, and Cedrych, and I forgive myself. Lockhart Edwards, I forgive the mistakes you have made." Exhausted and wracked with pain, I drift into sleep.

I am awakened by my guardian's gentle voice. "Lockhart." Barely able to open my eyes for the swelling, I know instinctively Wren's time to go is imminent. Low morning sun lights the room in pale-pink light, silhouetting the golden form of my guardian, casting away the shadows of night, welcoming a new day, a day Wren will not see.

She lies very still beside me, her eyes closed. "Don't leave me," I beg, but within moments a mist rises from her chest, particles of rainbow lights dancing. Terror grips me; tears blur my vision. "You said she would wait, Wren, do not leave me."

"Let go, Lock, it is time." Her voice in my head, her presence still in the room.

"I cannot, until I know I have done enough."

My guardian speaks, or is it Wren? "Lockhart, earth is a place for learning, you brought Wren happiness as you promised. You knew you would forget who you were, forget you are eternal, that all the power you needed was already within you, being human is about finding that out. If a soul remembered all the poor choices, it had made previously, it would influence the decisions made in this lifetime. Free will is the only way to learn. Before you incarnate, you see the potential of the human life laid out before you. You are aware of the challenges, the opportunities for the growth of your soul, but once the veil is in place, you forget. It is the same for all, but if you look within yourself, the truth is there. Everything is there. Remember you are immortal. This, just a lesson for your soul. Through the troubles and strife of earthly life. Remember you, are not your form."

"Will I return again, to put things, right?"

"You will get the chance, another time; this life is done. It is time to rest, time to come home to Annwn."

My guardian moves closer, holding out her hand. "I am always with you; you are never alone. Be still, listen, and I will guide you home."

Rainbow lights sparkle, her features finally visible. "Wren!" I struggle to understand. She lays beside me. "How can you be my guardian if you are Wren, who has been here, on earth with me?"

She smiles, revealing the dimple in her right cheek. "A soul is not solid Lockhart, nothing is. A part of the soul can be on earth, while another part remains in Annwn, or works as a guide. Let go, Lockhart, then you will remember, everything."

I try to reach out to her, but my body will not respond.

"Reach out to me with your heart."

Closing my eyes, I imagine stretching my fingers towards her, instantly feeling the warmth of her touch, running through me. Calm, peaceful, weightless. I sigh, a long slow breath. Realising I feel no pain, I open my eyes, surprised to see my form, laid out on the bed below.

"Lockhart." I turn to see my guardian, Wren, beside me. Her love, the warmth of a summer rain shower, restoring my vitality. I recall clearly now; the discussions shared in spirit.

"Is that all I had to remember?" I ask, askance. "I thought it was to make you my wife, to put right mistakes, that was only part of it, wasn't it?"

She smiles. "Humans always think they must do more, really it is quite simple. You asked to return, for the opportunity to follow your heart, and to love. All souls returning to earth are asked to do the same. However, most do not heed the messages from their guardian, dismiss their feelings, but to love all, to love themselves, is all they need to do."

I move closer, merging within her energy, no longer two, we become one, connected for eternity. For in the end… Love is all there is.

www.ingramcontent.com/pod-product-compliance
Ingram Content Group UK Ltd.
Pitfield, Milton Keynes, MK11 3LW, UK
UKHW010832310326
469528UK00004B/87